THE COURIER

A DAK HARPER THRILLER

ERNEST DEMPSEY

138 PUBLISHING

Hey Brad....

JOIN THE ADVENTURE

Visit ernestdempsey.net to get a free copy of the not-sold-in-stores short stories *Red Gold, The Lost Canvas,* and *The Moldova Job,* plus the full length novel *The Cairo Vendetta*, all from the critically acclaimed Sean Wyatt archaeological thriller series.

You'll also get access to exclusive content and stories not available anywhere else.

While you're at it, swing by the official Ernest Dempsey fan page on Facebook at https://facebook.com/ErnestDempsey to join the community of travelers, adventurers, historians, and dreamers. There are exclusive contests, giveaways, and more!

Lastly, if you enjoy pictures of exotic locations, food, and travel adventures, check out my feed @ernestdempsey on the Instagram app.

What are you waiting for? Join the adventure today!

1

Dak Harper stared down at the debit card on the hotel room desk, knowing he couldn't use the card until Colonel Tucker was dead. Next to the card, a stack of money sat on the desk's dark mahogany surface. To call it a stack was generous. All counted, he had $237 left in cash sitting next to his fake passport and driver's license.

He'd been careful, double-dipping at convenience stores or markets, shuffling money around to make it nearly impossible to track—not that the people chasing him were *that* good.

Still, he preferred to play it safe.

At his cabin back in the mountains of Tennessee, he had weapons, munitions, cash, and precious metals stored up for a rainy day, what others would say was a hitting-the-fan sort of contingency. The fan wasn't on yet, but it was plugged in with a fresh pile of manure sitting in a bucket close by.

Even the purchase of the cabin and its property had been concealed with the greatest of care. Dak used an LLC along with a subsidiary corporation to add two layers of anonymity to ownership.

The military had cleared his name and restored his benefits and his bank accounts, but Dak wasn't stupid enough to use them. He wasn't about to make it easy on Tucker.

The former officer had essentially been Dak's boss, though that term wasn't often used. Tucker was in charge of operations near Hamrin, in Iraq, and had made a series of career-ending mistakes, the first of which was wrongfully accusing Dak Harper of attempted murder and the betrayal of the men on his Delta Force team.

Even when Tucker learned the truth about what really happened —that Harper had been the one betrayed and left for dead in a desert cave—the colonel pushed ahead, unwilling to admit he was wrong. That vindictiveness cost him everything.

When Dak was cleared of all wrongdoing, Tucker was dismissed —given benefits, his pension, the whole nine, all in exchange for his quiet retirement. Dak knew the man did not intend to go silently. He blamed Dak for his fall from power, a collapse that blocked the colonel from climbing higher up the ladder. It was no secret Tucker had his eyes set on making general, and perhaps someday to even loftier positions within the government.

Now, none of that was possible.

Knowing Tucker, Dak figured the man was bent on revenge, and he wouldn't stop until his vengeance was fulfilled. With connections and resources all over the world, Tucker was more than capable of deploying mercenaries who were willing to exchange ethics and morals in exchange for thirty pieces of silver.

Dak knew there was only one way he would truly be safe. That would be when Tucker was dead.

Until then, Dak had to keep moving. That's why the job he'd discovered was so fortuitous. He'd saved up a few financial resources, but those reserves could run low if tapped too often, and he didn't want to risk going back to the cabin in the mountains more than necessary. Now, he needed money.

He turned his head and looked out the balcony door of the condo he'd rented in midtown Atlanta. It was one of the newer high-rises built in the last five years, contemporary and modern, with clean white paint and gray-brown hardwood flooring. The place had been purchased—he assumed—to be a rental, a common practice in the internet age, when people could rent out their homes on apps and websites.

Twenty stories below, the bustling city of Atlanta churned with activity. It was still dark outside in the early morning, but people were already in the middle of their commute or traveling through town to get a head start on the traffic.

In a few hours, Dak would meet his new employer, though he still had reservations about the in-person aspect of taking the job.

For all he knew, it could be a trap—an elaborate setup by the colonel.

Dak would take precautions. He always did. So far, everything checked out, but he wouldn't let down his guard.

He scooped up the money, cards, and identification on the desk and stuffed them into his front pockets. He spun around and picked up his black tactical bag; his few belongings having already been packed.

Dak traveled light, only carrying a few clean sets of clothes and the other necessities. He didn't like being on the run, always looking over his shoulder, but he was accustomed to it at this point. His former line of work had prepared him well for it. Dak only hoped that someday he could live a normal life—whatever that meant.

He turned and made for the door but paused when he saw a shadow move past the threshold on the floor on the other side. He frowned and ducked into the bathroom to the left, immediately wishing he'd grabbed one of the kitchen knives opposite him. They were fifteen to twenty feet away—so close yet so far.

Dak lowered his pack down to the floor, pressing his shoulder against the doorframe as he watched the shadow linger just beyond the entrance. He sighed. *So much for peace and quiet*, he thought.

The assassin didn't attempt to unlock the door. At least they were smart or aware enough to have seen the lights on in the apartment through the crack at the bottom of the door. Or so Dak figured.

Knowing that he was awake, the killer would loiter outside the entrance in hopes catching the target off guard as he left.

Dak only waited another ten seconds to make sure the assassin didn't try to come in, then he emerged from his hiding place and walked across the open corridor to the kitchen. There, he grabbed two large kitchen knives and two smaller ones. He also grabbed a dish towel from a silver rack by the sink.

Then he went back to the door, slipping the knives into his belt before reaching the entrance. Dak quietly looped the towel around the door handle and let it dangle. He paused for a second and then flicked the light switches. The condo went dark, only dimly lit from the city lights beyond the balcony and the faint glow in the east where the sun pushed toward morning.

Dak watched the shadows beyond the door shift. He knew the killer was getting into position, and if he weren't mistaken, a new shadow represented a firearm—probably with a suppressor.

There was no other way out than through the door. Dak would have opted for a balcony escape, but not twenty stories up.

With no other options, Dak crouched low near the door. The assassin would, most likely, be holding their weapon chest high. That's how he would do it.

Dak clutched one of the kitchen knives in a fist as he reached out with his left hand and twisted the deadbolt. The lock clicked. Then he grasped the towel tied to the latch, took a breath, and yanked the rag down and back.

The towel's knot held, and the door came free of the frame with another click. It swung wide open, pouring light from the hall into the darkened apartment.

Three muted pops accompanied the door's swoosh as the assassin fired blindly into the darkness. The bullets drilled through the glass balcony door, shattering it and sending huge fragments of glass down onto the floor.

A pause washed into the room. Dak knew the man had to be confused. He added to the confusion by letting go of the towel. The door's pneumatic piston at the top pushed it closed on the killer and forced the intruder to brace it with a free hand.

The assassin stopped the door before it had fully closed and quickly stepped into the room, sweeping to his left first to check the kitchen.

Maybe that was luck. Perhaps it was a tactical error. Either way, when the man turned left, Dak sprang from behind him and drove the kitchen knife up toward the back of the man's skull while wrapping his other hand around the killer's forehead.

It was a move he'd used several times on covert missions. The kill was always clean—momentarily—and most importantly, silent.

This assassin, however, was no ordinary opponent.

The man sensed the movement behind him. A split second before the blade tip reached his neck, he twisted his arm and fired the pistol under his armpit at the enemy.

Dak was forced to abandon his initial plan and twist to the side, narrowly dodging bullets as they popped out of the muzzle.

The counter move didn't completely deny Dak's primary attack, though, and the point of his knife slid over the back of the assassin's neck, cutting a wide slice into flesh.

The attacker seemed unfazed by the wound and continued turning until he faced Dak. He raised his weapon and met Dak's eyes. The man's short dark hair was in disarray, as if he'd just rolled out of bed and decided to go kill someone. The brown eyes were the color of dark cocoa, and they stared back without remorse or doubt.

The man fired two more shots. The bullets missed Dak's head as he twisted and backed into the door. He swiped the knife's edge down and cut a deep gash into the gunman's forearm. The weapon dropped to the floor with a clatter. This time, the man grunted in pain.

The assassin grabbed Dak's wrist with his good hand and twisted hard to the side while pulling him forward. The awkward angle forced Dak to let go of the knife, and he dropped to his knees in time to free his wrist, but also catch a knee to the face.

The dark room flashed with colors as the blow drove Dak against the wall. He clawed at the floor, dazed and desperate to get up.

The assassin grabbed Dak by the ankle and pulled him back toward the doorway. The man quickly stomped on Dak's back. The deadening blow nearly knocked the air from Dak's lungs, and he gasped to hold on to consciousness.

A fast foot swung around, directed at Dak's temple. He narrowly missed what could have been a fight-ending shot to the head by rolling drunkenly to the side.

His head cleared slightly, and Dak saw an opening. Without thinking, he swung his other foot up, striking the assassin in the groin with his shin. The man groaned and doubled over as Dak bicycled his other knee up into the killer's nose.

The assassin shrieked and drew back. Dak pulled another knife from his belt and stabbed up at the enemy. The man recovered despite watering eyes and a bleeding nose and managed to deflect Dak's strike with the swing of a fist that struck Dak in the forearm.

The second knife flew out of Dak's hand, and the assassin moved in.

Fists flew in a flurry of attacks and counters. The killer was fast, but he was also hurt. The man tried to grapple and get Dak into a compromising position, but Dak had seen every one of those moves before.

The two danced into the living room, feet and knees swinging, blocking, dipping, and kicking. Dak landed a punch to the man's right ear and momentarily caused him to step back, but the retreat didn't last. Dak pushed toward him but caught a right hook as reward for his careless attack.

The killer tilted and kicked, landing another blow with his heel into Dak's midsection. Dak reeled, stumbling backward over the coffee table in the middle of the room. He rolled over it, deftly landing on his feet despite the thumping ache in his gut.

He breathed heavily and glowered at the assassin. "You don't have to do this, you know," Dak muttered. "You can walk out of here and the colonel will never know."

"Weak," the killer grunted. "He said you had gone soft."

"Bold talk from a man who isn't brave enough to come after me himself."

"Perhaps," the assassin partially agreed. "But then again, if he was, I wouldn't be getting a big payday."

Dak smiled. "So, Tucker's found some deep pockets to help with his little project."

"Stop talking," the killer said. "Time to die."

He surged forward.

Dak whipped the first of the two smaller knives from his belt and flung it at the attacker. It tumbled by the man, narrowly missing his shoulder. The second the first knife was out of his fingers, Dak grabbed the second and thew it hard.

The assassin, preoccupied with dodging the first knife, didn't have time to miss the second. The point of the blade sank into the man's chest, close to his right shoulder. The killer grimaced and stumbled toward Dak, still unwilling to give up the fight.

Dak dropped one step back toward the shattered balcony door. The assassin winced with every stride as he charged, the blade in his chest cutting and pricking nerves amid the bumps.

Dak braced himself for impact. The assassin tackled him, running Dak through the jagged remains of the door with a crash. He grabbed at Dak's shirt, and Dak did the same, except Dak let himself fall onto the balcony floor. In one fluid motion, he rolled back and kicked his feet up, planting his heels in the killer's midsection.

When Dak pushed his legs out, the assassin vaulted over the railing.

The last thing Dak saw in the man's eyes was sheer terror as he felt nothing but air beneath him. Dak rolled over and watched the body tumble downward until it hit the street below—right in front of a parked bus.

Dak struggled to his feet and stumbled back through the broken door into the living room. He looked around the previously spotless apartment. He sighed and returned to the bathroom where he'd left his bag, scooped it off the floor and then picked up the dead assassin's pistol.

He stuffed the gun into his belt and pulled his Nirvana T-shirt down over it, then opened the door. Panning the room one more time, he shook his head. "No way I'm getting that deposit back," he grumbled.

Then Dak stepped out into the corridor and let the door close behind him.

2

Dak closed the door to his truck and stared at the house. From all appearances, it looked just like all the other homes on the street. The dwellings were nice, clean, and definitely had more space than he'd ever needed before, or would probably ever need, but hardly suited for someone who'd made more than ten million dollars in the last few years.

Perhaps that was just it. The owners of the home weren't the ones who'd made the millions.

It was their kid.

The McClarens were a fairly typical, hard-working couple. Mrs. McClaren worked as a family therapist, while Mr. McClaren worked in hospital administration. Together, they pulled down a good income, but it paled in comparison to their son's.

To say Boston McClaren had a knack for video games would be the understatement of the young century. It would be like saying politicians have a knack for lying. The kid was a savant, a prodigy of the gaming world, and he'd made a small fortune in a short amount of time with his streaming channels.

The uneventful drive took just under two hours from Atlanta to Chattanooga, though it felt like days with Dak looking in the rearview mirror every fifteen seconds or so to make sure he wasn't being followed.

He'd been fortunate Tucker's assassin had been alone, but Dak wasn't naïve enough to believe that would always be the case. This was, he knew, the first of potentially many attacks the colonel would send his way, and if he weren't ready, Dak would end up on the losing end sooner or later.

All the more reason to keep moving.

He trudged toward the front door and was surprised when it opened. He stopped and waited as a short blond boy with black glasses appeared.

"Are you Mr. Harper?" the boy asked with a curious expression on his face.

"Depends on who's asking," Dak replied coolly.

The kid looked around for a second, then back to Dak. "I'm asking. You're Dak Harper, right?"

Dak snickered. *Kids.*

"If you're Boston McClaren, then I'm Dak. Just Dak. None of that Mr. Harper stuff."

"Because your dad is Mr. Harper?"

"Something like that."

Boston's cool blue eyes met with Dak's jade ones, and then the boy grinned. "Awesome. Come on in."

Dak looked around one last time, a touch confused, and then ambled up the steps and onto the front porch. He leaned forward and peered into the entryway as if trying to find something.

"Do...your parents let you answer the door for strangers?" Dak asked.

"My parents are in the kitchen," Boston explained. "They told me to get the door since they knew it was you."

"Ah." In his mind, Dak considered it reckless to let their boy get the door for someone who—so far—was a stranger.

Boston motioned toward the interior. "Would you like to come in? Or do you want to just stand out here to talk business?"

"Talk business? That's a little direct for a kid your age, don't you think?"

"I'm twelve. Not stupid," Boston groused. "And I'm eager to see what you can do." Boston looked around Dak's tall frame, checking the street in all directions. "You weren't followed, were you?"

Dak snorted and shook his head. "No. I wasn't followed."

"Are you sure? We're going to be dealing with some potentially dangerous characters if you get the gig."

"*If* I get the gig?" Dak mused.

"Okay, you're probably going to get it. Come on. I'll let you meet my parents, then we can get down to business."

Impressed and still a little confused by the enigmatic boy, Dak nodded and followed him into the house. Boston closed the door behind him and locked it before leading the way to the left into the kitchen. A wide living room with white walls and black shelves to the right connected to a corridor that led toward the rear of the house.

Dak was immediately overwhelmed with the smells of onions and peppers, and something he thought might be beef, but slightly different.

"My mom is making veggie tacos," Boston said as he closed the door.

Dak frowned behind the boy's back as he led the way into the kitchen. *This has to be the most surreal thing I've ever done,* he thought.

He followed the boy into the kitchen, still uncertain if he should just walk in like this. Mrs. McClaren was the first to look up. Her golden hair hung in three knotted braids on the back of her head. She wore a light blue T-shirt with a white flower-covered apron over it. She busily stirred a pan loaded with what looked like ground beef but Dak realized was a vegetarian version. Still, the aromas hanging in the room caused his mouth to water.

"Oh hi," the woman at the stove said. "You must be Dak. Nice to meet you." She flashed a welcoming smile at him but kept stirring the meat. "Excuse me for not shaking your hand. Gotta keep this moving around so it doesn't overcook."

"Not a problem."

"Nice to meet you," Boston's father said from near the refrigerator. He chopped onions and peppers with a large kitchen knife, not unlike the one Dak had used earlier that morning. He figured that was a detail these people didn't need to know.

"Nice to meet you, too," Dak said.

"I'm John and this is Shelly. You're welcome to have lunch with us if you like. It should be ready in a few minutes."

"I'm not that hungry," Dak lied, trying to be polite.

"Well, if you change your mind, you're welcome to stay."

"Thanks," Dak said. "I appreciate that."

John was a few inches under six feet tall, slightly taller than his wife. The man had scruffy brown hair with hints of blond underneath it. His jeans and Tennessee Volunteers T-shirt completed a casual ensemble that could be worn comfortably at home or at the grocery store.

"Come on," Boston urged, reaching out to pull the newcomer through the house. "Let's go to my office."

"Office?"

"Yeah. I have an office. I know that must be weird for you to hear since I'm twelve. I get that a lot. Other kids have playrooms. I have an office."

Dak looked around as if lost for the first time in his life. He raised his eyebrows as if to say something, then lazily shook his head. "Lead the way, boss."

Boston chuckled a little and walked down a short hallway before turning left into a white room. Black shelves contained collectible action figures and objects from science fiction movies and television series. A few superheroes from the comics universe were also present on his desk in the middle of the left-hand wall. The room, however, was remarkably clean, and Dak had a difficult time believing it was really the boy's.

"So, just for future reference," Dak began, settling in a club chair near the door, "I don't think it's smart for us to meet a lot in person like this." *Actually, I can't believe your parents are letting you meet with a complete stranger you found on the internet.* He kept that thought to himself.

"First of all," Boston said as he took a seat in his white ergonomic desk chair, "I cleared everything with them. Second, I'm a good judge of character."

"Okay."

"I did my research on you."

"You did?" Dak sounded more surprised than he intended. The kid was disarming; Dak had to give him that.

"Of course," Boston spun around and hovered over the keyboard at his computer. In seconds, his fingers flew across the keys, pecking away rapidly. Then the computer monitor on the right flicked to life. Two others remained dark.

"You think you have enough screens there, kid?" Dak asked, joking.

"Any more than this, and it gets distracting," Boston said. "One is for my live-streams so people can see me while I play. I answer questions from other players, give tips, that sort of thing while they watch."

Humbled, Dak chewed on his lower lip.

"So, let's talk about your first assignment," Boston went on.

"Wait," Dak stopped him. "Isn't there anything else you'd like to know about me? Who I am? What I do for a living? Maybe I'm a serial killer."

Boston chuckled. "Like I said, I did my research. And my research is always thorough. I know you were Delta Force. That's no small feat to get in with those guys. That special ops group is the kind of team they make movies or television series about. I know that you were wrongly accused, based on some public info I found. And that your name was cleared."

Dak hoped the kid didn't know about his quest to exact revenge on the men who'd betrayed him. Then again, how would he know? That kind of thing wasn't the sort of stuff that made the papers.

Dak stumbled for words. "Um, okay. So, what does this gig pay, exactly?"

"Great question. It depends on the item and how hard it will take to get. This first one pays fifty grand. If that's okay."

Dak felt himself lean back in the chair at the statement. "Fifty? What are you wanting me to do, raid Fort Knox?"

"Nothing so crazy," Boston reassured. "Although Peru can be tricky."

"Peru? What's in Peru?"

The boy's eyebrows shot up, and he gazed back at his guest with wide open eyes. "What isn't in Peru? It's the home of Machu Picchu, the Nazca Lines, and tons of history. Not to mention Lima is perched right on the cliffs overlooking the ocean. I really want to visit there someday."

Dak stared at his host, still trying to process the conversation. "Sounds like you have a thing for Peru."

"History and travel in general." Boston replied.

"I see. So, what am I going there for... exactly?"

"An artifact that's been missing for almost five hundred years. It's a weapon, actually. You'll have to be careful. Not that I need to tell you. Peru can be a dangerous place, from what I hear. I mean, for tourists it isn't, but for what I'm looking for, you will likely see the worst of it. For a guy like you, though, it should be a piece of cake."

"You're not exactly selling the job very well. How do you know I'm interested in getting into a dangerous situation? And what cake, exactly, am I trying to get a slice of?"

Boston flashed a mischievous grin and turned back to his computer. He clicked on the mouse, the screen blinked, and a new image appeared.

A shiny sword appeared on the monitor. The long, slender blade occupied the screen from top to bottom, with an ornate, curling hand guard just above the grip.

Dak leaned closer to get a better look.

"That's a replica," he said, disappointment evident as he eased back in his chair.

"I know it's a replica," Boston said with an eye roll. "Of course it's a replica. Like I said, no one has seen the real one in almost five hundred years."

"I don't understand."

Boston took a breath and sighed. "This is a replica of the sword carried by the conquistador Francisco Pizarro. I want you to find it and bring it back to me."

3

Dak had to admit the kid had piqued his interest. There was no debating that.

"As in *the* Francisco Pizarro? The guy who tricked and massacred the Incas?"

"Yep. That's him," Boston confirmed.

Dak's concerned expression tightened, sending wrinkles across his brow. "So, if this sword hasn't been seen in five centuries, how do you know where it is now?"

Boston offered a grin in reply. "It's what I do."

"I thought you do video games."

"Well, yes. That too. But I also search the dark web in the antiquities black markets, looking for unusual items. Up until now, I haven't had any way to recover them."

Dak pressed his lips together before he spoke. "I don't think the dark web is any place for a kid," he cautioned. "I've heard bad stuff about things that go on there."

"I avoid that stuff and focus exclusively on artifacts or other historical items, sometimes art," Boston explained. "Don't worry. I know what to avoid." His face paled. "I wish I had never heard of some of it. There are really bad people out there in the world, Mr. Harper...Dak," he corrected. "I can't offer to buy any of the things I find in case they tracked the purchase here to my home. And I can't go to these locations in person to buy them."

"Because you're a kid."

"Because they're not for sale from the people who buy them," Boston clarified. "I find items that are up for auction, then track them down to whoever bought them."

"How do you do that? The auctions should be anonymous."

The boy gave him a look of pity. "On the internet, nothing is anonymous, Dak."

The statement from the young man sent a shiver up Dak's spine and pebbled his skin.

"I have several fail-safes in place so I can't be tracked," Boston continued. "I'm safe, so long as I remain an observer. And even that has its risks."

"Risks?"

"A gamer I know, in his twenties, told me about this one time he got on the dark web to have a look around. Said he saw some disgusting things there. I didn't ask what. He told me he was minding his own business when all of a sudden a black box appeared on his screen, and the words *I see you* appeared. He unplugged the computer and got a new one. Needless to say, he's more careful now."

"That sounds...strange."

"Scary is what it is," Boston said. "I have no intention of letting that happen to me."

"So," Dak steered, "you find these lost artifacts or relics and then what? You hire someone like me to go retrieve them from people who are clearly a different kind of bad?"

Boston's eyes shifted to the right for half a second and then returned to his guest. "Yeah, pretty much."

"And how many of these items have you located so far?"

"Twenty-one."

Dak's eyebrows nearly blew the roof off the house. "Seriously?"

"Yeah. Of course, some of those might change hands at some point. If that happens, they'll be lost again unless someone else posts them for auction."

Another question had been nagging at Dak, like a cat tugging on a loose sweater string.

"How can you verify these artifacts are real?"

"Good question," Boston said, crossing his arms over his chest. "This is one of those instances where the free market, or the underground one, takes care of itself. If you try to sell something that isn't legit, you don't stick around for very long."

"Self-policing, huh?"

"Something like that. I've heard stories of people who tried to sell forgeries on the black market. When they were discovered, it didn't end well for the sellers."

Dak's expression remained stoic. "That's kind of heavy for a kid your age to be hearing."

Boston shrugged. "I'm twelve, not five. You should see some of the cartoons I watch."

"Still. You're just a kid. Why all the interest in this stuff? You should be playing sports with your friends or—"

"Video games?" Boston cut him off.

"I was going to say school."

Boston beamed. "I do mostly homeschool."

Dak hadn't considered that option. He quickly changed the subject back to the job. "You're assuming I want to throw myself into a dangerous scenario like that."

Boston nodded. "True. Am I wrong?"

Dak thought about it for a second, weighing his options. He knew the kid was right. He just didn't want to admit it. And he didn't need to remind himself that Tucker was still out there on the hunt. His mind flashed back to the incident in Atlanta mere hours before.

"No," Dak finally agreed. "I need something that keeps me on the move. I can't tell you why."

"Don't want you to," Boston said, attempting to put Dak's mind at ease.

"From now on, our meetings need to be virtual if possible. I don't want these...activities," he said the word with a hint of cynicism, "to bring any danger to you or your family. Frankly, I don't think we should be having this meeting in person, but I'll confess: I'm intrigued. This gig is exactly what I need right now. And if you're serious about what you're offering to pay, well, I'm in."

"Great."

"So, who has the blade?"

Boston offered a condescending glare. "That's where the investigation really comes in. I can offer probable locations based on internet service providers. After that, you'll have to do some digging around. Every now and then we might get lucky."

"Lucky?" Dak tilted his head to the right.

"Yeah. You know how criminals really get caught, right?"

Dak released an easy grin. "They blab to someone about what they did."

"Exactly. Doesn't usually take too long for these guys to spill the beans. Thanks to social media, it's even easier."

"Criminals use social media?"

"More than you'd think. I believe it's their way of trying to look innocent and normal. They're also not too savvy when it comes to using VPNs. You know what those are, right?"

"Private internet service providers?"

"Yes, essentially. A VPN is like a tunnel into the web that only you have access to. They're not impossible to crack, but extremely difficult and time consuming. From what I hear." Boston added the last part quickly. "Most of these people in the auctions don't use those because they're not worried about the others in the auction. The ones who are careful will be much harder to track down. As my dad always says, we should start with the path of least resistance first."

Dak huffed. "I agree."

Boston beamed back at him. "Stick with me, kid. You might learn a few things."

Dak snorted at the joke.

The light mood in the room faded with Boston's smile. "This is going to be difficult, Dak. All of these are. But it's important. These are items that should be in a museum."

"Or your collection."

Boston shook his head, as if the barb didn't register. "No, I have a collection of things that were easy enough to acquire, at legitimate auctions. But I hope to open my own gallery someday. Would be cool to have a sort of museum of artifacts."

Dak had read the kid wrong, though he shouldn't have been surprised at that fact. The kid may have been twelve, but he didn't talk or act like someone that age. He wasn't preoccupied with stupid online videos, and despite the fact he played video games a good amount of time, Boston didn't seem to be obsessed with them. They were his job—at twelve—and had provided a good lifestyle for his family, a lifestyle Dak imagined the boy's parents were grateful to have.

"So," Dak said, ready to get started, "I'm going to Lima."

"Yes." Boston swiveled around and picked up a thin charcoal-black folder from the top of his desk. A white label on the top simply read "Pizarro."

He handed the folder to Dak, who took it and opened it. "What is this? Mission briefing?"

"Something like that," Boston confirmed. "In there, you'll find the details you need to get you close to the sword."

Dak looked through the details. The kid had narrowed down the search area to a few square miles, but that still left hundreds of thousands of people as potential targets.

"You'll be looking for someone with a lot of money," Boston said. "Probably a drug dealer. It's possible we could be searching for the head of a cartel."

"Most of the big cartels in Peru now are Mexican." Dak mused. "Last I heard."

He thought back to his old friend and ex-teammate who'd joined one of the most notorious cartels in Mexico. It was an episode from Dak's life he wished he could forget, but the past couldn't be changed. Only the future offered a blank slate, and he had to focus on that.

This job was going to help him shake Colonel Tucker, and eventually—maybe—make things right with the woman he loved.

He banished thoughts of her for now. They would only serve as a distraction.

"If there's a cartel boss buying up old artifacts," Dak said, "I think I know someone who can help me track them down."

Boston grinned at the comment. "I was hoping you'd say that. Otherwise, this whole operation would take a lot longer."

"Not saying it won't take time," Dak countered. "You're not putting me on a timer, are you?"

"No," Boston said, shaking his head. "Nothing like that. And I will pay you however you like."

"Obviously, cash is almost always best, but I also know it's not easy to get big sums like what you're talking about. Wire transfer is fine. I can send you the account information. You *do* know what a wire transfer is, right?"

Boston's head sagged as he put on a disparaging glare. "Duh."

"Hey, I have to keep reminding myself that you're twelve. Okay? This isn't exactly usual activity for anyone, much less a kid."

"That's understandable. But yes, I can transfer the money to wherever you say. And I will also take care of all travel costs. Flights, meals, hotels, the usual." The boy turned around and picked up a white envelope sitting on the corner of the desk. He handed it to Dak.

The man took it and opened the fold. He looked inside at several large bills.

"That's five thousand to cover anything you might need for the trip."

Dak blinked rapidly at the envelope's contents. He had to admit, the kid had his act together.

"Cool." Dak folded the file and stood up. "I guess I'll get started."

Boston stood as well and extended his hand. The guest shook it, his fingers wrapping around the back of the boy's meager attempt at a firm grip.

"I look forward to working with you," Dak said.

"Same here. And be careful."

Dak's eyes squinted as he grinned. "No promises."

4

"Lima? As in Peru?" Will Collins did nothing to hide his disbelief. "You know, I guess nothing should surprise me when it comes to your life."

"I was wondering when you'd catch on to that," Dak replied coolly.

"Oh, I caught on a long time ago. That incident with the desk chair at the beach pretty much solidified it."

Dak laughed at the memory. "Good times."

"Good? Me being strapped to an office chair with explosives under my butt doesn't exactly qualify as good. Good is sleeping in until nine in the morning, or having a good tequila on the beach, or the touch of—"

"Okay, I get it. Thanks."

It was Will's turn to laugh. "All right. All right. You get my point. So, what's in Lima?"

Dak stood on the edge of the rock, staring down at the valley below where the Tennessee River snaked its way through the lush green hills and mountains. A railroad also weaved its way through the bottom of the valley, connecting to several shipping centers that had been constructed over the years. The facilities, along with the small town around them, were the single blight on the otherwise pristine natural setting the view from Sunset Rock had to offer.

A breeze tousled Dak's hair, and a red-tailed hawk cruised on the air currents hundreds of feet overhead.

"I took a job," Dak said, aware that a rebuke would come soon after the statement.

"What? Are you crazy? What kind of job did you take down in Lima? It's security, isn't it? I bet you're going to be a bodyguard for some soccer player."

Dak snorted. "No. Nothing like that. My employer is American. I can't tell you anything else about them other than that. But it's a good gig. Pays well. And it keeps me on the move."

"Okaaay," Will said, elongating the word. Dak could tell he didn't fully accept the explanation yet. "So, what is it you'll be doing for this job?"

"Recovering artifacts for a private collector."

"Artifacts? Like old relics, pottery, that kind of stuff?"

"Sort of. More like things that have been acquired on the antiquities black market. We're talking extremely rare stuff, Will."

"Expensive too, I bet."

"Yeah."

Will considered the explanation for a couple of seconds before speaking again. "So, what do you need my help with exactly?"

"My employer can narrow the location of these artifacts to a pretty tight area, but he can't isolate them completely. I need you to help me find out who purchased these things so I can—"

"Go there and steal them?"

"I was going to say reclaim them."

"Reclaim? Did your employer own them previously?"

"No, but—"

"So, you're stealing them."

Dak sighed and rubbed the back of his head. "Yeah, but in a Robin Hood kind of way."

"Oh, you're giving them to the poor?"

"Uh, no. Not exactly. My employer is a multimillionaire."

"You do realize that is nothing like Robin Hood, right?"

"Look, it's complicated. Okay? The people I'm taking these things from are bad people. They're buying up priceless artifacts and relics from the black market. My employer wants to put these items in a museum or give them to the authorities. He's not doing it to keep them for his own collection."

"Ah," Will said. "So, it's a he."

"Yes," Dak confessed with exasperation. "I work for a guy. There. You just cut the population in half. Only a few billion more to narrow it down."

Will laughed into the phone. "Take it easy, big guy. I'm just messing with you. Of course I'll help."

"And I'm happy to give you a percentage of whatever he pays me for this gig."

"A percentage, huh?" Will sounded skeptical.

"Yeah. How does five grand sound for just doing a little internet snooping?"

Dak waited to hear the reaction. He wasn't sure if that was a lowball offer or if it was generous. From his perspective, it sounded like a lot of money. And he figured Will would feel the same, especially since there was almost no danger involved on his end.

"Just for doing a few Google searches?" Will chuckled. "Yeah, I think that could work."

Dak knew better than to think Will was serious for even a second about just using a public search engine. Will had resources, connections, and tools he could use to find almost anything, or anyone.

He'd been a gunrunner, primarily for nations run by corrupt governments or dictators. He supplied those who would stand up against tyranny, even though it still put him on several hit lists—not to mention the risks he took within the nations he called home.

Recently, Will had been lying low, though Dak suspected his friend was still working the grind and making money by the truckload.

"Good," Dak said. "Then we have an accord."

"Accord?" Will laughed. "What are you, a seventeenth-century pirate?"

"Okay."

Will bellowed through the phone. "Sorry, I couldn't resist. I'm sorry. What was it you were wanting me to find?"

Dak took a deep breath and exhaled, relieved to be back on task. "There's a sword. It's old."

"Figured that much."

Dak ignored him. "Apparently, my employer believes it was owned by the conquistador Francisco Pizarro."

A quiet whistle blew through the earpiece. "Wow. Your guy really is going big on that one."

"Why do you say that?"

"The sword of Pizarro? I mean, I don't know as much about history as you, but I would imagine that particular weapon would fetch a pretty handsome price on the black market—if it's authentic."

"Not up to us to decide if it's the real thing or not," Dak said. "I'm just supposed to collect. That's it."

"You make it sound so simple," Will huffed.

"We both know that won't be the case. I'll do some snooping around and see what I can find. I can't make you any promises. The kinds of people you're talking about aren't easily found."

"Hey, I can find someone else who wants to make an easy five grand." There was no reality behind Dak's statement, but he would have been remiss to not poke the bear just a little.

"Yeah right," Will said, not buying it. "We both know that's not true."

It was Dak's turn to laugh. "Yeah, you're probably right. Let me know when you have something. I'll be waiting."

"Sure thing. If you're talking about a sword that's a few hundred years old, I imagine there will be some chatter about that. Especially if it belongs to who you say. Pizarro was a famous historical figure."

"Not to mention that he died with that sword in his hand, the very sword he'd used to kill no telling how many indigenous people."

"I didn't know the part about him dying with it."

"Yes," Dak confirmed. "There was an assassination plot by some of his former supporters. They entered his estate, called him out, and killed him with a blade through the throat."

"That'll do it."

"Not before he took down a couple of them first. Pizarro was a strong swordsman. There was no way he would go down without a fight."

"So, the sword he died with—fighting off murderers." Will mused. "Yeah, I would say that weapon is worth some coin."

"And it's an important piece to my employer. I don't know what he has planned for it, but I imagine it's going to a museum."

"Sure," Will said, skeptical. "Look, I don't care what he does with it. I'm bored, and making a quick five will get me out of my funk."

"Glad to hear it."

"I'll call you when I find something. For now, maybe you should lie low and try not to attract any attention. I heard about what happened in Atlanta."

"That wasn't my fault. And Tucker should learn to leave well enough alone."

"We both know he's not going to do that."

Dak sighed. "Yeah, I know."

5

The eleven-year-old boy wiped the sweat off his brow with the loose sleeve of his ragged white shirt. Even though autumn in the Southern Hemisphere had arrived weeks before, the warmth of summer lingered.

His black hair was damp at its fringes, and beads of perspiration rolled down his light brown cheeks. The blazing sun overhead didn't help, and there were no signs of cloud cover anywhere on the horizon to offer relief.

He snugged the gray backpack tighter against his shoulder and continued down the sidewalk.

Hector Mamani didn't make eye contact with anyone. It was one of the rules he'd made sure to implement when he'd been recruited as a courier. *Recruited was a fine term*, he thought. He'd been forced into servitude, and there was no getting out. Well, there was *one* way. There had been others who'd failed the boss and abruptly disappeared. Hector had no intention of taking that route. He wouldn't disappoint Señor Diaz.

Hector continually scanned the streets and sidewalks, noting every passerby as they approached. He also kept a keen eye on the cops that loitered in front of various businesses now and then. Some days were worse than others when it came to the police. Sometimes, Hector would only see one or two standing watch. Other days, he'd pass no fewer than six.

Fortunately, most of them were on the Diaz payroll, seemingly more than not. Still, Hector knew enough not to cross or make contact with the police if at all possible.

He tightened the bag on his shoulder again, the weight in it pulling down on him with a constant, heavy drag. He didn't dare look inside or try to adjust the object within. Doing so would draw attention. He knew better.

So he continued down the sidewalk, doing his best to look like he was a boy on the way home from school.

He arrived at his destination on one of the street corners in the heart of the city. A bookstore called La Bonita Libro (The Beautiful Book) occupied the prime corner real estate. The smell of rich coffee drifted out of the building and into his nostrils. Hector had never really liked the taste of coffee—like most kids—but he did enjoy the smell of it, especially when being brewed.

The boy took a quick look around and then ducked into the shop. The door opened with a creak and he cringed, as he did every time he had to make a drop here.

He let the door close slowly behind him as he walked straight ahead. The clerk at the register—a muscular man with tattoos on his arms and neck, inclined his head at Hector. It was the same greeting the menacing man gave every time Hector brought his daily delivery.

With a nervous swallow and a nod, Hector continued into the aisles of books, heading toward the back of the store.

The scent of coffee grew stronger from the pot in the back where an array of pastries and treats was offered. Hector knew only a scant few people ever came into the bookstore for the food, and his employer usually allowed him to take some of the fare home for his efforts—if the man was satisfied with the day's haul.

Hector eyed the treats hungrily as he passed the display case, hoping today would be one of those good days. The *picarones* (sweet, sticky donuts) and *alfajores* (round sandwich cookies filled with a sweet caramel creme) were his favorite.

Whenever Hector was permitted to grab a few goodies on the way out of the store, the aches and pains in his muscles almost melted away. Almost.

Hector's father died when the boy was only five. It was, supposedly, a mining accident, but Hector had his doubts. Though he could never voice them publicly—and wasn't brave enough to in secret—he always felt that the accident that killed his father was more likely due to negligence than bad luck. The cartel, he knew, viewed peasants from the *tugurizadas*, or slums, as expendable. Hector's people weren't considered people at all, but more as beasts of burden to be used and disposed of when their usefulness diminished.

Two years after his father's death in the mines, Hector began working for the cartel at the age of seven.

His job wasn't as bad as some of the other children, but he knew that would change when he turned twelve. When he reached that age, the cartel would start using him down in the mines where he would no longer see the light of day until Sundays.

For now, though, Hector remained a courier. He carried illegally mined gold from underground mines hidden in the suburbs and slums or, in some cases, under businesses like this one on the outskirts of the cities. The cartel even operated mines beneath a couple of farms beyond the city limits.

Hector didn't have to go out there very often, and when he did, it was on the back of an old motorcycle since walking would take too long.

He and the other couriers—usually young boys—carried the gold ore to the drop spots where receivers would collect the haul. After that, the gold was refined and sold down at the port, where it could be taken overseas and resold.

The cartel's use for gold didn't stop there.

Money from cocaine would go toward buying legally mined gold bars, which the cartel would then sell for clean cash.

Using these methods, the Los Lobos cartel was able to launder their money while doubling their revenue simply by diversifying their business.

That's how Hector's mother described it, though she only did so at the boy's behest and warned him to never tell anyone about what she'd said. He recalled the night of their conversation and vowed to never share the information with anyone.

Hector entered the short hallway in the back, just beyond the bakery, and passed two bathroom doors before stopping at a black, nondescript door at the end of the corridor.

He took a deep breath before knocking, still thinking about the night his mother told him everything. She, along with many of the other women in the tugurizadas, worked in the cocaine processing facilities. Every day, they turned out bricks of white powder to be shipped to neighboring Colombia or to Mexico, where the cartel could move the product north into the United States.

Hector's mother loathed the cartels and how they treated the people, but the drug dealers paid better than any job she could take in the city—although not enough to allow her to leave the tugurizadas. Not yet.

One night, in a fit of tears, Hector's mother promised that someday she would save up enough money to move away, perhaps out into the country, where they could start a new life.

Such fanciful dreams barely registered to Hector. This was the only life he'd ever known.

A sliding panel at the top of the door opened, and dark eyes surrounded by smoke stared down at him.

The bushy-haired man offered a curt nod and then slid the panel shut again. A second later, three locks clicked and the door swung open. A pungent odor of cigarette smoke smacked Hector in the face a second before the actual gray haze wafted over him. He held back the urge to cough and stepped inside, just as he'd done countless times before.

The man at the door closed it shut behind him and motioned to the back corner of the room, where two men sat at a table. One counted stacks of money and coins, while the other sorted through gold ore much like the haul in Hector's backpack.

Another man sat in an office just beyond the table. The tiny workspace was separated by a large glass window and another door. The two men working at the table barely noticed Hector as he passed, walking toward the office.

The man inside turned his head and motioned for the boy to enter.

Hector was glad to get out of the smoke-filled room, even though the office only offered a partial respite from the dense tobacco fog.

The man in the office stood and indicated a scale on his desk. The man had a thick mustache and matching black hair. He was the person Hector reported to, and the one who paid him.

His name was Ricardo Flores, and he was second only to the cartel boss, Fernando Diaz.

Hector didn't need to be told what to do. He opened his backpack and carefully poured the ore out onto the scale to be weighed.

Flores watched with disinterest until the bag was empty. He'd overseen the process hundreds of times every week for years. Hector sometimes wondered if the man ever got a day off, other than Sundays when no one in the operation worked. It was the one quirk Diaz had. He always attended mass on Sunday and expected everyone within his operation to do the same.

Hector's mother said it was because the boss believed their business would be blessed. The boy had a difficult time believing God would bless a murderous drug dealer. He had a feeling his mother had the same doubts.

Flores adjusted the scale and made a note on a clipboard after reading the final tally. Then he nodded approvingly.

"Good work," Flores said with a hint of sincerity. He turned and plucked two bills from a stack near a computer and then took four coins from another pile. He extended his hands to Hector, who then held out his palm to receive his reward. Hector knew better than to ever put his hands out first. There were stories about how Flores had cut off one boy's hands because he expected payment before the man was ready. The rumor was that the violent and gruesome act was done to set an example, that all of the workers would be paid when the boss was ready.

Flores nodded, and Hector extended his right hand. The man pressed two, ten-sole bills into Hector's palm, and one, five-sole coin.

Hector bowed his head in thanks. "Thank you," he added on top of the gesture, doing his best to make sure that the man who paid him understood how grateful he was. It was one of his better paydays, though he'd made up to thirty before.

"You're welcome, Hector," Flores said.

The boy appeared puzzled. "You...you know my name?" he stammered.

The man smiled under his broom of a mustache. "I make it a point to know the names of anyone I deem worthy," Flores said smoothly. "You are a good worker, Hector. You're never late, and you are never short on your count."

Hector knew what he meant by the last part. Before he left the mine, a counter weighed his load before sending him out of the distribution house. That measure was sent to Flores, who would double-check to make certain nothing was missing.

Another horror story Hector heard was about another boy who'd accidentally lost a few grams of ore on his way to the bookstore. Rumor had it that Flores removed two of the boy's fingers, one for each gram he deemed "stolen." Hector wanted to believe that tale wasn't true, but he couldn't purge it from his mind.

"Tell me, Hector. How is your mother?"

The question caught the boy off guard. "She is well, sir."

"Good. That's good." Flores reached over to his desk and plucked a smoldering cigar from a black porcelain ashtray.

Hector didn't like the man's tone. It carried a sloshing bucket of creepiness that reeked of a lewd stench.

"I don't suppose she's remarried since the unfortunate passing of your father." Flores made the statement without regard for how it could affect the boy. The only effort he made to soften his words was a slight twitch of a smile at the corner of his lips.

Hector hung his head, then shook it side to side. "No, señor. Mama hasn't been the same since my father died. She's married to her job now."

The boy knew better than to combat the powerful man with his words. Hector wanted to spit at him for the insinuation. He was only eleven, but he wasn't stupid. Flores made a selfish inquiry, stepping on the grave of Hector's father in the process. Unfortunately, there was nothing the young boy could do about it. Not yet anyway. Deep down, in the shadowy recesses of his mind, a vengeful spark forged a plan. Someday he would be bigger. Someday he would have enough money and influence to take out Flores and his goons, and perhaps even the entire cartel operation.

Flores smiled fiendishly at him, though there was no way the man could read beyond the blank expression on the boy's face. It was a mask Hector wore often, especially in this place. He gave away no emotion, no concession of his private thoughts.

"She is a beautiful woman," Flores mused. He turned to the stack of cash on the table and lifted another bill from it. This one had a 50 on it. "Give this to your mother," Flores said. His words were tainted with both generosity and malice. He passed the bill to Hector.

The boy's jaw almost dropped wide open, and it was all he could do to keep his eyes from betraying his shock at the sum.

Without the slightest consideration, Flores had just handed him double the amount he'd been paid for the job. Nerves started tingling inside him, causing his flesh to pebble and his gut to tighten.

He'd never carried that much money before. His mind swirled with the possibilities, ideas that he had to quickly usher away.

"Thank you," Hector managed. "I am grateful."

"I'm sure you are. Now, tomorrow, I don't want you hauling from the mines."

"No?" The comment surprised the boy, and he wondered what devious plan Flores might have for him.

"No. You're too valuable to merely be used as a mule. You are trustworthy, reliable. You have never come up short on your hauls, and you're always on time. Some of my other carriers get distracted by candy carts or pretty girls on the sidewalk. Others are tempted with football in the streets or sandlots or playing in the park. They think only a few minutes won't hurt. But when they're late, I'm late. And I don't like being late. Señor Diaz does not appreciate tardiness. Nor do I."

"Señor Diaz?" Hector stuttered the moniker, as though saying the sacred name of the Almighty.

"Yesss," Flores said, elongating the word so it carried extra weight. "He has issues, on occasion, with deliveries not arriving in a timely matter. But that's something I've never had to worry about with you."

"I do my best, sir."

"I know you do, Hector." The man flashed his nicotine-stained teeth. "Which is why I'm not going to allow you to become a miner."

The statement sent a spear of hope through the boy's chest. "You're not?"

"No. I can't have my best, most trusted courier down in the tunnels chipping rocks all day. I have a more important task for you, my boy."

Hector waited for the man to continue. He didn't want to say anything lest he invoke a change of heart from Flores and incite the man's wrath.

Flores inclined his head, looking down at the boy just over the bottoms of his eyelids. "As I've said, I need someone I can trust. The gold is just one part of our business. You've taken a few items to the docks for me before, yes?"

Hector nodded. "Yes, sir. A few times."

"Well, those occasions were another in a line of tests. You have no idea what you were carrying in those backpacks, do you?"

Hector's head swiveled back and forth.

"Again, why you're the perfect man for the job." Flores turned and grabbed a tanned backpack from a table against the back wall. He lifted it with only slight effort and handed it to Hector. "Take this down to the Port of Callao. Dock 79. A man named Chocho will meet you there."

Hector took the bag and realized immediately how much weaker he was than Flores. He slipped it over his shoulders and felt the weight nearly drag him back onto the floor. He fought for his balance, though, and was able to maintain it enough to keep steady.

"How will I know what he looks like?" Hector asked.

"He will be looking for you. When you get there, Chocho will take the bag. Understood?"

Hector responded with a sharp nod. "Yes, sir. Thank you."

"Good. He will be waiting for you."

Hector turned and walked out of the office. He passed the money counters like a ghost, as if they didn't even notice he was there. They continued running cash through machines that flipped the bills in rapid succession, posting red digital numbers on a display counting up into the hundreds within seconds. The machines made a whirring sound over top of the paper flicking.

The man at the metal security door saw Hector coming and stood up from his stool. He pulled the door open and tipped his head up once, as if to say goodbye, then closed the door again once Hector was back in the bookstore.

The boy looked down at the money in his hand. He just now realized how tightly he'd been squeezing the cash. He couldn't afford to lose that kind of money. It was several days' wages and would help his mother immensely.

He considered stuffing it in one of his pockets, but paranoia gripped him and he feared it might fall out onto the sidewalk. Hector knew, even at his young age, that his precious bills would either be scooped up by passersby or blown away by the coastal breeze within seconds. He couldn't risk keeping the money in his pocket.

Then again, if he tripped on his way to the wharf, he might stumble and fall, and in the process brace himself with his hands, thus losing the money that way.

Standing in the back of the bookstore, alone, he decided to stuff the money into the sock on his right foot. That way, he'd be protected from his two greatest fears, along with securing the funds from bullies he might run into along the way.

He'd had his pockets turned inside out three times on his way home from making deliveries to Señor Flores, but never while actually carrying the man's goods. The thugs and pickpockets of Lima knew better. To steal from Flores was to steal from Fernando Diaz. No one survived making that mistake.

Satisfied with his security measures, Hector strolled through the bookstore, waved to the man working the register, and stepped out onto the sidewalk.

He did so without looking and nearly got bowled over by a tall gringo with hair as dark as midnight shadows and eyes the color of emeralds.

"Excuse me," the man said in perfect Spanish. "I didn't mean to run over you."

Hector looked up at the man, mesmerized for a second. "It's...it's fine. I should watch where I'm going."

"Perhaps we should both be more careful," the man said. "I hope you don't bump into any more clumsy tourists." The words came with a kind smile. Then the man bowed his head and walked away.

Hector watched him for far longer than he intended—until the man vanished into the crowds of people walking along the sidewalk. When the gringo was gone, Hector turned toward the oceanfront and began the long walk down to the port.

6

Dak swam through the tide of people flowing in the opposite direction on the sidewalk. He glanced back over his shoulder a couple of times to make sure the boy he'd nearly collided with was okay, but the kid was already gone.

He shook his head at the thought of being so small and yet out on his own in a big city like Lima. There were more dangerous cities for a kid to be alone, but it still bothered Dak. When he was young, he'd grown up running around his suburban neighborhood with other children, playing in the park, walking down the streets without fear.

Things were different back then. And so was the location.

He couldn't imagine leaving a child on his own to run around the suburbs—let alone a big city—with the current climate of crime and abductions seemingly happening every day. The thought of it made him sick, and also glad that he didn't have any kids.

He and Nicole had talked about it once, about starting a family when he was done with the military, but neither of them had been ready to settle down. She wanted to live abroad, work in new places, and experience the cultures of foreign lands. So Dak went with it since he didn't care either way about having a family beyond her, but his work and hers had slowly unraveled their relationship until there wasn't a thread left.

Since arriving in Lima earlier that morning, Dak had seen dozens of kids on the streets—all of them unsupervised or unaccompanied by an adult. There'd been several carrying backpacks, much like the one the boy he'd just bumped into bore on his shoulders.

Based on the time of day, the kids should have been in school, but Dak knew from his short research of the area that many kids from the tugurizadas didn't go to school. They were resigned to a life of poverty, scraping by in the dumpsters or stealing from local vendors for just enough sustenance to survive one more day in squalor.

Dak hadn't visited the slums of Lima yet, and he wasn't sure he wanted to. The tugurizadas were filthy from what he'd heard, and he doubted they were a safe place to be. The safety issue didn't concern him much, he could handle himself, but there was no reason to tempt fate if he didn't have to. He'd spent enough time in the slums of other big cities to know that sometimes even the most battle-hardened soldier could get caught off guard.

The thought reminded him to stay alert and he let his eyes drift over the swarms of people to make certain he wasn't being followed or watched.

By now, Colonel Tucker surely knew of his assassin's fate—how the man had fallen from the top of a building. Dak reasoned he'd left town soon enough to be impossible to track, but Tucker wouldn't let up. Sooner or later, Dak knew he'd face another of the colonel's mercenaries.

At the next intersection, Dak double-checked the street names and then turned left. Dozens of signs hung over the sidewalk ahead—each promoting a cantina or café or restaurant. Some had a few tables reaching out onto the promenade, effectively cutting the walkway in half. As a result, pedestrians were forced to skirt around the tables that awkwardly took up space with nothing separating them from passersby but an imaginary boundary.

Dak continued walking, his eyes constantly darting back and

forth in search of trouble. His gaze locked on to a red-and-black metal sign with a bull engraved into it, and he quickened his pace.

He stopped under the sign and looked into the cantina. No words adorned the tinted windows or brick walls. Dak knew it had to be the right place. Will had told him to find a bar called El Toro Cantina, a place that only had a picture of a bull on the sign to identify it. Apparently, it was a known place for locals, and without the trappings of the other cantinas, it remained somewhat off limits to tourists—a fact Dak believed to be by design.

He took a breath, looked both directions down the sidewalk, and then pulled the door open.

The smell of cigars smacked him in the face. He grinned at the scent. It reminded him of his days with the team, back before they'd betrayed him and left him for dead in a cave. They smoked cigars together after every successful mission. Dak wondered if they had smoked one after attempting to kill him.

That line of thought wouldn't help. It was a rabbit hole he knew not to go down, and so he focused on the moment.

The door eased shut behind him with a creak as Dak took in the surroundings. Few people occupied the cantina. Two men sat at the bar with a stool between them, their heads drooped over mugs of beer. Off to the right, another man and a woman—both locals—munched on pieces of roasted meat and rice. Their worn and weathered faces betrayed years of hard work in the sun.

To his left, Dak spotted the man he'd come here to meet.

Peter Davenport sat alone in a booth farthest from the entrance. He noticed Dak standing in the entryway and immediately motioned for him to come over with a flick of his hand.

Dak glanced around one more time and then sauntered over to the booth. He stood over the table for a few seconds, waiting for an invitation to sit.

"You Doc Davenport?" Dak asked.

The man huffed, busily sprinkling pepper onto a piece of grilled chicken and rice. He set the pepper down and scanned the room deliberately—a sardonic look in his eyes. Then he lifted his gaze to meet Dak's. "You see some other old gringo in this joint?"

Dak made a show of checking the room again, then shook his head. "No. I suppose not."

"Then stop standing there like a putz and sit down."

Dak liked the man immediately.

He sat down across from Doc and waited for the man to chew a piece of chicken before swallowing it.

Crow's-feet stretched from the man's tanned face, the lines twitching and stretching with every movement of his jaw. His gray hair was swept to the right. He wore a light gray windbreaker and khakis. His white sneakers looked like he'd worn them right out of the store.

Dak folded his hands on the table and waited for the man to speak. Being a quick judge of character, Dak knew better than to interrupt a man like Doc when he was eating. This was a guy who was accustomed to being in charge and had a process for everything he did.

Will had skimped on the details regarding Dr. Peter Davenport, but a few key items helped fill in the gaps. Filling in gaps about people helped Dak understand the best way to communicate with an individual.

A retired naval physician, Davenport had spent most of his adult life in medicine. Then he'd abruptly moved to Lima, leaving the States behind just over eleven years ago. Dak knew the man was in his mid-sixties, but outside of that, Peter Davenport, or Doc as he liked to be called, was something of a mystery.

Dak sat in his seat, never pressing the conversation. He waited patiently as Davenport chewed through everything on his plate and then downed half a glass of golden lager. Then, when he was finished with the meal, Doc picked up a napkin, dabbed his mouth, then exhaled audibly.

"So, tell me how I can help you, grunty."

Dak's right eyebrow reached for the ceiling, but he said nothing at first.

"Oh," Doc huffed. "You didn't think I would do a little research on you before you showed up? I'm sure you did the same. You served in the army. Delta Force. Had some things go awry, got blamed for something you didn't do, then were cleared. Single. No children. Parents still alive. Blah blah blah."

"Yes, sir. All correct."

"I know it's correct, son. I did the research. What do you know about me?"

Dak shrugged. "Naval medical officer. After you retired, you left the States. My sources didn't tell me why you moved to Lima."

"You're a bit thin on my backstory, son. You got some of it right, though." The older man's face darkened with a distant pain—a memory that scratched at his steeled nerves.

Dak drew in a deep breath. He'd already passed the man's first test—an exercise in patience. Now Doc was throwing another trial Dak's way, and the younger man understood it clearly.

"Something happened," Dak said. "You were hurt. Not physically but emotionally. Whatever it was had to be pretty big for a tough guy like yourself, someone who worked their way up through the ranks and then applied all that discipline to the field of medicine." Dak's eyes fell to the wedding band on the man's ring finger. "I don't know that I should tread there, sir. But if I had to make an educated guess, I would say you lost your wife. Because you're still wearing your ring, that means she didn't leave you. And you didn't leave her. It's none of my business how she died, sir. And I don't want to be disrespectful."

Doc inclined his head slightly, driving away the painful memories with the mental whips he'd always used to focus on the present. The swallow in his throat gave away that he was losing the battle, and probably always lost it.

"Brain tumor," Doc said finally. "They diagnosed her with it just over eleven years ago. She was dead a month later." He noted the pity in Dak's eyes and scowled. "I don't blame myself, if that's what you're thinking, son. No physician could help her. Not me, not anyone. Sometimes people get sick. It always hurts someone. I suppose it was just my turn to lose the one person in the world I truly loved; the one person who understood me."

"Yes, sir," Dak said. "Sooner or later, we all have to take our turn in that bitter dance."

"Indeed, grunty. Indeed."

Doc raised his glass and tipped it toward Dak, then downed the remaining contents.

He slammed the glass back on the table with a satisfied "ah" and then leaned forward, folding his hands on the table to mirror Dak's.

"Will says you're looking for a sword," Doc said, casting a wary glance around the room. He spoke in a secretive voice, as if the walls themselves would betray the conversation to someone of ill intent.

"Yes, sir. That's correct."

"Not just any sword," Doc went on. "The fabled blade of Francisco Pizzaro, the infamous conquistador."

Dak merely nodded.

"Well, there are a few things you need to know before I help you out with this."

Dak waited, again exercising patience with the man.

A slight twitch in Doc's right eye betrayed his unspoken approval at another test passed. "First of all, in no way are we ever going to be known as some kind of team. None of this Doc and Dak malarkey if you were even thinking it."

Dak chuckled. "I wasn't." *Although now I am*, he thought.

"Good. Second, you need to understand the severity of the situation here. A few of the Mexican cartels have set up shop here, and they are a greedy, nasty bunch. They started moving in years ago. Felt like this region was an untapped resource. They were right. Now they're working with the Colombians in the cocaine business, shipping heroin from Mexico, and they've gotten into the mining industry here in Lima."

"Mining?"

Doc huffed and motioned to the waitress with two fingers, indicating how many beers he wanted brought to the table. The dark-haired woman in a red dress and white apron smiled and nodded, then walked behind the bar to pour the drinks.

"Gold mining," Doc clarified. "Big business in these parts. The government's got their sticky fingers all over it, too. Good to see some things are the same as back in the States."

Dak laughed at the statement. "Corruption knows no borders."

"Got that right."

The server brought the beers over and set them on the table. She left, and Dak waved his hand. "No, thanks. I don't drink while I'm working."

"I wasn't offering. These two are for me."

Dak snorted, only slightly embarrassed.

"Anyway," Doc continued after another long sip, "the cartels have several illegal mines here in the city, most of them in the suburbs underneath existing houses. They go in through the basements. These mines are deep, mind you, and extensive. The ore is extracted and brought into the city where it's weighed and then shipped out to who knows where to have it refined."

"They don't do the refining here?"

"A few of them do, but too much of that would draw attention from the local authorities. They don't want that."

"Sounds like a big operation."

"It is." Doc stole a look at the door as it opened. One of the men from the bar slogged through and out into daylight. Then the door closed again and the room fell back into its dreary, artificial light. "They get poor people from the tugurizadas to do the work. The ones down in the mines suffer the most. The cartels don't exactly care much about workplace conditions. They just want the ore. People die all the time down there. And if they don't die in the mines, they die from damaged lungs later on."

"Cartels are ruthless. There's no doubt about that."

"You're telling me. When I lost Maggie, I moved here to get away from the memories that lurked like ghosts around every corner. Lima was a place we'd never visited, but she'd always wanted to, mostly to head over to Machu Picchu. When I got here, I discovered what was going on behind the scenes. So, with nothing to lose, I made it my business to make life difficult for the cartels, as safely and as responsibly as possible."

"You don't seem like the safe and responsible type," Dak joked.

"Hey, I'm a doctor, son. Don't forget it." Doc hefted the first beer and drank half of it in seconds. "Anyway, I know how their operation works, how they move the gold, the money, and the drugs. There is a big problem, though."

"You need more manpower."

"Exactly. The cops are undermanned. And I'm only one guy. Not to mention I'm just some gringo from America. I don't have a ton of pull around here, and I'm not stupid enough to go out recruiting people to join some harebrained vigilante crew looking to knock off drug dealers."

Dak could already see where this was going but he decided to lead Doc to the finish line.

"So you can't just retire peacefully, hang out down here in Lima eating whatever it is that smells so good in here?"

"Those are the cigars," Doc said with a face so straight it could have been stone. "The food here is subpar. And to answer your question, no. I can't just sit idly by and watch innocent people be treated like expendable shell casings. They need someone to help."

"And I'm that someone?"

"Don't get cocky, kid. We're both that someone."

Dak chuckled again and nodded. "Fair enough."

"And this is one of those two-birds-with-one-stone kind of deals," Doc added. "The head of the biggest, baddest cartel in town is a guy by the name of Fernando Diaz. Cops can't touch him, and no up-and-coming magistrates would, either. His reach extends all over the city."

"Sounds like a tough guy to reach."

"It gets worse." Doc crossed his arms and held Dak's gaze. "No one knows where Diaz actually lives."

"How is that possible? Someone has to know." Dak wondered.

"Diaz keeps everything a secret, except for the boasting he does to his close associates, which is how I'm guessing your employer learned about the sword. Sooner or later, big egos love to show off. My point is, we're going to have to track him down, and that won't be easy. The man doesn't show his face in public often, and for good reason."

"You trying to convince me to walk away?"

"No. Just getting you prepared. I know you're not the type to walk away. You came for the conquistador's sword. My guess is you're going to get a pretty hefty sum for your efforts."

"And you want some of that payout?" Dak hedged.

"Nope. I have money. What I don't have is peace of mind, the kind that comes with killing a man like Diaz and razing his entire organization to the ground."

"You don't want anything?"

Doc looked indignant. "Are you hard of hearing? I just said the only thing I want is that cartel taken out. You must have been in too many firefights. How long were you over there in the Middle East, anyway?"

"Long enough," Dak said coolly. "And I heard you. I'm happy to pay you for your help, though, if you like."

Doc waved a dismissive hand. The thin haze of cigar smoke swirled around his fingers. "Not necessary. I appreciate your generosity, but I'm good."

Dak's mind switched gears to planning mode. Doc studied him as he schemed. "You said you know a lot about how the Diaz operation works."

"Yep." The former naval officer took another swig from his glass, nearly finishing the first.

"How do they move the ore?"

Doc coughed a laugh. "It ain't just ore they're moving, kid. The ore doubled the cartel's profits, sort of diversified their portfolio. Thing about it is, they can sell it to legit distributors all over the world. When that happens, there's currency exchanged. Money slides through more hands than you can imagine."

"Which gives them an easy way to clean their drug money."

"Bingo." Doc pointed a finger at Dak. "As to how they move the money, the ore, the cocaine, you've seen those kids walking around the streets with the book bags on their backs?"

Dak felt his stomach turn as the realization struck. "The kids are mules for the cartel?"

"Yeah." Regret and sadness filled Doc's response. "They have them use those book bags to make it look like the kids are going to or coming from school. Not that the cops are going to stop a bunch of kids. Sure, every now and then one of them gets caught shoplifting or doing something stupid. When that happens, the kid gets arrested, and whatever loot they have on their backs is taken into lockup. I don't have to tell you how that gets divvied up by the cops."

Dak nodded his understanding. His face darkened at the thought of the cartels using the children like that. His memory returned to the boy he'd nearly trampled as the kid left the bookstore earlier. That boy had worn a book bag. *Was he carrying drugs or illegal gold or laundered money?* There was no way to know for sure, but Dak's gut told him the answer was a yes. And that answer dug into his chest like a knife point.

"I can tell from the look on your face you don't approve of their methods," Doc said.

"Something along those lines." Dak paused for a second. "What do we do first?"

"Now you're asking the right questions. We can't get to Diaz directly, but his empire is built on stilts. Knock out the stilts and the whole house comes tumbling down."

"Who are these stilts?"

"I've been observing the operation for a while, and I still don't know who all is involved. Diaz has done a good job in keeping a tight lid on things, and if any of his men, or couriers, get caught, they're erased before they can turn on him. Very few people outside the organization know many details about the hierarchy within the Diaz operation."

The way he used the term *erased* sent a chill up Dak's spine. He knew what that meant.

"You got somewhere I can start?" Dak's right eyebrow inched upward.

"Of course. I wouldn't send you out into the dark without a flashlight. Start with a man named Antonio Boldega. Runs a brothel on the other side of the city. The area is full of lowlifes, and there are tons of underground operations there. The place you're lookin' for is called Tortuga Roja."

"The Red Turtle?"

"Well, look who took eighth-grade Spanish. Yes, the Red Turtle. When you get inside, you may not like what you see."

"Not much bothers me."

"You say that. But this brothel's employees," he said the word with disgusted sarcasm, "are brought in via human trafficking. Boldega drugs them to keep them docile. Then he pimps them out until they're no longer useful."

A sickening tendril snaked through Dak's gut at the thought.

"Sounds like this Boldega character needs to die."

"Easier said than done, but I agree. Find him, and you'll find the next breadcrumb to Diaz. Boldega is connected. And with the right amount of leverage, you should be able to get him to cough up that information. Heck, he might even know where Diaz lives, though I doubt it. When Diaz has guests, most of the time they're brought in with hoods over their heads."

"Sounds like a strange way to treat one's guests. As to the leverage, I know how to apply that," Dak said with cool menace.

"Good." Doc picked up the second glass of beer and chugged it until the thing was half-empty. He set it down with a refreshed "ah" and nodded to Dak as he slid a white business card across the table. "Let me know when you're done with Boldega. I'll help you any way I can. That address is the place you're looking for. The phone number is mine. Don't drop it."

Dak picked up the card and inspected the number. He flipped it over and found an address on one side and a number on the other. He met Doc's gaze. "Will do. Thanks, Doc. Nice to meet you."

"Pffft," the man spewed. "I'm a grumpy old has-been. Nothing nice about it."

"Actually," Dak countered, "I find your honesty refreshing."

He set a twenty down on the table and then walked away without looking back. He wondered, as he stepped out into the warm air again, what the old man thought, what he felt in his heart. There must have been severe pain there for him to be as grouchy and thirsty for beer as he was.

Dak never wanted to feel that way; to be so attached and emotionally hung up on someone. Despite his desires, Nicole's face popped into his mind more often than he cared to admit, and he couldn't deny how he felt for her.

He shook off the memory and took to the sidewalk with long strides to make his way to the other side of the city, where he hoped to find Antonio Boldega and his operation.

I came for a sword and found myself in a war, he thought. A young boy walked by him with a black backpack on. The kid's eyes dripped with fatigue. His sagging face displayed a lack of nutrition and sleep. His clothes were dirty and tattered, and the shoes on his feet were worn through. One didn't have a shoestring.

Dak watched the boy disappear around the corner. When the kid was gone, Dak set his jaw and swallowed away the sadness his heart oozed.

His thoughts cleared with a newfound determination. He'd get the sword for his employer, and along the way Dak would take down the entire Diaz cartel.

7

Hector marched down the long hill toward the pier. The walk from the bookstore to the Port of El Callao took more than forty minutes on such short legs. With every step, the tall red cranes, towering stacks of steel shipping containers, and enormous ships on the water drew ever nearer.

The boy kept the dock number at the front of his mind. He repeated it silently, over and over again. *Dock 79. Dock 79. Dock 79.* There was no way Hector would forget that, not if he had anything to do with it.

He wasn't going to let down Señor Flores. Especially not after the pep talk the man had just given him. He made Hector feel good about himself, about his work ethic, though deep down the boy also felt disgusted. The man clearly had dark intentions for Hector's mother. Even though he was only eleven, the boy knew exactly where the Flores inquiry about Hector's mom was going.

She was a pretty woman, still in her mid-thirties. She worked hard at the cocaine manufacturing facility, but Hector knew she did it only because if she refused, the cartel would put her down in the mines or worse. *If there was something worse than being down in those hell holes.*

The men in the tugurizadas had never approached his mother, Lisbeth, after her husband died. Some of their timidity came from respect. But as the weeks and months slipped by, their reasons for staying away from her muddled, though Hector told himself it was because he was her protector now, and any man who tried to take his father's place would have to go through him.

He didn't know if that was true, but he chose to believe it. Hector didn't want a new dad. He wanted his real father back.

The thoughts dredged up memories that he didn't want to think about right now, not while he was working. He especially couldn't let the other kids on the street see him crying. They sensed weakness; like predators on the hunt, they always picked off any who showed the slightest sign of vulnerability.

Hector clenched his teeth and kept walking. He distracted himself by focusing on his destination. *Dock 79. Dock 79. Dock 79.*

It felt like forever between the bookstore and the docks, but Hector finally arrived with beads of sweat rolling down the sides of his face. His stomach grumbled, and the temptation to dip into one of the many bakeries or cafés on the way back to the tugurizadas swelled in his mind.

Those thoughts were rapidly swallowed in the chaos that surrounded him. The Port of Callao was the busiest in the nation, and while it looked massive from a distance, it was downright overwhelming when standing next to it.

Hector had never really visited the port before, and nothing could have prepared him for the flurry of activity surrounding him.

Huge trucks rumbled by with black smoke spilling out of their pipes. Moving vans rolled by, too, carrying smaller loads than the 18-wheelers. Beyond the fences, forklifts zipped around, moving heavy crates—sometimes more than one at a time. Cranes towered over the entire site. Some sat dormant, while others lifted bulky steel containers and hoisted them onto ships docked nearby.

Hector swallowed back his fear. They probably wouldn't even let him in the facility, and even if they did, he worried he'd be run over by one of the many vehicles rushing about.

A portly man by the fence stood guard in a white hard hat. He wore an orange vest and held a tablet to document who was coming and going. Down the street to the right and left were several more entrances and exits where similarly dressed guards kept a record of who came and went at their entry points.

Hector sighed and tightened the bag against his back. He looked both ways down the street one more time and, with no vehicles coming at that moment, hurriedly crossed the street.

He trotted up to the guard and stopped a few feet from him on the sidewalk. The gruff man looked down at the boy with scorn in his eyes.

"Get out of here, kid," he spat. His neck fat jiggled as he spoke. He motioned with a firm finger, pointing back up the road toward the city. "You could get hurt or killed walking around this area."

Hector choked back his insecurities and stiffened his shoulders, emboldened by the kind words Flores had given him. "I am here to deliver something to Dock 79," he said, glad he hadn't forgotten the dock number.

The man tilted his hard hat back an inch and scratched the side of his face. Suspicion oozed out of squinty brown eyes. "Dock 79? Who sent you? What are you delivering?"

"I can't tell you what it is, sir," Hector explained.

"Oh? And why is that?" The man crossed his arms as if that demand would shake the boy from his grip on the secret.

"Because my employer doesn't want anyone else to see what's in this bag other than Chocho."

The man's narrowed eyes widened at the sound of the name. "Chocho?"

"Yes," Hector confirmed. Confidence throbbed in his chest at the sight of the fear written on the man's face. "And my employer doesn't like it when his deliveries are delayed."

The guard shook his head, flapping the fat around his jowls like a bowlful of *mazamorra morada*, a popular pudding-like dessert.

"No, of course not." The man looked around nervously as if searching the buildings on the other side of the road for signs of snipers who might take him out for even delaying the courier for more than a minute. "You said Dock 79, yes?"

"Yes, sir."

"Right. So, go through this gate here." The guard pointed through the opening in the fence. "Follow the white painted lines to the left and keep going until you reach the water. Dock 79 will be down that last row on the left. Just look for the number on the building. It's a long walk from here." The statement gave the guard an idea. "Would you like me to get someone to take you over there? That way you won't have to walk."

For a second, Hector considered denying the request. He could walk. Then again, he'd been walking a long time already, and the sooner he could get to the dock, the more pleased his employer would be. Not to mention if he saved some minutes, he could use the spare time on his way home to grab something nice for his mother with the extra money he'd earned.

"Yes," Hector said, brimming with confidence. "A ride would be helpful. My employer will be glad I saved time."

"Of course. I'm sure he would be." The words virtually spilled out of the man's thick, sweaty lips.

The guard plucked the radio hanging from his overworked belt and pressed the button. He ordered a cart to the gate, using some expletives that Hector only heard when he was picking up deliveries from the mines or from some of the older kids in the slums.

When the man was done making his request, he clipped the radio to the belt again and smiled nervously at the boy. "A cart will be here in a moment to take you to the dock. Please, if you don't mind, be sure to mention to Chocho that José Ruiz helped you. I would appreciate it."

Hector nodded as if he were a benevolent king giving mercy to one of his lowly subjects. "I will."

"Thank you. Thank you very much. I apologize for barking at you before."

"It's okay. I'm sure you don't get kids my age bringing things to the port very often."

"No. We definitely don't. You must have impressed Señor Flores."

"Perhaps." All Hector offered was a shrug.

A dingy white golf cart appeared from around the corner of a stack of shipping containers. The driver was a thin man with an equally thin black mustache and a mop of black hair under a blue hard hat. The bright green vest flapped in the breeze overtop a flannel shirt and blue jeans.

The cart stopped next to the gate as another semi growled by on the street. The wind from the huge truck blew Hector's hair around for a second before it settled once more.

The guard motioned to the cart. "That's Raul. He will take you to Dock 79. Please remember to tell Chocho that José Ruiz helped you. Yes?"

Hector grinned, finding the man's desperate need to be recognized somewhat funny. "I won't forget."

The boy walked over to the golf cart and climbed into the passenger seat. Raul reached into the basket on the back and grabbed a blue hard hat that matched his own, then handed it to his charge.

"Put this on," Raul ordered in a gravelly voice.

Hector took the helmet from the man and placed it on his head. The thing was way too big for him and slid around on his skull, barely hanging on through the power of gravity alone.

"You can tighten it here," Raul said, taking the hat off the boy and pulling on a plastic strap inside the dome.

He handed it back to Hector. The boy propped the hat back on his head, and this time it felt tighter, more secure.

"Better?" Raul asked, as if he had to.

"Yes. Thank you."

"Good. Hold on."

The driver stepped on the gas pedal and the cart's engine growled to life. It accelerated quickly but topped out at a steady fifteen miles per hour, which wasn't fast, but much better than walking.

Hector watched the symphony of the shipping yards pass around him. The huge stacks of steel containers made it almost like a maze, and the boy was certain he could get lost in all of it if left to his own devices.

Enormous metal warehouses stretched all the way to the waterfront to the west. The buildings were so long, Hector could barely see to the end of them.

Raul apparently wasn't in the mood for chatting, a fact Hector was glad for. He'd expended enough energy trying to keep it together at the gate. If the cart's driver started asking too many questions, he wasn't sure if he could keep it up.

Fortunately, Raul only spoke after they arrived at one of the more dilapidated-looking warehouses. "This is you over here," he grumbled while pointing a bony finger down the row.

He turned down the row the first guard had described. Hector looked at the numbers painted on the gables near the top of the cloned warehouse structures and counted up from the number *51*.

He spotted 79 painted in peeling white paint over what appeared to be a derelict building. The window below the dock number was cracked, and one pane had been chipped away completely. Rust covered portions of the window frame.

The massive sliding doors were closed, and a man stood outside them wearing a red T-shirt and blue jeans. Hector knew the guy was probably armed, likely carrying his weapon in the back of his pants and tucked into the belt to stay hidden. The boy had seen several of the cartel's men with weapons hidden in this manner when he was at the mines, or on the rare occasions he visited the cocaine plant where his mother worked. Although in that place, there were far more guards and most of them held their weapons out in the open—most of which were AR15s or AK-47-style rifles.

Raul stopped in front of the door and the guard—a hulking, muscular man with a clean-shaven face and short-cropped hair—stepped toward the cart, reaching toward the back of his belt as if in warning.

"Got a delivery for Chocho," Raul said coolly. There was a distant fear in his voice, akin to a priest uncertain if the gods would accept their sacrifice. To be denied would mean death.

The guard extended his right hand, palm up, and rapidly curled his fingers, beckoning Hector to come forward.

The boy hesitated, but only for a second, then summoned every ounce of courage he could before stepping out onto the blacktop. He strode confidently around the front of the cart and then paused before he reached the guard.

Hector looked back over his shoulder and asked, "Will you wait here to take me back to the main gate?"

Raul, in turn, looked to the guard for permission. The guard nodded once and then motioned for Hector to approach the door. Hector noticed the gun in the man's belt, just as he'd suspected. The pistol's grip stuck out with part of the T-shirt tucked in behind it.

The guard pulled on a handle riveted to the side of the door. He tugged the heavy metal until the opening was wide enough for the two of them to pass through, then he ushered Hector inside.

The interior of the big space was mostly empty. Dim fluorescent lights hung from the ceiling. Wire coverings protected them, from what Hector had no idea. Once they were in, the guard slid the door shut again, removing the outside daylight from assisting the artificial light above.

Only the window in the front allowed rays of sunlight to pour in, fixing into a broken, glowing square in the center of the room.

A few tables sat next to the walls, along with various tools and machinery Hector didn't recognize. He'd never been around boats much. In fact, this was about as close to a ship as he'd ever been. Most of the objects around him were foreign, except for the more common tools such as hammers, screwdrivers, and wrenches.

"Back here," the guard said, pointing to an office in the back-left corner. The office occupied six hundred square feet of the building's interior, made from the same metal siding as the warehouse walls.

Hector followed the guard toward the office's closed door and stopped a few feet behind the man while he knocked.

"Chocho," the guard barked. "Delivery." He stepped back away from the door and waited. Seconds ticked by before the two heard the sounds of locks clicking open.

After the last deadbolt was unlocked, a man appeared in the doorway. His darkly tanned bald head and face were surrounded by a thick haze of cigarette smoke. Chocho was thick, built of half muscle and half fat. He was bigger than the guard, but not fitter, though if Hector had been forced to choose who would win in a fight, he'd have probably gone with Chocho, simply due to the man's mass.

He looked down at Hector with eyes so brown they were nearly black. He had a white tank top undershirt on and a pair of dark blue jeans. A necklace with the Virgin Mary dangled from his neck. Over his left eye, the eyebrow had two neat lines trimmed into it. Five teardrop tattoos dripped away from the corner of the same eye, and several more were on display on his chest and arms, amid a tapestry of other ink work.

"Who are you?" Chocho asked in a sharp tone.

"Um, my name is Hector, sir. Señor Flores sent me." Hector slid one strap of the bag off his shoulder and started to loosen the other, but Chocho stepped back and drew a pistol. He glowered down at the boy with wild eyes. It was only then that Hector noticed the red vessels in the whites of the man's eyes. The boy had no idea why they looked that way, but he had a bad feeling it had something to do with drugs. A mountain of white powder on the desk ten feet behind Chocho confirmed that suspicion.

"What are you doing, boy?"

Hector froze, terrified by the weapon pointed at his face. "Just giving you the delivery Señor Flores asked me to bring."

Chocho's head tilted slightly, and his eyelids narrowed in suspicion. The guard stood back with a hand on his pistol in case Chocho's insane paranoia proved to have a foundation.

"Take the bag, Corrito," Chocho said to the guard.

The other man took a cautious step forward and jerked the bag off the boy's shoulder. Corrito held it for a second, waiting for his next order.

"Check it," Chocho barked.

The guard set the bag on the ground and unzipped it. He stuffed his hand inside and felt around for a good thirty seconds before he looked up and nodded, much to Hector's relief.

Chocho grinned on the left side of his mouth and nodded. "You're early; what was it you said your name was?" He wagged the gun around nonthreateningly, but it still unnerved the boy.

"Hector. My name is Hector."

"Yes, Hector. Good. I can see why Ricardo uses you. You're punctual. He likes people who don't waste time. Hard to find good help these days, no?"

"That's what I hear," Hector said as coolly as possible.

Chocho looked down at the boy, then up to Corrito, then back to Hector. He broke out in laughter and took a step forward to slap Hector on the shoulder. "That's what he hears, Corrito. I like this kid. Come in. Come in." The man motioned with his pistol like it was a crossing guard's flashlight. Corrito lifted the book bag and handed it over to Chocho, who slung it over his shoulder.

Hector didn't want to go into the office, but he also didn't feel like he had a choice. He stepped inside, passing Chocho to wait in the corner.

"Watch the front," Chocho said to the guard.

The man nodded and turned, then headed back to the front door while Chocho closed the office door behind him.

"So," Chocho said, making his way over to the mound of white powder on the desk. He set the bag down and tipped it over, spilling stacks of bills onto the surface next to the cocaine.

"Looks like business is good, my friend," Chocho said with a laugh.

"Yes, I guess so."

"You guess right."

Chocho stacked up the bills and then nodded at his handiwork. "Good. Looks like it's all there. Lucky for you, huh?" Chocho smacked the kid on the shoulder again, sending a stinging pain across his skin.

"I don't steal," Hector said with a tremble.

"That's what they all say, but not everyone is as honest as you."

Chocho inclined his head and peered down at the boy. "Did Flores pay you yet?"

"Yes, sir," Hector admitted. "Before I left his office."

"Good. That was another test. If I called him and asked him the same question and he said no, I'd probably have to kill you and dump your body in the sea."

Hector's face washed pale.

"But you didn't, so you're good." The man turned to a different stack of money on a side table to his right and plucked a twenty from the top. He held it out toward Hector.

The boy stared at the proffered money hesitantly.

"What's the matter with you? Take the money. You did good today, kid. There's plenty more where this came from, too, if you work hard and stay trustworthy to us."

Another twenty? Hector couldn't believe it. These guys threw money around like it was nothing. He timidly reached out and pinched the bill. Chocho pulled back on it for a second, and then smiled and extended it to the boy once more.

"I'm just messing with you. It's yours. Go on. Take it. Job well done, Hector."

The boy stretched his arm out again and gently squeezed the bill with his fingers. He expected the same trick again, but this time Chocho let it go.

"There's more where that came from if you keep working hard, kid. Señor Diaz can always use good help in his organization."

"Thank you, sir."

"Sure. Sure. Now get out of here. I'll see you again."

The man unceremoniously turned and sat back down at his desk to resume cutting up lines of blow right in front of the boy.

Hector, afraid he might linger too long, walked back to the door, opened it, and stepped through. He shut it behind him before Chocho could tell him to and then made his way back to the front entrance.

He knocked on the metal panel and a couple of seconds later, Corrito tugged it open.

The golf cart still sat there with Raul waiting patiently behind the wheel.

Once he was outside in the shipping yard again, the guard closed the warehouse door with a bang.

Hector adjusted his hard hat and climbed aboard the golf cart again. He unconsciously stuffed the new bill into his pocket and sat back as Raul steered the cart back toward the port's entrance.

He couldn't believe how much money he'd earned in the last couple of hours. Plans formulated in his mind about getting something nice for his mother, a bouquet of flowers perhaps. She loved flowers, but she couldn't afford to buy any, and there were too few wild ones growing in the tugurizadas.

Hector made up his mind, and even picked out the place where he would make the purchase. Deep down, though, his joy was tempered by the overshadowing feeling that he was being sucked into something he didn't want to be a part of.

8

Dak stood on the street corner, leaning up against a retail shop selling women's clothing, cheap perfume, and even cheaper jewelry. He thought it ironic, or perhaps just good business to be positioned across the street from the bordello where so many men sinned. Conveniently, they could walk across the street when they were done and pick out something nice for their wives or girlfriends to make themselves feel better about whatever they'd done in the brothel.

Down in his gut, Dak felt a sickening knot twist and lurch.

He'd been watching the entrance to the brothel for the last twenty minutes. Since he'd been there, only one man had entered—a middle-aged guy with thin black hair and matching glasses.

With the sun still out, Dak doubted the place was in its prime time for business. Most men were probably too aware of onlookers to be willing to risk being recognized on the way into the joint, but once darkness fell, Dak figured the building would be packed with clientele.

He figured the best thing to do was to go in through the front door and pretend to be interested in a little business. A quick walk around the back had provided him with good recon. The rear door was closed tight, and he guessed it would be locked. Checking it would be a dumb idea since the only people who would go through the back were either expected visitors, or perhaps VIP clients who preferred discretion.

There were no guards, but security cameras hung in the corners between the buildings that extended out beyond the brothel on both sides.

That made his decision to go in through the front much easier.

He sighed and pushed his sunglasses a little closer to his face to help conceal his identity, then when the light changed, he walked across the street and over to the brothel entrance.

Dak paused in front of the white brick building and looked around. No one seemed to be paying him any attention.

The bordello looked like it had been a house of ill repute for the better part of a century. Tarnished brass handles hung from the double doors. The glass portion of the doors was covered from the inside, as were the windows on either side. A red turtle painted on the glass of both doors, along with one hanging over the entryway on an old metal sign, told Dak he was at the right place.

He grabbed one of the handles and yanked the door open, then stepped inside.

A nauseating aroma of incense and cigarettes smacked him in the face. A faint twinge of weed also laced the air, along with something he couldn't place. The latter, he reckoned, was probably some kind of synthetic drug. Crystal meth, perhaps. Dak winced at the assault on his senses but quickly acclimated to it.

The light from outside vanished with the closing of the door behind him, and with the sunlight gone, the lobby plunged Dak into the dim red glow of corner table lamps. A ceiling fan overhead also contained a glowing red bulb. The color bathed the room, and Dak felt dirty, as though the light covered him in something tangible and disturbing.

A man who looked to be in his late forties stood behind a counter in the corner. A series of box shelves hung on the wall behind him. Another red lamp sat on the counter next to an old cash register.

There were no signs of computers or any kind of traceable technology, which made perfect sense for a place like this. All transactions were done in cash, some of which would go to paying off the cops. Dak wondered about their system for greasing the tax collectors' palms, too, but he wasn't here to theorize on how the operation worked. He just needed information.

"Hello, *amigo*," the man behind the counter said. "You looking for a good time?"

"Something like that," Dak demurred.

"Well, you've come to the right place. What's your flavor? We have a fine selection to choose from." The manager grinned, flashing his crooked, yellow teeth under a bushy, black mustache.

Dak looked around, scanning the room one more time. The dark purple curtains added to the sleazy ambiance, along with the antique upholstered couch over in the sitting area.

"What do you recommend?" Dak asked, returning his gaze to the proprietor. "Señor Diaz told me that a man named Antonio Boldega would take good care of me."

The man's face stiffened for a second, then cracked with the same stupid smile once more. "You are a confidant of Señor Diaz?"

"I guess you could say that."

"A business associate then?"

"You're getting warmer. Let's leave it at that."

"Understood. I'm sure Señor Diaz appreciates your discretion." The man paused as if considering what to say next. "I am Antonio Boldega. This is my establishment. And any friend of Señor Diaz gets the best treatment here." He held up a finger. "I think I have the perfect girl for you. Come, let me take you to her."

Dak choked back his disgust as the proprietor ambled around the corner of the counter. The man pulled back a purple curtain that blocked a corridor to the back and leaned in. "Marta, get in here and watch the front desk. I have a special visitor."

Boldega let the curtain fall again and resumed his faux friendly expression until a young woman with long black hair appeared through the curtain. She wore a sheer white gown over red lingerie.

Her cheeks were drawn and pale despite her tan, and deep circles hung under her eyes. The girl looked young, perhaps twenty or twenty-one, but the fatigue on her face made her appear much older.

"Watch the desk," Boldega barked, his kind expression gone in an instant. "If someone comes in, just tell them I'll be right back."

She nodded, though Dak wondered if the girl even heard the man's words. The vapid look in her eyes betrayed a mental vacancy that could only be the result of heavy sedation or fatigue, or both.

Dak noted a few needle tracks on the girl's left arm and figured there were probably more between her toes. *Heroin.* This place had a cornucopia of illegal activity going on, and it seemed no one was going to do anything about it. The immediate trust of nothing more than words and a name from a total stranger had not even caused Boldega the slightest twinge of doubt or concern. That told Dak that the man believed he could get away with anything, which most likely meant he had Diaz's protection.

Whenever he'd encountered people doing illegal things with reckless abandon, Dak knew it usually meant a higher power protected them from the shadows.

"Come with me," Boldega said, motioning to a staircase on the other side of the room. The stairs rose to a landing and then turned and disappeared behind the wall going up to the second floor.

Dak didn't like the idea of going up there, not without some recon or at least knowing if there was another way out, but he didn't have much choice. So he nodded and kept his right hand ready in case he needed to draw the subcompact pistol from his hip.

He followed Boldega up the stairs to the landing and continued at the turn. Boldega's skinny frame climbed the steps easily. The man wasn't in peak physical shape—scrawny with a pooch for a belly that caused his red button-up shirt to protrude over his belt—still, he was in good enough shape to not be bothered by the climb, and soon the two were on the second floor.

The hall ran sixty feet to the back of the building. Five doors lined the walls on each side: most of them open. The second one on the left was only slightly ajar, and as the two men walked down the corridor,

Dak looked in and saw the man he'd spotted from the street. The guy was standing at the foot of the bed, staring down at a young brunette girl with curly tangles splayed out onto a white pillow. Her underwear was barely hanging on, and from the look of it, neither was she. Her glazed eyes stared up at the ceiling, seeing and unseeing the black fan overhead as it swirled slowly in endless circles.

Dak felt a stab at his heart. That twitch of pain and sympathy quickly morphed into rage at the sight of the man unbuttoning his shirt slowly, methodically, as if savoring every second. Even in the brief moment Dak passed by, he could see the look from the side of the man's face. It was a look of someone who wanted not only sex, but control, unabashed power over another human being. Whether they were drugged up or not didn't make any difference to him.

Dak felt himself slow involuntarily as he passed, his mind wandering to dark places where he could almost feel his fingers against the man's throat as he choked the last breath from the john's lungs.

At the next pair of doors, Dak cast sideways glances into both rooms and found similarly clad young women lying on the beds. One was on her side, asleep, while the second lay on her back, eyes closed. Their breaths came in shallow, labored bursts. Neither of them looked healthy. They were undernourished, and both displayed multiple bruises on their arms, legs, and necks.

Dak again had to swallow back his anger.

They passed two more sets of doors before arriving at the last one on the right. It was closed.

Dak assumed that another client was inside with a host, but Boldega twisted the doorknob and pushed the door open.

Inside, a young redheaded woman sat in a leather chair in the corner next to a bed. The disheveled sheets looked like they hadn't been straightened in weeks. The girl, probably twenty, stared back languidly with her head drooped to the left.

"You like, yes?" Boldega asked proudly, extending a hand as if the girl was on display at an auction.

Knowing what he did about human trafficking, Dak realized with a dizzying sickness, that was probably how the woman came to be here.

Dak nodded while he clenched his jaw. "Yes." He turned to Boldega. "What's wrong with her? All these girls look sedated. You keep them drugged?"

Boldega shifted nervously. "Of course, *amigo*. We have to keep them like this so they don't try to escape. They like being high, and we like to keep them that way, in case they ever have any thoughts of trying to leave."

"Smart," Dak said with an approving nod. "Wouldn't want them running back to their families."

"Exactly." Boldega slapped Dak on the shoulder. "Take a ride for free this time, *amigo*. On the house. Any friend of Diaz gets a complimentary first time. Do whatever you want with her, just don't kill her. Huh?" He nudged Dak on the shoulder as if they were college buddies. "She's so spaced out; she won't know what's going on."

"They all like that? Won't remember who comes and goes?"

"*Por supuesto*," Boldega said. "They never remember anything."

"I couldn't do it for free," Dak said, his mind already shifting to putting his plan into action. "You're running a business here." His feet shuffled deeper into the room while his shoulders guided him toward the door. Dak had already spotted the assortment of needles festooned on the nightstand to his left.

Security for the business was minimal, at best. Dak had seen no security guards, no armed men standing watch over the rooms or even in the lobby. Boldega had complete faith that Diaz made him untouchable. Dak intended to show the man he had misplaced that faith.

"You got anything else in the way of drugs? I'm more of a cocaine guy, personally."

Boldega stared blankly back at his guest for a couple of seconds. Dak noticed the white residue around the man's nostrils and the wild, almost rampant look in his reddened eyes.

"Sure, *amigo*. Got some prime stuff right here."

The change in tone wasn't lost on Dak; he knew immediately that Boldega's friendly demeanor had flipped to one of suspicion.

Boldega stepped over to the nightstand and pulled open the first of two drawers. Plastic baggies of white powder filled to the brim. Boldega plucked one of the bags out and tossed it to Dak, who snatched it out of the air with his right hand.

He noticed the pistol tucked into the back-right side of Boldega's belt, and his senses tingled a warning. Boldega was on to him, or at the very least no longer trusted the visitor.

Dak subtly pricked the side of the baggie with his fingernail. "Thanks." Dak's eyes shifted to the bag for a second, then back to the proprietor.

"You need anything else, *amigo*?" Boldega's hand was inching toward the pistol tucked in his belt. Had he known Dak's background, the man wouldn't have done anything so obviously foolish, but he didn't know who he was dealing with.

"I'm good. *Muchas gracias*," Dak offered in Spanish.

"*De nada*." Boldega said, his eyes narrowing.

Dak knew that was a tell, just like he'd seen in poker rooms when another player would blink too fast, or scratch their nose, or rub their hair, or shift in their seat. Boldega was about to draw down.

9

In a blur of movement, Dak twisted. His right hand flashed in front of him, flinging the bag of blow at Boldega's face. It struck the target just as Boldega reached for his pistol.

The powder exploded from the tear in the bag, covering Boldega's face like a bad makeup job. A cloud puffed around his head.

Thrown off guard by the abrupt attack, Boldega reacted incorrectly, reaching both hands to his face to either defend or to wipe away the drug.

Either way, he wasn't prepared for what came next.

In a split second, Dak covered the distance between the two men and pounced on Boldega like a mountain lion. He wrapped his fingers around Boldega's throat and slammed the man's skull against the wall, then dragged it deliberately down to the floor.

Boldega kicked and squealed like a stuck pig, but he couldn't free himself from the powerful visitor's grip. One of his feet struck the nightstand and sent it toppling over, spilling needles full of heroin to the floor in the nearby corner.

Dak pinned the man down with one hand. He used his other hand to raise a finger to his lips. "Shh," Dak urged. "We wouldn't want you to wake the girls, now would we?"

The proprietor tried to say something, but all that came out was gurgled spittle.

"Now, I'm going to loosen my grip, but only if you calm down. You're turning very red, *amigo*. Pretty soon, that's going to start going blue. After that, you die. Understood?"

Boldega nodded furiously as best he could with so much force on his throat.

"Good. If you scream, I kill you right now." To show he was serious, Dak took the man's weapon from the belt and pressed it to Boldega's head. "You going to be quiet?"

The man's face was already starting to darken. He tried nodding again.

"Okay then." Dak took his fingers away from Boldega's throat but kept the gun's muzzle firmly pressed against his temple. "Let's get started, shall we?"

"Do you have any idea who you're dealing with?" Boldega spat. A flurry of obscenities accompanied the question, including one rather creative one regarding Dak and his mother.

"That's not very nice. I don't think Mom would appreciate that. I know I certainly don't." Dak punched the man squarely in the nose for the offense.

Boldega howled in pain, and Dak covered his mouth as blood started trickling out of the nostrils.

"I warned you. Don't be loud. And I also asked if you were ready to help, which you clearly weren't." Dak caught a glimpse of one of the needles close by.

"You can't shoot me," Boldega was saying. "Everyone will hear it. The cops. The people on the street. Someone will come looking for you. And when that happens, you'll be dead."

"Depends on what I shoot you with," Dak said calmly. He reached over and picked up a syringe, then without warning, jammed the needle into the man's right arm that Dak had pinned down with his knee.

Keeping his thumb on the plunger, Dak stared into the man's

soul. "Now, if I shoot you with this, I bet this might be enough to cause an overdose for someone with an obvious cocaine problem."

True fear filled Boldega's eyes. His head trembled, begging mercy of the interloper.

"Now, let's start again." Dak glanced over his shoulder at the girl, who still sat in the chair as if nothing had happened.

"If you didn't know already, I'm not a friend of Diaz. But I'm looking for the man. Word is, you know how to find him."

Boldega shook his head violently. "No, please. I don't know anything."

Dak rubbed the plunger with his thumb and flashed a look at it. "Too bad."

"No, wait. Please. I'm telling you the truth. Well, part of the truth."

Dak's eyebrows shot up at the almost funny moment of honesty.

"I can't get you a meeting with Diaz."

"Then you can show me where he is."

"He's too paranoid," Boldega said, his head tossing back and forth. "Only his personal bodyguards know where he lives. The only times I've been there, I was taken in a hood. At first, I thought they were going to execute me."

That statement jibed with what Doc had suggested, so Dak prodded for more.

"When does he come by for payment. I know he uses this place as one of his laundering fronts. At the very least, he takes a little, mostly an insurance payment from you for his protection."

At that, Boldega nodded. "Yes. But he doesn't come by in person. He always sends one of his men. They were just here last week, so they won't come around again for another three."

"So, you can't get me a meeting with Diaz. Can't get me into his compound. And you said I have to wait three weeks until one of his men comes by to make a pickup? You're not very useful, Antonio. And do you know what I do to useless people?"

"No, please. Wait!" The man's begging disgusted Dak, but in a way he almost found humorous.

To see Boldega go from being a man in total control over the lives of others, to completely out of control of his own fate, was a truly beautiful thing.

"I'm waiting," Dak groused.

"I can't get you in, but I know someone who might."

Dak stared blankly into the man's eyes, waiting.

"His name is Raul Piñeda. He runs the cocaine manufacturing facility just outside town. It's on a farm. Not far from here. Maybe twenty minutes. I can take you if you like."

"What's the address?"

"What?"

Dak twisted the needle, and Boldega grimaced. To his credit, he didn't let out a yelp.

"The address. What's the address?"

Boldega forced the pain away long enough to give the information to his tormentor.

"You sure that's the one?" Dak pressed. "I'd hate to leave only to find out you gave me a fake address. Seems awfully convenient you have it memorized."

"No. No I swear. Please, just don't kill me. That's the real address. You have to believe me."

"How old are you?" Dak asked.

The seemingly random question caught Boldega off guard. "What?"

"Say 'what' again, and I will inject the full contents of this syringe into your bloodstream."

"Sorry. It just...seems like a random thing to ask. I'm forty-seven."

"Good. And what was the address you gave me before?"

Boldega's eyes looked up at Dak, confused by the question. Then Boldega repeated the same address from before.

"Excellent," Dak congratulated. "I've found that if you really want to get the truth out of someone you think is lying, you have to give them a question they can't lie about between the other questions. Studies show that forces people into a truthful situation, and if they were lying before, they won't be able to recall the lie. Unless, of course, it wasn't a lie."

Boldega nodded, only half listening at this point. "Yes. See? I told you I wasn't lying. Now, please, let me go."

Dak shook his head, an expression of sincere disappointment on his face. "No. I'm afraid I can't do that."

"What?" Fear flooded Boldega's face. "Why not? You said you wouldn't kill me if I helped you. I did what you asked."

"That's true. I did say that. And you did help. But I just can't get past what you've done to these poor girls." He looked back over his shoulder at the young woman still sitting in the corner. He returned his judging gaze to the man on the floor beneath him. "But I did tell the truth. I'm not going to kill you."

A sliver of hope sliced through Boldega's eyes.

"But this heroin probably will," Dak added. His thumb depressed the plunger quickly, injecting every drop of the drug into Boldega's veins.

"No! Please!"

It was too late. Boldega felt the hot surge of liquid flow into his bloodstream. It crawled up his arm and into his chest. Within twenty seconds, Boldega's face paled and his eyes rolled back into his head. Dak released the man when his body started to twist. Boldega retched onto the floor nearby, then doubled over, curling up into a fetal position.

The veins on his neck bulged as the drug coursed rapidly through his body.

He rolled onto his back and continued vomiting. In his new position, however, he could only inhale the bile with every involuntary convulsion.

Boldega choked and jerked around on the floor as Dak stepped away and turned to the girl in the corner. She continued to stare at the door with an empty gaze.

No words of hope or encouragement would help her right now. She would neither hear nor remember them.

Dak took out his phone and called the number on the card Doc had given him. The older man answered after one ring. "What do you want?"

"It's me."

"Of course it's you. Who else you think I'd give this number to?"

Dak would have laughed if the circumstances were different. "The Red Turtle is cleaned. But there are some workers here who need medical attention and a safe place."

"I see." Doc remained quiet for ten seconds, then said, "I know who to call. I have a friend with access to medical supplies and another one who runs a research ship close to here. I'll get them on that boat where they'll be safe from Diaz and they can get the help they need."

"Sounds good. Thanks, Doc."

"You bet. You okay?"

Dak nodded as he watched Boldega's movements slow to offbeat, random twitches. "Yeah. I have to go. There's another appointment I need to keep."

He ended the call and slid the phone back into his pocket. Dak looked over at the girl with sadness filling his chest. He sighed and walked over to her. After he waved a hand in front of her unseeing, dream-filled eyes, Dak scooped up the half-naked girl in his arms and placed her gently on the bed. *At least that way she wouldn't fall over and hurt herself.* There was no need to say anything to her. When she snapped out of it and became aware of her surroundings, she'd be free. He didn't know how long that would take, but he figured more than thirty minutes depending on the drug that had been used to sedate her.

Then Dak remembered the girl down the hall with the afternoon client. The same anger that roared through him a few minutes before returned with a wave of fiery indignation.

He left the room without looking back at Boldega's body or the girl and walked on down the hall.

Dak stopped when he reached the room where he'd seen the client undressing. The door was closed now. Dak knew there were no locks. He'd scoped that little detail a few minutes before in the other room. It made sense. If a client were doing something they weren't supposed to—as thin as those rules appeared to be in this joint—the manager could come to the rescue. Dak figured that was probably the reason for the firearm in Boldega's belt.

After a deep breath and a second to mentally prepare himself for what might be on the other side of the door, Dak twisted the doorknob and pushed the door open.

To his surprise, the hinges remained quiet.

He continued to open the door until the client came into view. It was a visage Dak could have done without, but he pushed aside adolescent-fueled nausea and closed the door quietly behind him.

Inside, the man stood at the foot of the bed wearing nothing but his boxers, and he was about to remove those. He was saying something to the girl, telling her the things he was going to do, and none of them were good.

Dak reached down to his ankle and drew a knife from its sheath, then took a step toward the man.

The floor creaked under his weight and the man spun around, eyes wide with shock that turned instantly to fear at the sight of the blade. The girl on the bed didn't move as Dak grabbed the client by the throat and shoved him toward the wall.

"Hey!" the man whined. "Get out of here. It's my turn. Go take one of the others—"

"I'm not here for them," Dak sneered.

"What? I'm sorry? I don't work here."

Dak snorted at the misinterpretation. "No, *amigo*. Not that."

The man cowered against the wall and slumped to the floor in the most helpless, defensive position he could muster.

"Do you want money? I can give it to you. It's in my pants over there. Take it. It's yours. Just don't hurt me."

Dak denied the man's request with a slow twist of his head. "Not here for money, either."

"What do you want, then? Name it. Just leave me alone." His voice quivered, realizing that there were few other things an intruder could want of him.

"Stand up."

The client shook his head, but after a kick from Dak's boot, found the strength to straighten his legs, though he remained fixed to the wall.

"Now," Dak said, holding the tip of the blade out. "What were you going to do to that girl?"

"Nothing. I wasn't going to do anything."

"Really?" Dak cocked his head to the side. His eyes oozed mocking disbelief. "Because I heard some of the things you said a minute ago. It didn't sound like nothing. Sounded like you were going to violate that poor girl." He pointed the knife at her, but she remained perfectly still. The only movement came from her chest rising and falling in a shallow, steady rhythm.

"I was just talking. You know. Getting myself in the mood."

"You were going to rape her."

"What's it matter to you? I paid good money," the man jabbed, suddenly indignant. "It's none of your business. She's just street trash, hopped up on drugs. No one misses her. And when she's gone, no one will miss her. She's here for one purpose."

Dak had heard enough. "Is that so?"

He stepped toward the man and ripped down his underwear before the guy could stop him. Then in one fluid movement, Dak slid the razor edge of his knife up through the man's groin.

The client screamed in a delirious combination of horror and agony as blood poured from the wound. He dropped to his knees, clutching the bloody patch with one hand while grasping desperately at his severed manhood with the other.

"They are not just street trash," Dak said.

He stood over the bleeding man for half a minute amid the groaning and writhing. Then, after Dak thought the man had suffered enough for his sins, he reached down, grabbed the client by the hair on the back of his head, and jerked him upright onto his knees once more.

Without fanfare, Dak slid the blade across the man's neck, feeling the metal sink deep enough into the throat to cut through the esophagus, carotid artery, and jugular. The man's eyes looked back up at

Dak as the American let him fall to the floor to connect with a growing pool of his own lifeblood.

Dak walked over to the man's pants and wiped the blade on them. Then he fished through the pockets until he found a wad of cash. He left everything else where it was, then exited the room, wiping down the doorknob on both sides just in case the Lima police actually bothered to show up and conduct an investigation.

He walked casually down the stairs, and when he reached the bottom, strolled over to the counter where the girl named Marta stood smoking a cigarette.

Dak placed the wad of cash from the dead client on the counter and smiled at her. "Thanks. I think I got everything I needed. By the way, you and your friends are free. If you need a place to go, I have someone on their way here now to help. Or you can just take that money and do what you please. Choice is yours."

He didn't wait for her to ask questions. He simply turned and walked to the door, pulled it open, and stepped out into the waning sunlight.

10

Dak kept his eyes peeled as he walked down the sidewalk toward the cantina. No one had paid any attention to him leaving the Tortuga Roja. From what he could tell, the only people who noticed him now would probably think him a tourist, though he wasn't dressed in anything fancy—a black T-shirt and light brown trousers. Being unmemorable was key when it came to carrying out operations like this. The fewer people who could recall details about him, the better. He knew the girl, Marta, was one who could pick him out in a lineup, but he also knew she wouldn't go to the cops. She'd been treated like a slave, and there was little doubt that Boldega used her for his own personal entertainment.

She'd probably taken the money and slipped out the back door. If, on the off chance, she'd gone upstairs to see what happened, Dak doubted the young woman would have called the police. They would implicate her before some mysterious American.

As he walked, Dak felt something deep down that he'd not felt in a long time—since his early days in the military. Those were the times before he felt like he was just a tool of a faceless government, back when he believed he was actually making a difference in the world.

He still believed he did some good, and his faith in the United States hadn't wavered, but questions abounded, and Dak knew he would probably never have those answers.

He'd been wrongfully accused, pursued, and threatened by the very leadership that was supposed to have his back. It was impossible for him not to wonder how far up the ladder that betrayal went.

All the more reason he was glad to be on the move with his new job.

Dak wasn't necessarily an adrenaline junkie, someone always looking for danger or excitement, to the contrary, he enjoyed relaxing and taking it easy. The quiet time he spent in his tree stand on the mountain afforded him all of that, and with no distractions except for the sights and sounds of nature around him.

Until Tucker was out of the picture, though, Dak knew he would never be able to truly let his guard down.

He crossed the street at the next intersection and continued on until he felt far enough from the scene of the crime to stop and get something to eat. He paused and looked around, spotting a café a couple doors down. The place looked good enough, with a dark green awning over the door and a matching one that extended out over a narrow section of the sidewalk for two tables.

Dak dipped into the eatery and ordered two beef empanadas from the young man at the counter. A few minutes later, Dak stepped back out onto the sidewalk with a white paper bag in one hand and a wrapped, steaming hot empanada in the other. He scanned the street out of habit, paying close attention to the windows in the buildings across the way, then made his way across the intersection. He took a bite as he neared the curb. The combination of the slightly crispy, sweet pastry with the savory meat, peppers, and garlic on the inside, slammed Dak's palate with flavor.

He stepped up onto the curb as he chewed, looking down at the empty section of pastry where he'd taken a bite.

"Man, that is one good empanada," he whispered to himself.

Unexpectedly, a short figure beneath him came into view, and Dak tried to sidestep to avoid bumping into the person.

The kid twisted sideways but still bumped into Dak's leg and nearly toppled over. Dak reached out and steadied the boy with the hand holding the bag, almost dropping it.

"Easy, kid," Dak said in Spanish. "Sorry about that. I need to watch where I'm going."

As the boy stared up at him, Dak realized it was the same boy he'd nearly run over earlier that day.

"I guess we need to stop bumping into each other like this," Dak joked, hoping to disarm the frightened kid.

The boy stared back through confused, narrow slits for a few seconds before he realized the stranger was joking.

"Yes, I'm so sorry, sir," the boy spewed. "I tried not to bump into you."

"Hey, take it easy, kid. I was only kidding. Besides, it was my fault. I was eating this empanada and not watching where I was going. Don't worry about it."

"Yes, sir," the boy said.

Dak noticed him eyeing the empanada in his hand with a ravenous stare. From his scrawny looks, Dak figured he didn't get two decent meals a day, much less three. And the drawn skin on his face sagged more than most of the kids he knew. Looking at the boy, Dak's mind drifted to Boston. The two were probably the same age, but the external difference in their health was easy to see.

"Not sure if you remember," Dak ventured, "but I think I almost ran into you earlier today. You were coming out of a bookstore."

"Oh," the boy said. The realization hit his eyes a second later. "Oh yes. I remember you."

"Seems like you have a lot on your mind," Dak said. "Sorry to pry, but shouldn't you have been in school earlier, and home by now?"

"I don't get to go to school," the kid explained. "I have to help my mother."

"I see," Dak said with a disapproving stare. The kid was probably from the tugurizadas and never given the opportunity to attend school. His clothes looked dirty, and Dak wondered if they were the only set he owned.

"You hungry?" Dak asked.

The boy shook his head, lowering his gaze to the sidewalk. Dak looked out over the street. Cars drove by, some honking at others. People strolled past them, either ignoring the two or simply not seeing them due to other distractions.

"It's okay," Dak said. "I have two, and I really only need to eat one of them."

He dug into the white paper bag and pulled out the second empanada. "They're really good."

The boy looked around, as if he should be suspicious. In reality, he probably should have been. Random stranger on the street handing him food from a nondescript bag. Then again, Dak figured beggars couldn't be choosers.

"I can't take that, sir," the boy refused.

"Okay, but I'm just going to throw it in this trash can over here if you don't eat it."

"No," the boy snapped, more forcefully than he wanted. "I mean, if you're going to throw it away, I'll take it."

Dak could tell from the kid's reaction that he was desperately hungry. He handed the boy the foil-wrapped empanada and smiled. "Enjoy," he said. "It's the least I can do to make up for running into you like that."

He charmed the boy with a kind smile. "What's your name?"

"Hector," the boy said before he realized it.

"Nice to meet you, Hector. Run along, now. I don't want your mother wondering where you are."

"Yes, sir. Thank you. Thank you."

Dak watched the boy stumble away down the sidewalk. As hungry as the kid appeared to be, he didn't immediately tear open the foil and devour the empanada. Either Dak's assessment of the kid's hunger was way off, or maybe the boy was saving it for when he got home.

With other children out and about, it was certainly possible bullies might try to take the meal from the boy. Perhaps he wanted to take it home to his mother to share.

A car growled by; the busted tailpipe spewing exhaust in great plumes.

Dak remained undistracted by the noise. The people around him blurred out of focus, his sniper instincts kicked in, and he zeroed in on the boy as he walked away, weaving in and out of the foot traffic.

Then it struck Dak—the kid's backpack was missing.

In seconds, Dak rewound his memory to a few minutes before when he inadvertently bumped into the boy. *No,* he thought. *The kid didn't have his backpack then either.*

It hadn't been stolen while the two talked, and Dak was certain both he and Hector would have noticed that happening.

The kid definitely had a backpack on earlier that day. And by his own confession, Hector admitted he didn't go to school.

That could mean only one thing.

Dak's mind steered back to the conversation he'd had with Doc earlier that day, about how the kids with backpacks were the ones who delivered illegally mined gold, laundered money, and probably even narcotics.

The epiphany sent a shiver through Dak's body, and he exhaled slowly. *So much for getting a good meal.*

He stuffed the rest of the empanada into his mouth with three huge bites and chewed as he strode down the sidewalk behind the boy.

If Hector were a mule for the cartel, then maybe there was something Dak could do to get the kid out of his abysmal situation. And maybe, with a little luck, the kid could steer Dak a little closer to Diaz.

11

Against his better judgment, Dak followed the boy along the streets of Lima. What he thought would be an easy tail job turned out to be trickier than he suspected. The boy dipped in and out of crowds like a fox through trees. One second, Dak had the kid in plain sight. Then Hector would speed up, cut left or right, and disappear from view for several seconds.

Dak found himself trying to speed up to catch the boy, only to have to slow down because he'd nearly caught up.

Once they neared the sketchy streets of the tugurizadas, though, Dak had to play things differently. He hung back, dipping into side streets, hiding around corners, or sliding into the alcoves of closed shops.

Darkness descended over the city only a few minutes into the journey, which made staying concealed easier but tracking his quarry more difficult. Dak couldn't believe that the boy was permitted to roam the city streets alone in the day, much less after dark. Then again, it probably wasn't allowed—it was required. He'd seen several other kids making their way back to the slums—a sort of disturbing rush-hour of child laborers hurrying to get back to their derelict homes.

The abject poverty of the tugurizadas struck Dak hard as he and Hector left the city-proper behind. A faint smell of garbage littered the air. Children played on the sidewalks and between the shacks that lined the streets. The dilapidated homes filled almost the entire hillside to the left and were likewise packed together on the right. Some of the structures were built from metal siding, while others featured a mixture of earth, rock, and tin.

Tiny lights flickered on the hillsides all around, and Dak could see in the faint glow of early evening moonlight that the slums covered the surrounding mountainsides. Dak's heart twisted at the sight, and it only got worse.

Two children—a boy and girl, both under five—sat on a makeshift porch sixty feet away, staring with hungry, hollow eyes at the gringo as he passed.

Dak wished he had more empanadas to give to them. There'd been no way he could have anticipated this, though, and he reminded himself that he'd decided to follow the boy on a whim.

He still didn't entirely know why he'd tracked Hector back to this place. Perhaps it was a feeling, a hunch that the kid might need his protection just to get home safe. Or was it merely intense curiosity that pushed Dak to follow the boy. He wasn't sure, but one thing Dak knew was that something in his gut tugged at his instincts and forced him to continue tailing the unsuspecting Hector all the way here.

The area reminded Dak of the *favelas* in Brazil, a similar place where the poor were kicked by the boot of modern society. There, too, drug cartels ran much of city life, using people as expendable resources until their usefulness ran out.

It wasn't like the people had much choice. For most of them, they didn't know any other way. The slums were their lives. They'd been born into hopeless poverty, and they would die in it. For them, no light shimmered at the end of the tunnel. Few were able to find work that would pay enough for them to climb out of the hole that had sucked in so many. Because they'd lived in the tugurizadas or the favelas their entire lives, they didn't get the education that could get them better jobs, and many of the businesses wouldn't pay well for unqualified labor.

Hector climbed the rickety wooden ladder to the top where a narrow wooden porch encircled his home.

The tiny shack was built on top of a lower level of slums. Made of aluminum siding and roofing, his mother had painted the exterior walls a bright blue in an effort to bring some sense of joy to their lives.

Hector walked around to the other side of the humble dwelling, and Dak had to skirt over to the other side of the road—if it could be called that—to see the boy enter through a rickety wooden door. That side of the home was built of cinder blocks, perhaps the most stable part of the shack.

Many of the homes filling the tugurizadas displayed similar engineering, being built from whatever had been available. Dak knew that the people here did the best they could with what they had available. They weren't able to drive into town to the big hardware stores and buy lumber, insulation, roofing, siding, or any other proper construction necessities. Dak wondered how some of the places were still standing.

He pulled up the collar of his jacket and zipped it so he could keep a low profile. Not that people were paying much attention to him. The slums were full of people disinterested in the misery of others. It was all they could do to eke out some form of survival, much less a living.

Dak huffed at the thought. *No one is living here. They're just not dying. Not yet anyway.*

He felt his chest tighten as the vision of Hector's face appeared in his memory from earlier in the day. No kid deserved to grow up like this.

He'd never been wealthy growing up, but his parents put food on the table and kept a decent roof over his head.

Dak noticed a narrow side path, more like a half alley between two buildings. The house on the right—constructed from an assortment of bricks and metal siding—appeared to be unoccupied, though he knew that such structures often served as drug pits for addicts to use to get their daily fixes. He peeked through the doorway of the abandoned building and immediately realized why no one was home.

The roof had collapsed in the center of the house, allowing the elements to do as they pleased throughout the interior of what passed for the living room. From the looks of it, the incident happened well over six months ago, maybe more. Water damage was everywhere, and the place reeked of must and filth.

All that remained were a few pieces of furniture: a couch with torn 1970s-style upholstery, a coffee table with a broken wooden leg and its surface covered in dust and grime, an old lamp in the back-right corner with a dingy yellow shade, and an olive-green rug that had been ravaged by rain.

Ignoring the sensory overload, Dak called on his focus the way he had so many times in battle and stepped in through the half-open door. He crept over to the nearest window and dipped his hand into his backpack.

He pulled out a small microphone with a black dish attached to the back. The dish folded to save space, and when expanded only boasted a diameter of four inches. Dak took the wire that dangled from it and placed the earpiece in his right ear. Holding the microphone up to the window, but careful to stay back enough so he wasn't noticed, Dak aimed the device directly at Hector's house and turned it on.

"Where did you get all this, Hector? You are better than that. I told you we are not thieves." The woman's voice came through the earpiece, slightly muted but clear enough for Dak to understand everything she said in Spanish.

"I didn't steal it," the boy protested. "I swear it, Mama. A nice gringo on the street gave me the food. And the extra money was from Señor Flores. He said I was a good worker; someone he could trust to always be on time."

The woman sighed. "Hector, Ricardo Flores isn't someone you

want to impress. And you certainly don't want to be one of his favorites. That's how you end up in the cartel for life."

"I know you tell me they're evil, but look at the life they live. They have nice cars, food, clothes. And you should see the money, Mama. They have these machines counting bills faster than I can think."

"Hector," she snapped. "These are evil people. Their drugs ruin people's lives."

"But you help make the drugs, don't you?"

Dak could hear the confusion in the boy's voice, and he had to admit the kid had a point.

"I don't want to do it, Hector. But I don't have a choice. Your father," she faltered, choking back the pain. "They said it was his fault what happened in the mining accident. Now we owe them a debt."

"A debt for what? It was their mine. You told me it was their fault."

"It was, Son. But no one argues with the cartel. But I promise, I will get us out of here, out of the tugurizadas, out of Lima forever. Then we will be free."

"How are you going to do that?" Hector's confusion melted into childlike curiosity.

"I've been saving some money. As much as I can. It isn't a lot yet, but when we have enough, we're going to Santiago."

"Santiago? Why there?"

"I can sell my jewelry there," she said. "We can start over, Hector. It won't be long. I promise. Just a few more months, and then I'll have enough money to rent a flat in the city; a proper apartment."

Silence settled into the conversation like fog in a cemetery.

"Then this money will help make that happen faster," Hector offered. "Please, Mama. Take it. I think there might be more where that came from, too. Señor Flores—"

"I want you to stay away from Señor Flores as much as possible, Hector. He is an evil man, a manipulator. He may seem generous, appreciative even, but he is the devil." Her voice lowered to a whisper. "Just like Señor Diaz. Tell me you will do what I ask."

"Okay, Mama. I will."

"Swear it," she demanded.

"I swear."

She drew a deep breath in and exhaled. "Thank you."

"What about the money?"

"I don't want their dirty money, but all the money we earn is dirty. From their drugs or their mines or whatever else the cartel has their fingers in, it's all dirty. But I won't sell my soul much longer, Hector. You are such a kind, unselfish boy, sharing this food and this money with me. Your selflessness has, perhaps, taken the dirt off it. We will use it to make our new life. And we will never help the cartel again."

"Okay, Mama."

Dak could almost see the boy's smile through the response in his earpiece.

"Now," she changed subjects, "tell me about the gringo who gave you this food. I hope you weren't begging, especially after receiving such a sum of money."

"I don't know," Hector said. "He was just a man. It was funny, though. That was the second time I bumped into him today. I saw him earlier outside the bookstore."

"He wasn't following you, was he?"

Dak noted the sincere concern.

"No, he wasn't. I always make sure no one follows me. I would have noticed a tall gringo like him. There was something about his eyes. They were green like mountain grass in the summer. He seemed kind. I don't know why he offered me the food. I wasn't going to take it, but then I figured this would be a good way to celebrate the extra money I earned today."

"Yes, well, it was very kind of this stranger to offer you something to eat. And you do look hungry." Sadness swelled in her tone. "Yes, my love. Let's eat. We are celebrating, after all. And soon, we will be in a new home, in a new place, safe from all of this."

Dak lowered the mic and switched it off. After tugging the earpiece from his ear, he folded the dish and stuffed the device back in his rucksack. He stared at the shack for several minutes, more time than he'd intended. His chest stung, and his gut remained tight from the conversation he'd heard.

Fortunately for Hector and his mother, a plan continued to evolve in Dak's mind that would solve both their problems—and complete his assignment at the same time. The name and location of his next target reverberated in his mind.

Raul Piñeda, you're next.

12

Fernando Diaz stepped out of the white Mercedes SUV and peered around the street corner through black sunglasses, even though night had fallen more than an hour before. His white suit jacket and pants ruffled in the breeze.

Two police cars blocked the lane nearest the sidewalk, but there was no crime scene tape, no flashing lights, no sign of trouble other than two cops standing guard at the entrance to the Tortuga Roja.

Diaz's entourage wrapped around him like an armored glove. Each man carried pistols in holsters, all in plain sight. The cops said nothing. They were, after all, working for the same team.

Diaz removed the sunglasses and ran his fingers over his shaved head. He stared at the door for several heartbeats, as if he would tear down the entire building purely with his outrage.

He glanced over at his lead bodyguard, a man named Paco, and nodded.

At six foot three, Paco towered over Diaz who was a full six inches shorter. Paco bowed his head in reply and ventured forward with Diaz tucked in behind.

The other four bodyguards followed them, each checking the perimeter as they proceeded into the building.

Diaz only gave a vague nod to the two cops as he passed them. Even with them on the payroll, the head of Lima's biggest cartel didn't trust the police. They were turncoats in their own organization, which meant they could just as easily be persuaded to turn back.

So far, no one had been foolish enough to do such a thing.

A strange smell washed over Diaz as he entered the brothel. The usual scents of incense, tobacco, and weed were fainter than usual. Another thing he noticed upon entry was the sticky feel of death hovering in the lobby.

No one manned the front desk, and the halls and upstairs didn't allow a peep. Diaz turned to Paco for answers. "Where are the girls?"

He'd been told there was an incident at the Tortuga Roja that needed his immediate attention. When he declined, telling the cop who made the call that Boldega could handle it, the policeman went on to inform Diaz that Boldega was dead.

The cop had, apparently, gone into the brothel during a break on his shift when he discovered the place empty, except for two bodies. One of those corpses belonged to Antonio Boldega.

Paco sighed and answered the question. "They're gone. No one knows what happened to them. The cop who called said they were gone when he got here."

"Which cop?"

"The one on the left of the door outside. He's the one who found the place empty."

"Bring him in here."

"Yes, sir."

Paco turned and disappeared through the door while Diaz ambled over to the desk and looked over the barren shelves and lower counter that held the register.

As Paco returned with the cop, Diaz kept his back to the door, knowing that his four guards would allow nothing to happen to him.

"Here he is," Paco said, presenting the cop as if he were some sort of animal at auction.

Diaz kept his gaze down at the counter surface. "Where are the girls?" The question was simple enough, but it came with an unstated threat, a threat that if Diaz didn't get the answer he wanted, there would be a third body in the bordello.

"I'm sorry, Señor Diaz. They weren't here when I arrived."

"And you saw nothing?"

"No, sir. The place was empty, except for...." He hesitated to go on.

"Except for the two dead men upstairs? Yes, I've heard that account." Diaz paused for three long breaths then rounded on the man. "I'm sorry, but I find it very difficult to believe that every single girl managed to get out of here without being seen."

The dumbfounded cop shook his head. "We don't know, sir. We called you as soon as we found out. We figured you would want to be the first on the scene so you could tell us what to do."

Diaz licked his lips and nodded slowly. The cop *had* done the right thing, and Diaz definitely wanted to be there. Someone had hit one of his businesses. It was mostly a front for cleaning cash, just like most of his ventures, legitimate or otherwise. But whoever did this took all of his stock. It would take weeks for him to get more girls, not to mention Diaz would have to find a replacement for Boldega.

Admittedly, that was the smallest of his losses. Antonio had been a sleazeball, but what other kind of person operated a brothel? On top of that, he was Diaz's cousin, so he felt a faint obligation to provide his relative with employment. As idiotic as he could be, Antonio never shorted Diaz on the week's take, never cheated him. Difficult attributes to find in an employee in Diaz's world.

"Paco," Diaz said, slowly turning to face his bodyguard. "Check the video footage from the camera in the back. I want to know who did this."

"Right away, sir." Paco burst into motion, striding across the floor to the purple curtain covering the corridor.

As Paco disappeared into the back of the building, Diaz stared at himself in the mirror over the lounge chair on the far wall. He straightened his neck and turned his attention to the cop.

"Show me," he ordered.

The cop's head snapped down. "Yes, sir." Then he stepped forward, heading to the stairs. Diaz and the remaining four guards followed him up and around the corner, then up the main flight to the second floor.

A new odor struck Diaz's senses, drowning out those downstairs. This one was bitter, acrid, with a hint of something metallic.

When he reached the door on the left where the cop stood, he discovered the source of the odor.

Inside the chamber, a naked man lay prostrate on the floor in a pool of congealed blood. His head rested on its side; unseeing eyes fixed on some random point halfway across the room. Diaz could see that the man's neck had been slit, deep and wide. Cartels executed people in such a way, always making sure the blade went deep enough to make the death quick and efficient.

But who had done it? None of the other cartels had the cojones to hit one of his operations. Diaz considered the notion. It *was* one of his smaller businesses, with almost no security to speak of except the cameras and the pistol Antonio carried. Perhaps they'd all been too confident in the Diaz brand scaring away potential threats.

"Show me my cousin," Diaz asked, staring without regard at the dead man on the floor.

"Yes, sir." The cop motioned toward the end of the hall.

The group walked down the corridor, Diaz slowing to inspect each room briefly along the way, before stopping at the last one on the right.

Another new odor. Diaz found himself struggling against the urge to cover his mouth or turn and empty his stomach at the wretched smell. He clenched his jaw and fought off the reflex. He could see on one of the guards' faces that he was fighting the same battle.

Diaz stepped into the room and looked over at the dead body against the wall. His cousin's face was covered in vomit and a needle stuck out of his arm—plunger fully depressed.

Diaz took a slow breath through his mouth to keep as much of the smell at bay as possible, then analyzed the scene. He knew his cousin had been a screwup. Antonio dipped into the family's product more than occasionally. But most of them enjoyed cutting up a rail and snorting it every now and then. Heroin, however, was not one of Antonio's vices.

"He was murdered," Diaz stated out loud as he crouched low and stared into his dead cousin's vacant eyes.

"Sir, it was an overdose. The needle is still in his arm. They're all over the place. It has to be heroin."

Diaz whirled on the cop with flames in his eyes and nostrils flaring like a raging bull. He raised a finger and shoved it at the cop's face, stopping just inches from the man's nose.

"My cousin wasn't a smack head. He did a lot of things, had his vices, but heroin wasn't one of them. Understand?"

"Yes. Of course. It's just that—"

"Just that you forgot your place? He was murdered, and I want all of our resources available to find out who did it."

"Yes, sir. We will."

The cop lingered nervously for several seconds, to which Diaz put his hands out demandingly.

"Well? Why are you not moving? Is there something else you want to tell me?"

Heavy footsteps outside the room interrupted them, and a second later Paco appeared in the open doorway. He held up his phone so that Diaz could see. "Two vans came by earlier this afternoon. We have footage of the girls being taken away by two men."

"Can you identify them?" Diaz peered with narrowed eyes at the device.

"No. Their faces were covered. But we were able to get a number off the side of the second van. Whoever was using it tried to paint over it, but the black numbering is still barely visible."

"Can we track it?"

"I believe so. I have two men on it right now."

"Make it four," Diaz said, motioning to two of the guards still in the hallway.

The men nodded their assent and marched away.

"If there are numbers on the side, that means the trucks are rentals. We should be able to track down the place that rented them. Then we'll have our killer."

The quick detective work brought Diaz's attention back to the cop. "Why are you still here?" he roared. "What is it that you need so badly to tell me?"

"Sir?" The cop looked terrified.

"Would you just spit it out?" Diaz barked. He drew his pistol and aimed it at the cop's nose. "Speak quickly, or I will put a bullet through your head. It's not like we don't already have a mess to clean up here."

The cop nearly soiled himself. He felt his knees buckle, but he didn't give in to the weakness. He turned his head slightly and pointed at the doorway.

"What?" Diaz asked. "Speak, man."

"The other room, sir."

"What about it?"

"The victim."

"I don't know who they are."

The cop swallowed his fear and countered. "Yes, you do, sir."

Diaz peered at the man through a haze of confusion. "Who is in the other room?"

The officer hesitated, then said, "The mayor's husband."

"You're certain of this?" Diaz peered into the man's weary, fearful eyes.

"Yes, sir. Without a doubt."

Diaz's face darkened for a few breaths. Then a thought swept away his concerns. What could have been trouble had just been turned into an opportunity.

He rounded on Paco. "Get me any footage of the mayor's husband coming into the brothel. And take pictures of his body. It looks like my cousin's untimely demise might be just the stroke of luck we never anticipated."

13

Dak walked into the cantina and looked over at the back corner where he'd met Doc earlier. The man was sitting in the same spot, just as he said he would be. Dak strode over to him and slid into the booth across from the older man.

Like before, a glass of lager sat on the table in front of Doc.

"Before you ask, I wasn't followed," Dak stated.

"Took you long enough to get here," Doc remarked, gripping the glass with his right hand.

"I detoured a few times, doubled back, you know the drill." It was only sort of a lie, a misleading, really. Dak had taken a big detour, and if anyone had followed him into the slums, it would have been obvious.

"A few times?" Doc groused. The question overflowed with incredulity. "You're an hour and a half late."

"Can't be too careful," Dak said coolly. "Especially with the cartel."

"Yeah. I suppose you're right, but next time don't make me wait. I was just about to leave after I finished this beer."

The soccer game on the television roared with the cheering of thousands of fans and the elongated "Gooooooooaaaaal!" from the broadcaster.

Dak turned and looked at the screen for a second, using the moment to sweep the room for trouble as he'd done upon entering.

Slowly, Dak returned his focus to the man across from him. "The girls okay?"

"Yeah, well, as good as can be expected. A few of them were in rough shape—needed medical attention. Some fluids will set them right, at least for now, but they were all drugged. Will take weeks, months more likely, to get them off that stuff."

"They're going to crash emotionally, too," Dak added. "They'll need mental health care as soon as possible. You think you'll be able to find their families?"

"Some, yes. Others, maybe not." Doc decided to change the subject. "Did you find what you needed?"

Dak rubbed his chin and pondered the question. "Funny you say it that way."

"Oh?" Doc waved off the waitress who approached from the bar. He disarmed her with a cool grin, and she smiled at him before returning to the bar to get back on her cell phone. "She gets paid to look at Instagram all day and sling five beers an hour. Not a tough gig."

"I doubt she's well paid."

"Probably not. But it ain't digging ditches."

"I suppose not," Dak conceded.

"Where was I?" Doc asked. "Oh yes. What you needed."

Dak leaned back against the vinyl behind him and exhaled. "That's another conversation for another time." He ignored the curious expression from his new friend and went on. "Raul Piñeda. Ever heard of him?"

Doc didn't take long to think on the question. "Yeah, I know Piñeda. Or I know of him, rather. He's a piece of work, that one. Runs his operation like a sweatshop on steroids. It's borderline slavery what he does to his workers. The single difference is that they get to go home to their crappy shacks every night, but only after being worked to the bone for twelve or more hours."

"I guess the cartel doesn't worry about labor laws."

"That supposed to be a joke?"

Dak shrugged. "Was it funny?" He held Doc's gaze with ease.

The older man snorted. "A little. But that's beside the point. Piñeda is a first-class piece of you know what. Been processing blow for the cartel for five years. He got that gig after he bumped off his predecessor. And by bumped off, I mean that literally. As in, off a really high bridge into a ravine."

"Sounds like ancient Roman politics," Dak mused.

"That's not too far from the truth. Bump off your boss, get a promotion. Anyway, if you're going to try to get to Piñeda, it'll be trickier than the brothel. You won't be able to waltz onto that farm with a million-dollar smile on your face. You'll have to sneak in."

"I'm okay with that."

Doc huffed. "Yes. I'm sure you are. I don't have a schematic of the place, but I can get you there. It's just outside the city, so you don't want to walk."

"I have a vehicle."

"Yeah, but you don't want to leave a car sitting around outside the property. One of their patrols will notice it and get suspicious. Better to drop you off and come back for an exfil."

Dak nodded. "That's a good idea. But I don't want to bring you too deep into this."

"Son, I just stole a bunch of girls from the cartel's bordello. I'm already in deep."

"Yeah, but no one saw you."

"Someone is always watching. Sure, we took precautions, but I guarantee you this: Diaz's men are looking for us right now. They may not know who they're looking for yet, but they will not stop hunting until they find us, or we're out of Peru."

"I bet you're the life of every party you walk into," Dak joked.

"Life does that to you. Maybe not everyone. But it did it to me."

Doc downed the rest of his beer and stared absently at the empty glass, a distant pain flooding his eyes and sapping the life from his face. "I'll get you to Piñeda. And I'll get you out of there. Once Piñeda is out of commission, then we'll get the full brunt of Diaz's wrath. He will comb the city for whoever did this."

Doc's eyes drifted up to meet Dak's once more. "They'll start with rival cartels. It will be a bloodbath. I figure they'll take out the heads of the other families just to make sure the message is loud and clear. After that, they'll widen their search throughout the city."

"That will make getting to him much more difficult, too," Dak realized. "Increased security all over his place."

"When we make things too hot in the city, he'll head to his mountain retreat about thirty minutes from here. It's remote, and a friggin' fortress."

"You've seen it?"

"Once. I got curious one day, and probably a little stupid. I followed Diaz's caravan out into the country. When it was impossible for me to tail him without being noticed, I backed off, but I already knew where he was going."

"So, the home we talked about before?" Dak asked.

"When things get hot enough, I don't think he'll stay the city. Too many variables. Any ordinary citizen could be the one picking off his men and destroying his inventory. Like those poor guys in 'Nam. The Vietcong would send children and women, strapped with explosives, into the midst of infantry columns. Of course, our guys couldn't do anything about it until it was too late." His voice trailed off.

"I'm too young to have been there, but I remember reading about that." Dak let his statement be his condolences and left it at that.

"Well, now Diaz can fear the same kind of covert attack. But first, we have to get to Piñeda."

Dak nodded. "When?"

"I say we scope it out tonight. We can get a better idea of the patrols, how they move, how many guards he has. That sort of thing."

"Sounds good." Dak glanced down at the empty glass. "Maybe I should drive."

Doc followed Dak's gaze, inspected the glass for a couple of seconds, then nodded. "Yeah, you're probably right."

14

Fernando Diaz sat at the wrought-iron bistro table in the center of his inner courtyard. Three stories of beige stucco walls surrounded him, along with iron gates in the front and back of the area.

This was his quiet place, and one of the few spots he could find peace in what was perhaps the most dangerous line of work a person could choose. Not that he had a choice.

Diaz's rise to power was well known among his men, and many of the cartels who dreamed about becoming a rival. He started as an errand boy for Don Miguel Esperanza, working his way up the ladder with grit, determination, and an utterly ruthless way of handling the dirty side of business.

Growing up in the tugurizadas, Diaz knew what it was like to live in abject poverty, and he hated it. He loathed it so much he decided that he would never allow himself to fall back into that state. That motivation had led Diaz to do unspeakable things. His reputation for brutality rivaled some of the most infamous gangs and cartels on the planet. It was his belief that to maintain order, and the lifestyle he'd grown accustomed to, a firm and often cruel hand had to be shown to everyone within, and outside of, his organization.

He mulled over his history briefly, only giving it a few passing thoughts as he guided his mind to the issue at hand—his cousin's killer. So far, the last few hours had brought no new insights to the mystery, save one. The murderer had come through the front door. The security camera in the corner had captured only part of the man's face, though, and nothing that could be used to identify him other than his clothes. Diaz knew that by now the suspect had already changed his attire, leaving Diaz's investigators only one detail to go on—the man was a gringo, probably an American.

The way he'd kept his face out of direct view of the camera either meant that he knew the camera was there, or he'd been lucky. Based on the way the man moved, Diaz was inclined to think it was the former. If he was a visitor to Lima, there was a good chance the killer had already skipped town, flown back to his native land perhaps.

He raised a glass of rum to his lips and took a sip. The mild burn vanished quickly, but the vanilla and oak aftertaste stayed with him long after he'd swallowed. It was one of his favorite rums, and difficult to get in this part of the world. *Except for a man like me,* he thought.

Diaz wondered what the killer's motivation was for taking out his cousin. Antonio was a low-level functionary, with only tertiary connections to cartel operations. So, why? Why would someone kill Antonio?

It wasn't some random customer, unsatisfied with the product or pricing at the bordello. No one was ever disappointed there. No, this man came specifically to kill. The fact that he'd killed the mayor's husband only deepened the mystery, but it might have given some insight to the crime.

If the murderer had only killed Antonio, then Diaz figured it was a hit, perhaps by a rival cartel getting a little too brazen. But the killing of the second man threw a wrench into that.

The mayor's husband had no connection to Antonio other than on a transactional basis. Perhaps the answer was right under Diaz's nose. *Is it possible this was one of those crimes of passion? Did the mayor find out about the man's infidelity and have him and anyone fueling his desires killed?*

Diaz considered the possibility, and the more he dwelled on it, the more it made sense. The way the killer had entered the lobby, kept his face diverted from the camera. It had to be someone who'd been there before, or at least knew the setting well. Or the killer was a professional assassin, someone who knew how to do things with enough stealth to remain unidentifiable.

Diaz raised the glass to his lips and took another swig. The more he considered it, the more he believed that the latter was a logical explanation, and that Antonio had either truly overdosed, or been collateral damage.

What that didn't explain was what happened to all the girls.

Diaz didn't believe the assassin had taken them, although it was possible the man returned with a mask on and helped the girls into the vans. But where they'd gone, he had no clue. Still, there was more than one person involved, and judging by the timeframe between the killings and when the vans arrived, it seemed unlikely the killer had returned. More likely, he called in the other two men when the targets were eliminated.

DIAZ GRUNTED from the mental effort required for solving this. He ran his fingers down both sides of his face in exasperation. It was getting late, and Paco hadn't reported back yet.

With a sigh, Diaz leaned forward and picked up the metal straw next to his glass. He hovered over a line of cocaine he'd cut up earlier and snorted it in less than a second. He tilted his head back, pulled in a huge breath of air through his nostrils, then shook his head one time.

Free product was one of the perks of being on top.

He knew that many other cartel heads didn't indulge. They were unwilling to eat where they worked, but he wasn't an addict. Diaz primarily used the drug for moments like this, when he was stressed out and tired, needing a boost to keep him awake while contemplating a serious issue.

He set down the straw and picked up the glass of rum just as Paco walked in through the front gate. The imposing bodyguard carried a smartphone in one hand and a dark, emotionless expression on his face as he passed the two armed guards at the entrance.

"Tell me you have something," Diaz said, forgoing any pleasant greetings.

"I do." Paco stopped at the table and set the phone down in front of his boss. The screen displayed a car rental business specializing in vans and moving trucks.

"This is where they got the vans from?"

Paco nodded.

"Then I assume you know who owns this establishment," Diaz hedged.

"We have the owner in our custody as we speak."

Diaz's eyebrows shot up with surprise; partially from the ecstatic high of the rail of snow he'd just inhaled. "Really?"

Paco's even lips creased only slightly on one side. "You pay me to get things done, sir. That's what I do."

Diaz's expression changed to one of approval, and he nodded. "That's very true, my friend. Very true. Bring him to me."

Paco picked up his phone and stuffed it in his pocket, then turned to the guards at the gate and ordered them to bring in the prisoner.

The guard on the right stepped through the gate and disappeared. He returned less than a minute later with two other guards dragging a skinny man in a cotton polo. The brown and white striped shirt showed a smattering of bloodstains, and one look at the man's beaten face revealed the answer as to where the blood had come from.

Ten feet from the table, the guards shoved the prisoner forward, where Paco caught him and held him by the back of the neck to the point it appeared the bodyguard's grip was the only thing holding the captive upright.

Paco held up his phone and switched images to display the scene of the two vans parked behind the brothel. "These are your vans, yes?"

The man nodded helplessly. "Yes. I rented them earlier today. Please, I don't understand what is happening. I'm just a lowly businessman. No one pays any attention to me. I didn't do anything wrong."

Diaz held up his hand. The man took the cue and shut his mouth. "Who did you rent the two vans to?"

"Just a guy, sir. I swear. A gringo." The man chattered the words through busted lips and an overwhelming sense of dread.

"An American?"

The prisoner's head bobbed like a rotten apple on a pencil. "Yes. Yes, sir."

"What was his name?"

Paco reached into his back pocket and produced a folded piece of paper. He handed it over to his boss, who accepted it without comment.

Diaz opened the paper and read the information on the rental sheet. "This says you rented the truck to a man named Peter Davenport." The statement also sounded like a question.

"Yes, sir. That was his name. He had identification and everything."

Diaz held up his hand again as he studied the paper. The captive shut his mouth once more and watched, hoping with every passing second that he'd provided the most dangerous man in Lima with what he wanted.

After a long minute, Diaz folded the paper again and handed it back to Paco. "Find this Peter Davenport," he ordered. "Bring him to me."

"Of course, sir."

"What about me, Señor Diaz?" the captive asked, desperation overflowing in his words.

Diaz cocked his head to the side and inhaled deeply. The smells of sage, lavender, and salty air wafted into his nostrils and tickled his senses. He nodded appreciatively. "You have been a great help to us."

Diaz twisted his head to face the bodyguard. "Paco? Let this man go."

Paco acknowledged with a single nod. "Yes, sir."

"Oh, thank you, Señor Diaz. Thank you so much. I appreciate it."

Diaz smiled meekly back at the man and nodded, waving his hand to dismiss the two.

He watched as Paco escorted the man back through the gate and to the left. When they were gone, Diaz picked up his glass and downed the remainder of the rum. He might sleep better tonight, knowing that they could locate the man responsible for his cousin's murder. Or if Davenport weren't the killer, he certainly would know who was responsible for Antonio's death.

PACO LED the prisoner down the dimly lit corridor. Electric candles burned in sconces along the light brown walls, their false flickers dancing on the ceiling and rippling the shadows of the two men on the walnut floor as they walked.

The two turned down another hallway, which featured paintings of various landscapes in Mexico: mountains, farms, and valleys. Some contained colorful sunsets and sunrises.

The captive looked around in bewilderment. "Your employer has excellent taste in art," the man said nervously.

Paco remained silent, continuing to usher the man forward with a firm grip on the prisoner's arm.

"I'm sorry, but we didn't come in this way," the captive clarified his confusion. "Is there another exit we're going to use?"

No answer.

"Will you be taking me back to my house? I'm not married, and all of my friends are asleep right now, or will be soon." The man looked at Paco, his eyes digging into the side of the man's skull as if they could bore the answer from his skin.

Again, Paco said nothing. He wore the same grim look on his face he'd been wearing since he encountered the henchman.

Before he could ask another question, the prisoner noticed the strengthening scent of the ocean. Between their footsteps on the hardwood floor, he also thought he detected the sound of waves crashing on the shore.

They turned right at the next corridor, and the man realized where the smells and sounds were coming from.

A single armed guard held a door open, which led onto a balcony. A strong ocean breeze blew through the opening and down through the corridor, circling the two men as they approached.

"What are we doing here?"

Once more, Paco didn't respond. The prisoner started to resist, stiffening his legs as if that could slow the huge bodyguard. "I think we took a wrong turn. Perhaps we should go back the other way."

"I was told to let you go," Paco said, his voice dark and cryptic. "That's what I'm doing."

"So, is there a staircase here?" A sliver of hope shimmered in the words.

"Something like that."

They stepped through the doorway and out into the night. The rhythmic crash of waves a hundred feet below filled the wet, salty air.

The captive looked around, frantically searching for the stairs. Then he felt the hand on his arm shift to his neck, and another grab him by the belt.

"What are you..." Terror filled the man's eyes. "What are you doing? You said you were going to let me go."

Paco's cold response sent a chill through the prisoner. "I am."

"What? No! Please! Please! Don't do this!" He screamed as Paco lifted then tossed him over the railing. The man's screams faded into the abyss, vanishing forever on the foamy rocks below.

Paco turned and faced the other guard at the doorway. "Boss wants to pick up another one. An American named Peter Davenport."

"American? We don't usually mess with them." The guard's look of concern mirrored the question.

"It's personal."

15

Dak peered through the lens of his night-vision scope. The scene before him was little of what he expected to find, and a lot of the unexpected.

Doc crouched next to him against the embankment, digging his shoulder into the earth as he also looked through a night-vision scope.

"That's a lot of guards," Dak noted.

"If twenty's a lot," Doc joked.

Dak snorted. Part of him wished Doc had been younger and in his special operations unit in the Middle East. The guy would have fit right in. Or one of the team might have gotten tired of his snark and shot him in the desert. Dak grinned at the thought. It was fifty-fifty in his mind.

But he liked Doc. The man was no nonsense, no fluff. He didn't say anything he didn't mean, and if you didn't like it, he would lose exactly zero seconds of sleep over it.

"Won't be easy," Dak admitted. "But I've seen worse."

"Yeah," Doc said, taking his eye from the scope and turning to face Dak. "I'm sure you've seen some pretty rough situations."

"Yes, sir," was all the man would get from Dak.

"Well," Doc returned to his scope and swept his view across the ten-foot chain-link fence surrounding the compound.

The property was nestled in a valley where an old farm merged into a sparse forest. A metal building that looked like it was half barn, half warehouse stood in a clearing in the middle of the woods. A dirt road ran through the gate at the fence and stopped at the processing facility where, even at this late hour, the lights were on.

"Working the late shift," Dak hissed in disgust.

"These people are little more than slaves," Doc said in response. "It's terrible."

"Well," Dak said, "maybe it's time someone busted up this little operation."

Doc looked at him again with concern in his eyes. "I thought you said we were going to recon the situation and come back at an optimal time."

"I did say that. Now I'm changing the plan."

"A little quarterback audible, huh?" Doc said. "Well, aren't you a regular Peyton Manning." He put the scope to his eye again and peered at the fence. "You're not wrong, though."

Dak took the half concession.

Doc went on, keeping his voice low. "This is as good a time as any. Probably the best time, actually. Those guards are going to be tired, even if they just started their shift, which they didn't. My guess is they've been on duty for at least a few hours. They'll be getting bored, but that doesn't mean they won't be jumpy."

"Yep," Dak said, lowering his night-vision scope. He stuffed it into his rucksack and shoved the bag toward Doc. "I guess that means I'll have to be quiet."

"What do you want me to do with this?" Doc asked, motioning to the bag.

"Hold on to it until I get back."

"I thought you wanted me to leave and then meet up with you."

Dak shrugged. "You can do it that way if you want to. But I'd hate for you to miss the show."

"Heh. You're brimming with confidence, that's for sure."

"Thank you," Dak said, standing up and checking the pistol on one hip and the knife on the other.

"It could get you killed."

"Sooner or later, I'm sure it will. Gotta go sometime, right?"

Doc shook his head. "Don't be cliché, kid."

Dak grinned at him and then climbed over the embankment and took off toward the left side of the fence. As Doc watched him through the scope, he noticed a pair of wire cutters in Dak's left hand.

The older man shook his head and grunted. "That boy is going to get himself killed," he mused. "But I like him."

Dak skirted the clearing in the forest and stopped at a collection of SUVs parked away from the gate in a gravel lot. He maneuvered around the vehicles and continued through the trees, using the trunks for cover. Two guards armed with submachine guns stood at the gate. Four more were inside the fence at the doors to the dilapidated facility, about fifty yards from the gate. Only a few trees could be used for cover once Dak was inside, but there were other ways he could stay out of sight. Old farm equipment littered the fence's confines: three tractors, a big military-style transport truck, a combine, and several stacks of old wooden crates.

Dak froze behind one tree the second he spotted one of the patrols making his rounds along a path just inside the fence. Another guard passed him walking the other direction. Dak retrieved his scope again and peered through it. From this vantage point, he could see most of the fence except where it disappeared behind the processing building, and the random spots blocked by the farm equipment.

He waited patiently for the men to continue farther along their path. When the one walking away from him reached the corner of the fence and turned right, Dak sprang from his hiding spot. Keeping low to the ground amid patches of tall grass and shrubs, he crept over to the corner where a tree stood just fifteen feet from the fence. Dak paused for a few breaths, then scurried over to the barrier.

He clipped the fencing, one section after another, looking up after every snip to look for the next patrol guard coming his way. He was halfway done with his circular hole when another guard came into view near the gate.

The man ambled mindlessly past the entrance, looking out at the road and the forest as he moved.

Dak immediately abandoned his task and returned to the shadows of the trees. He waited patiently, hoping the guard wouldn't notice the fruits of his labors. The cut section of fence wasn't easily noticeable, but if a guard were checking for that sort of thing, only an aloof idiot wouldn't see it.

He wasn't given to nerves often, but at the moment, a lot was riding on this guard not spotting Dak's handiwork. There were people in that facility, working in some degree against their will, and for an organization that caused harm to others in myriad ways. The last thing on his mind was the payment from Boston.

Dak leaned against the tree's rough bark. He deftly slid the pistol out of its holster. Holding it high and tight close to his right shoulder, Dak peered around the tree trunk, watching the gunman like a wolf stalking its prey.

The guard continued his steady pace and walked all the way to the corner, then paused. Dak watched intensely as he hoped the man wouldn't see the clipped wiring of the fence. For a second, he thought the man might have noticed. The gunman appeared to be inspecting something close to where Dak had been working, but then the static of a radio crackled, and the guard reached for his receiver and responded to the call as he proceeded down the path in the other direction.

When the man was out of earshot, Dak hurried back to the fence and rapidly cut away the rest of the fencing. Then he crawled through the hole and onto the grass on the other side. After checking both directions for trouble, he replaced the fence, carefully balancing it against the uncut portion. It wouldn't even remotely pass a close inspection, but by the time Dak was done with them, none of the guards would know what had happened.

He hurried across the open area to one of the tractors and waited. He pulled out his scope again and peered across at the entrance to the facility. He lowered the device when the light pouring out of the building bathed the lens, making it difficult to see. The same guards he'd seen before were at the front door. He swept around to the left and noted a closed side door. That might be an option for entry, but it could also be a death trap. He suspected another guard would be waiting on the other side, but fortunately he didn't have to guess.

He retrieved another device from his belt and raised it to eye level. A dark blue scene appeared on the LED screen. He could see the outline of the building, along with colorful waves of orange, red, and yellow seeping out of the windows along the roofline and from the front door. The bodies, too, came into view, filling the screen with similar warm colors.

The thermal scanner gave him a view into the building that he wouldn't have had otherwise and allowed Dak to count the exact number of guards and workers within the facility's confines.

Workers sat at a long table, from the looks of it, going through monotonous motions. Dak didn't need to see with his own eyes to know what they were doing. They were cutting and packaging cocaine. Other figures stood around the gigantic room, each holding darker objects that contrasted the brightly colored body-heat signatures.

Dak recognized the guns hanging from the men's shoulders, held in front of them in a threatening manner. If one of the workers so much as sneezed wrong, they would receive immediate and terrible punishment.

Dak counted the number of guards inside the building, making sure he had the correct tally. A miscount in this kind of situation would be a lethal mistake. The last thing he wanted was to catch a bullet in the back from a guard he'd failed to account for. Thanks to the guards' spacing, it was easy to spot them all.

In his peripheral, Dak caught movement to the left and ducked down into the shadows. Another guard sauntered along the fence, lazily carrying his weapon at his waist. His focus was outward, toward the trees and surrounding hills. It made sense. Why would any of them look for a threat inside the confines?

Dak knew better than to take out those guards first. With them overlapping and constantly passing by the gunman at the gate, it would only be a minute or two before the enemy realized something was wrong.

The plan was simple, in theory. Get into the building, take out the guards inside, which would cause the perimeter guards to storm the building. Sure, he would be outnumbered and outgunned, but he'd have the advantage of creating a bottleneck in all the entrances to the facility as the men poured in.

The downside was that there could be collateral damage of the human kind. The workers could be accidentally—or worse, intentionally—shot. The more he considered his initial plan, the more Dak didn't like it.

What he needed was a distraction.

He rose slightly from his crouching position and looked through the gap in the tractor between the seats. Just as he figured, no key was in the ignition, not that the old machine would have run anyway. Based on its appearance, the tractor hadn't been used in years, and the engine block was likely locked up.

Dak scanned the immediate area, inspecting the farm equipment until his sweeping gaze stopped on a dark green golf cart parked near the back corner of the building. He'd noticed the cart before but hadn't thought much of it. Until now.

Stealthily, Dak slid under the tractor's chassis and waited until the next guard passed by. Like clockwork, the man ambled along the fence path toward the back of the property. With the guard safely walking the other direction, and out of earshot, Dak hurried to the next tractor twenty feet away. He paused only for a second, then slipped through the tall grass and over to a combine.

There, Dak pressed his shoulder against the inner part of the front-right tire and waited, watching the fence for the next guard. With no sign of the patrol, he crouched down and crawled under the huge machine to the other side. Once there, the golf cart was in clear view only forty feet away.

Only forty feet, he complained in his head. That normally

wouldn't be a huge distance, but without any cover between his current position and the cart, he'd be out in the open and easily spotted if someone were to look the right way.

He surveyed the area to his right and left and made up his mind. Now was as good a time as any.

16

Dak burst from his hiding spot, and sprinted toward the golf cart as fast as he could while keeping the lowest possible profile. Half the distance to the cart provided the tall grass that appeared to have never been cut, so he could at least keep mostly out of sight until he reached the bare dirt surrounding the building.

Once there, Dak sped up, knowing he only had seconds before the next patrol came around the back of the facility. Or the front. Or both.

The moment he reached the cart, he ducked under the floorboard and stayed down. He didn't dare look out through the windshield or the back. Based on the timing of the patrol, Dak knew there would be another guard or two appearing any second.

He forced himself to be patient and waited, looking out through the passenger side of the cart while holding his pistol in front of his chest.

Dak only allowed himself to be distracted by a single item—the key dangling in the ignition to his left.

He grinned at the stroke of luck, but also knew he wasn't just lucky.

Anyone Dak had ever known who owned a golf cart almost never took the keys out, even if the machine weren't kept in a garage. He figured that if someone wanted to steal an electric golf cart, it would be a slow getaway, or the battery would eventually run out, thus stranding the thief. He'd heard of instances where people stole them with trailers or ramps onto pickup trucks, but that hadn't deterred the owners he knew from often leaving the keys in plain sight.

So when he darted across the clearing to this golf cart, it was more strategic than hopeful.

Waiting in the cart exercised every ounce of patience he could muster. It reminded him of a mission he'd completed in Afghanistan —minus the golf cart and cartel goons.

In that episode, he'd been forced to hide out in a farmer's cart full of hay, waiting for Taliban sympathizers to emerge from a barn where they were conducting a secret meeting.

Fortunately, on this mission, he didn't have to wait for hours like he did in Afghanistan. The guard he'd seen when cutting the fence emerged around the corner of the building, taking the same path he had before. Dak had no misgivings as to whether or not the man would miss the damaged fence this time around. He'd been lucky before, but the odds of the guy not noticing now were much slimmer.

Dak lowered his weapon and turned the key into the on position. Then a voice from behind froze him where he crouched.

"Hey," a man said in gruff Spanish. "What are you doing?"

Dak didn't look up, instead, he lifted the seat and pretended to fiddle with the wiring. As he rifled through the cart's internals, he concealed the pistol on top of the battery, then shifted his hand down to the knife on his left hip. "Sorry," he replied in perfect Spanish. "The boss wanted me to have a look at this thing. Said the motor was sluggish. Probably just needs to be charged, but you know he wouldn't appreciate being asked if he'd plugged it in."

Dak risked his response on a common male theme. Most men he knew, including himself, didn't like being asked the obvious. It was one of the few things that annoyed him in his relationship with Nicole. Whenever they'd had an issue with anything electrical, her go-to question was always, "Did you check to see if it's plugged in?"

"I know what you mean," the guard said as he approached from around the back driver's side of the cart. "Probably a smart move."

"Yes," Dak agreed. The gunman hadn't seen his pistol yet, and he definitely hadn't seen the knife he gripped in his left hand. "Could you hold this seat up for me? It's such a pain to try to prop it up while I check this stupid machine."

The guard chuckled and stepped around into full view. The stocky gunman stood close to the golf cart, displaying a single gold tooth in the middle of his vacuous grin. Tattoos adorned his neck, and from the looks of it, they continued down to his chest. He was probably in his late twenties, strong, full of ambition. He didn't realize he had only seconds to live.

The guard grabbed the seat by the bottom and held it up easily.

"Thanks," Dak said.

Before the guard knew what happened, Dak twisted and thrust the knife up through the back of the man's chin until the hilt stopped it from going farther. The guard's eyes froze. He gurgled for a couple of seconds, but Dak knew the knife point had already struck the brain. All the wide eyes could see now was the cold, black embrace of death.

Dak jerked the knife out as the man dropped to his knees and then over onto his side. After another quick look around, Dak slid off the cart and hefted the body into the seat. He propped the dead man up as best he could, then took the guy's belt from his pants and looped it around a piece of the seat frame behind him.

Satisfied the dead guard wouldn't fall off, Dak positioned the man's foot over the accelerator, lined up the wheel, and pushed the foot down.

The golf cart lurched forward on a beeline for the gate.

Dak didn't remain in the open for long. He hurried back to an old wooden barrel near the corner, sitting in the building's shadow, and watched.

The cart rumbled on the rough terrain as it rolled toward the gate. The ghastly occupant's head bounced and jiggled like a bobblehead doll. Halfway to the entrance, the guards at the gate noticed the cart, but they didn't think much of it, that is until the men realized its passenger was dead.

Shouting ensued. The confused guards seemed caught in a no-man's-land between a decision to shoot it or just let it crash into the fence.

They chose the latter, jumping out of the way as the cart smashed into the fence and came to a stop.

The patrol guard farther along the fence noticed the commotion and immediately rushed to the scene. More hurried over to assist, appearing from various points on the premises.

The commotion also drew the attention of the two guards at the front of the building. The men ran across the yard and down the driveway to the gate to get a look.

It was the best Dak could hope for. There were still several gunmen inside, but now the numbers were more in his favor.

He sprinted to the front of the building, around the corner, and over to the open doorway in the middle of the front exterior wall.

He stopped for only a second, still holding the knife, and slipped inside out of view.

Dak froze the second he was inside, nearly bumping headfirst into another of Piñeda's goons.

The tall gunman's surprised expression became blank when Dak thrust the knife up into the man's skull the same way he'd dispatched the previous guard. The hulking figure fell forward as Dak withdrew the blade and stepped to the side.

Dak didn't wait to check the corpse. The man was no longer a threat.

Moving forward through a short foyer-like corridor, Dak stopped at another doorway that separated him from the processing room. There were still at least four guards on the main floor and two above, and he knew there was no way he could take all of them out with his knife.

He'd have to resort to shooting. Suppressor or not, the second he shot a single bullet, the other men would open fire. It wasn't ideal, but there was no choice.

Hating the idea, Dak twisted the worn doorknob and flung open the door.

He stepped into a nightmare.

Thirty people sat at a long, wooden table, fifteen to each side. Some were chopping up solid white blocks, while others poured liquid into pans to cut the pure cocaine, diluting its strength but increasing the quantity—a common practice by the cartels.

The people went about their tasks in monotonous, zombie-like movements. Their hollow, vapid eyes stared blankly down at the product, almost as if they didn't see it. Short stacks of leaves sat next to the right of each worker.

It took Dak one second to realize what they were. *Coca leaves.*

He'd heard that some organizations gave their workers coca leaves to suppress appetite. No appetite, no need for the workers to eat. And from the looks of this group, they hadn't had a decent meal in a long time.

It took just seconds for Dak to take in the plight of the workers, and now his focus moved to the armed guard in the corner across from him—thirty feet away.

Without pause, Dak moved forward with calculated, deliberate steps. He raised his pistol and fired a single shot through the gunman's forehead.

The loud pop stunned everyone in the room. The workers froze and looked up with shock in their eyes. A guard to Dak's left, six feet away, clutched at his ears from the sudden explosion.

Dak used the knife in his left hand and drove the tip through the man's hand, right ear, and into his skull before turning the pistol to the guard in the far-left corner. Two rapid shots to the torso dropped that gunman before he could muster a retaliation. The one in the far corner lifted his gun, but Dak ended any ideas he might have had with a burst of three rounds—one in the shoulder, one in the center of his chest, and one that sailed a little high and struck the man in the throat.

The guards on the catwalk above scrambled, desperate to get to the other side where they could get off a shot at the interloper.

Dak didn't wait for them to catch up.

Moving to the center of the room, he took aim and fired, sending a round through the base of the first target's jaw. The bullet exited through the top of the skull in a pink eruption. Another gunman on the opposite side opened fire, sending the room into a chaotic clatter of automatic gunfire. Dak darted toward the left end of the room as bullets rained down behind him. Momentarily safe from the shooter's aim under the catwalk, he ejected the magazine and replaced it with a full one.

The guard above yelled obscenity-filled pleas in Spanish, begging for reinforcements.

Dak noticed the man was shouting at a closed office door on the second floor. *Piñeda,* he realized.

The gunman crept around toward the far wall, hoping to get a clear angle, but Dak burst from his cover and twitched his finger rapidly six times, unleashing a volley of hot metal at the target.

Five of the six shots missed, piercing through the flimsy wall's siding. One shot, however, burrowed into the guard's chest on the right side. The man flung back against the wall, stunned. Dak didn't need another opportunity. He stood straight, took aim, and squeezed the trigger.

The bullet hit the man just below the neck. The gunman staggered forward toward the railing, then toppled over it, dropping to the floor below.

To their credit, none of the workers screamed. The second the shooting commenced, they merely covered their ears and ducked under the table as if trained to do so in this type of situation. Dak wondered if they assumed this was a hit by a rival cartel, but he didn't have time to open that conversation.

Instead, he ordered them to stay under the table, then returned to the front door, knowing that the men at the gate would be on their way to reinforce the guards inside.

Just as he suspected, Dak could hear the angry shouts from beyond the entrance. Someone issued orders in loud, sharp barks. They were going to fan out and surround the building, covering both exits. He wasn't sure what would come next, but assumed they would unleash a barrage of gunfire, potentially killing everyone inside—even the workers and their own men.

He hoped he was overestimating their ruthlessness.

If that were the plan, though, Dak would have to come up with a way to counter it.

His eyes drifted up the metal staircase to the catwalk, and the closed office door. The idea blossomed in seconds. While it was certainly risky, it was his best chance at getting himself, and the workers, out of here in one piece.

17

Dak's legs pumped quickly as he ascended the stairs. He reached the top in a blink, and he stopped at the office door with his back against the near wall. A second later, gunshots rang out from inside. Bullets tore through the flimsy wooden door.

Understanding the shooter's intent, Dak grunted and thumped his boot on the catwalk floor. The entire framework shook under his weight.

He remained close to the door, waiting. The men outside would be in position now, or close to it. Time was running out, and if his overestimation proved correct, everyone down below would be cut down in a barrage of gunfire.

A click from the doorknob signaled the man inside was unlocking the door. That was the only invitation Dak needed.

The second the door opened, he reached around and snatched the gunman by the throat before he had a chance to react.

Dak squeezed the man's throat with one hand while snatching a pistol out of the shooter's grip.

"Hello, Raul," Dak said.

The brown eyes that stared back brimmed with fear.

Raul Piñeda was thicker, and easily four inches shorter, than Dak. The fingers clenching Piñeda's fleshy neck sank deep, nearly cutting off the artery.

"I need you to tell your men to stand down. Tell them everything is okay. Understand? If you don't, you're not going to get out of here alive. Got it?"

Piñeda nodded rapidly as panic set in.

"Good. You do anything stupid; I kill you. Diaz isn't a man worth dying for. Neither is his business. Survival is your only concern."

Another nod.

Dak loosened his grip and motioned to a walkie-talkie on the desk. "Tell them to stand down and that everything is under control inside."

He ushered Piñeda over to the old metal desk and shoved him toward it. One of the outside guards was repeatedly asking if everything was okay inside or if Piñeda needed their assistance.

Dak knew the source of their hesitation. If they charged in with guns blazing, they could be cut down in a deadly volley of bullets. They had no idea how many people were inside, or if the interior guards had taken care of the problem.

Piñeda reluctantly picked up the walkie-talkie and pressed the button on the side. "All clear inside," he said with a tremble in his voice. "Stand down and return to your posts. We'll take care of the mess."

"Are you sure?"

"Yes," Piñeda spat, a touch too eagerly. Then, more calmly, he added, "Everything is under control."

"Understood."

Nothing else came through the speaker.

Dak took the walkie-talkie from the man and set it on the desk, then leveled his pistol at Piñeda's face. "We need to talk."

"You're making a big mistake, gringo," Piñeda sneered, albeit timidly.

"Seems like I've been doing that a lot lately," Dak countered. "Sit down."

Dak shoved him into a cheap upholstered chair that reminded him of chairs he'd been in during job interviews in the past. He noticed the open vault to the left, behind the desk. It looked like a gigantic gun safe and contained tall stacks of bills, several gold bars on the top shelf, and two AR15-style rifles.

He returned his attention to Piñeda, knowing the men outside would only believe the ruse for so long.

"You want the money?" Piñeda spoke first. Beads of sweat rolled down his forehead from the buzzed, black hair on his skull. "Take it. It's yours."

"Sure," Dak said. "I take that money, and then Diaz comes after me. I'm not stupid." In the back of his mind, however, he fully intended to take the money. But not for himself.

"I won't tell him. I swear."

The man's desperation overwhelmed any lingering resemblance of common sense he might have grasped.

"We both know that won't work," Dak said. "Forget the money. I'm not here for the money. And I'm not here for the drugs, either."

Fear washed over Piñeda's face. "So, you're here to kill me? Did Diaz send you?"

Dak shook his head. "I'm looking for Diaz. I heard you might be able to help me find him."

"What do you mean, find him?" Piñeda twisted his face in confusion.

"I need to know where he is. Can you take me to his home?"

Piñeda spat out a laugh. "I don't know where he lives. No one does. Anybody who is taken to his place doesn't come out alive."

"Surely you've been there, a trusted lieutenant like you." Dak pressed the issue.

"I'm telling you," Piñeda insisted, "the only people who go to his place and come out alive are his personal guards, and any entertainment that he might bring in."

"Entertainment?"

"Girls." Piñeda shot him a disparaging glare, as if Dak should have known what he meant.

Dak hardened his expression. "Well, you're not much use, are you? Do you know what I do with useless people?" He tensed his finger on the trigger and did it in such a dramatic way that there was no chance Piñeda didn't notice.

"No, please. Wait. Chocho will know where he is."

"Chocho? What is that? One of his dogs or something?"

"No. Chocho runs our operation at the docks. He'll know where the mansion is."

Dak arched one eyebrow. "So, you know it's a mansion."

"Of course. Everyone knows it's a mansion, but no one knows where it is. Diaz keeps all of us connected to each other, but the secrets he harbors are for his personal protection. I think it's because of how he got to where he is."

"And how is that?" Dak sincerely wanted to know.

Piñeda looked surprised. "You don't know?"

"Why would I know? I'm not from around here."

"True." Piñeda considered his next words. "Diaz killed a lot of people to get where he is. The former boss knew he was ruthless and would eventually come after him."

"So, he killed the previous boss?"

"No," Piñeda said. "The old man was clever, he knew that Diaz would try to kill him and take over the organization. He promoted him, making him the second most powerful man in the entire cartel."

"Keep your enemies close, huh?"

"Yes. When he died, Diaz was given the keys to the kingdom. But he is paranoid, afraid that the sins of his past will eventually catch up to him."

"Heavy lies the crown," Dak quoted.

"He's taken extreme measures, even down to the servants who work for him. They almost never leave the compound. I hear they have their own rooms on the property."

Dak realized the man was stalling and forced the conversation forward. "You're telling me a lot without really telling me anything at all." He stabbed the pistol toward the man's face, causing Piñeda to retreat deeper into the chair, if that was possible.

"I'm giving you everything I know. Please. You have to believe me."

"I don't have to do anything, Raul." Dak eased his grip on the pistol. "But you did give me a name. I can work with that."

Piñeda's posture slackened and he let out a relieved sigh.

"You said his name is Chocho?"

Piñeda nodded.

"Where at the docks can I find this Chocho?"

"Number 79. The guards at the port gates can tell you how to find it."

"The port is on the other side of the city," Dak said. "That's a long way to go to find out you were lying to me."

Piñeda put up both hands innocently. "It's not the wrong place. I swear. Dock 79. You'll find Chocho there, along with a few of his men, but he's never surrounded by more than four or five guys."

"Sounds careless."

"Perhaps." Piñeda shrugged.

Another thought occurred to Dak, and he wondered if he could squeeze one last bit of information out of Piñeda.

"There's a bookstore in town," he said. "Who runs it?"

"What?" Piñeda tried to look ignorant, but the lies seeped out of his eyes.

"You know which one I'm talking about. Your organization uses it as a front. Who is in charge there?" Dak cocked his head sideways.

"Flores. His name is Ricardo Flores. He's...Diaz's right hand. But you'll never get to him. That place is well guarded."

"What's the layout?" Dak pressed.

Piñeda glowered at him. "You mean, what does it look like inside?"

Dak held his grim expression.

"The bookstore looks like any bookstore. But there's a door in the back. It leads into the manager's office. That's where Flores runs things. They have money counters there. It's the center of the distribution channels. Most of Diaz's money runs through it."

This guy was giving up all the goods, and Dak couldn't have asked for more, other than the exact location of Diaz's hideout, but that appeared to be a dead end. The only thing Dak could figure was that the man believed if he gave the American enough information, he might let Piñeda live, which Dak found amusing.

Dak glanced over at a black duffle bag and nodded. "I want you to fill up that bag with cash and a couple of those gold bars," he said.

Piñeda fired a scathing glare. "I knew you weren't too pious to take the money."

"It isn't for me. It's for the workers downstairs, the people you've been treating like slaves for who knows how long. Now, stand up."

Piñeda did as instructed and waited.

Dak shifted over next to the desk and removed the two rifles, one by one, while keeping his pistol trained on Piñeda. He leaned the guns up against an old leather couch, then motioned to his prisoner again. "Now, fill the bag, please."

Piñeda moved slowly over to the safe. Once there, he began lifting stacks of paper currency and stuffing them into the proffered duffle bag until there was almost no room left.

"Now, one gold bar," Dak said, indicating the shiny yellow metal with a wave of his pistol.

"Diaz won't let you get away with this. You know that, right?"

The threat did nothing to change Dak's mind.

"So I've heard. The bar. Now."

"Okay. Okay. Take it easy."

Piñeda lifted the first heavy bar off the shelf and carefully laid it in the duffle bag within a sort of cradle he'd made from the cash stacks. Satisfied the brick was secure, he zipped it shut.

"There. Anything else you want me to pack for you?" Piñeda asked, irritated.

"No. Now, move over by the door."

Piñeda shuffled over to the doorway and waited with his hands held high.

Dak reached down and lifted the heavy bag, quickly reminded at just how heavy gold bars could be.

Then he looped the two rifle straps over his opposite shoulder and slung the guns down to his side. The combined weight of his own gear and the new additions was almost overwhelming, but he'd carried that kind of burden before, and then some.

"Down the stairs," Dak ordered. "Nice and slow."

Píñeda obeyed and gradually made his way down the stairs, one step at a time. Dak stayed close behind, keeping the pistol aimed in the middle of the man's spine. One wrong move, and Piñeda would never walk again—if he survived the gunshot.

On the ground floor, Dak shifted Piñeda's stance, forcing him to look toward the front door. Dak took a step backward and addressed the workers still hiding under the long table. Their confused faces housed eyes full of fear. Two of the women kept their heads down, as if they knew they were about to be executed.

"I need all of you to listen," Dak said in Spanish. "Upstairs, in that office, is a vault. The money and gold in it are for all of you to divide among yourselves. If I hear of any bickering or arguing, I will kill the troublemakers." He lied about the last part, but he figured it was one of those rare instances where deceit could prevent trouble.

No one moved.

"I also need you to stay in the office until I tell you to come down. Understand?"

A few of them nodded weakly.

"Good. Now, go on up there. And divide the money equally."

At first, no one budged. Then a pencil-thin man who might have been in his thirties or forties crawled out from under the table and stood up straight. He was a couple of inches shorter than Dak. His tattered gray T-shirt and worn olive green trousers displayed multiple holes and stains.

He met Dak's gaze for several breaths, then nodded.

"Thank you," the man said in accented English.

Dak only gave a nod in reply.

Then the man slowly rounded the bottom of the stairs and began his ascent. Others followed, one by one, until all thirty of the workers were up on the catwalk. Not all of them could fit in the office, but up there they would be safe from what was going to happen next.

Dak returned his attention to Piñeda. "Okay, Raul. Let's take a walk."

"What?"

"Is there a problem?" Dak asked.

"No," Piñeda hesitated. "No problem."

"Good."

Dak shoved him forward, and the man stumbled through the short corridor toward the exit.

Piñeda caught himself when he slammed into the door, nearly smashing into it with his face.

Dak raised his weapon and aimed it at the man. Piñeda stared down the barrel with terror in his eyes.

"Open it," Dak ordered.

Piñeda shook his head. "No. Please. Don't make me go out there."

"Why?" Dak asked. "Did your men stick around the exits, just in case I tried to get out?"

Piñeda shook his head, but his eyes couldn't lie.

"Here's the thing," Dak drawled, "if you stay in here, I'm going to shoot you. That's a certainty. If you open that door, maybe your men outside see it's you and don't shoot. One way is a gamble. The other way is not. It's your call. But I'm only going to give you to the count of three to make your choice, then I put a round through your head. And I don't miss often. Especially from this range."

"They will kill you," Piñeda hissed. "All the people upstairs, too. They're expendable. Diaz will replace them before sunset tomorrow. And what will you have achieved? Nothing!"

"One," Dak said, ignoring the rant.

"You don't understand. You'll all be dead!"

"Two."

"Okay. Okay," Piñeda said, holding out his hands, pleading. "I'll open it."

He turned his back to Dak and put his hand on the doorknob. Piñeda swallowed hard, fear gripping him in a nearly paralyzing embrace.

"One," Dak said.

"No, please."

Piñeda turned the doorknob and eased the door open. Several flashlights shone brightly on the entrance from outside. Those lights were the last thing Raul Piñeda saw.

Gunfire erupted from the yard.

Dak ducked back around the corner as Piñeda's body shook and gyrated from the impact of dozens of bullets hitting his body.

The guards outside continued firing several seconds until most of their magazines were spent.

Piñeda dropped to his knees and then fell forward onto his now unrecognizable face.

Dak left the duffle bag on the ground, raised one of the rifles, and whirled around the corner.

He stalked forward to the doorway, taking aim at the flashlights pointing into the building. With every squeeze of the trigger, one of the flashlights wobbled and then vanished as the guards fell.

Clear moonlight also helped Dak see his targets more easily, and he was baffled at the fact that all these armed men were standing out in the open, without any kind of protection whatsoever.

The remaining guards, having spent the contents of their magazines, scrambled and split up, desperately trying to load fresh magazines into their weapons.

A few scattered and started to run. Dak focused on those staying put and took them down in rapid, brutal succession.

Then a distant, thunderous boom echoed through the valley. Dak saw one of the runners fall to the ground in midstride. Another collapsed in similar fashion, only twenty feet away from the first. More booms followed, slowly and methodically, as a mysterious sniper took out the cartel thugs trying to escape.

Nice work, Doc, Dak thought.

One of the remaining gunmen raised his weapon and fired wildly in Dak's direction. The bullet whizzed by to the left, hitting the metal wall with a plunk. Dak narrowed his eyes and fired two shots, landing one of them in the gunman's abdomen. Dak squeezed the trigger again, taking aim at another man lifting his gun, but his rifle clicked.

He cursed himself for not doing a better job of counting how many rounds he had left in the magazines, realizing he'd already gone through thirty in a matter of seconds.

The last three shooters outside fired their guns again, sending Dak sprawling back to the inner corner for more protection. He made sure a round was chambered in the rifle and waited.

Another loud boom rolled through the facility. The gunfire outside shifted, and the bullets no longer flew through the building.

The men were aiming at Doc.

They would never see the sniper hidden in the dark.

Dak stood up and stepped around the corner. He raised the rifle and fired a round straight through the man's back standing on the left, then through the back of the other's skull, exiting by way of his face.

The men fell in a heap on the ground, and then the world went silent.

Dak steadied his breathing and looked up at the people on the catwalk. "Anyone hurt up there?" he asked in Spanish.

The skinny man from before looked down at him with several stacks of money in his hands. "No," the man said with a single twist of the head.

"Good. Take that money, get your families if you have them, and leave Lima. Understood?"

"Yes," the man said. "Thank you, sir. You are an angel sent from God."

A dozen witty comments flew through Dak's brain, but instead he simply said, "I don't think angels do this sort of thing."

"They do when the innocent can't fight for themselves."

Dak felt humbled by the comment. "Just make sure everyone gets out of here safely. Okay?"

The man nodded and turned to start issuing orders to the others. When he looked back down at the ground floor where the gringo had been standing, Dak was gone, along with the black duffle bag.

Outside, bright headlights poured through the damaged gate.

Dak surveyed the meadow, checking to make sure all the cartel goons were dead. He detected no movement, and no threat.

The energy he'd spent, and the adrenaline of battle, caught up to him. He slumped his shoulders and breathed heavily, watching as Doc climbed out of the truck and stalked toward him.

Dak sucked up his fatigue and trudged to the gate and pulled it open.

Doc scanned the battlefield with a grim but impressed look on his face.

"I thought you said you were leaving," Dak hedged.

His comment received a humph. "You said I was leaving. I don't recall saying anything."

Dak chuckled, then looked back to the building. "There's a big safe in there. Lot of cash, and some gold bars. I told the workers to divide it among themselves. I figure they earned it."

"Nothing for yourself?" Doc sounded unconvincingly surprised.

Dak shook his head. "Nah. I got you a gold bar for your trouble, though. And I'm taking some of the stash to a family in the tugurizadas. They need it more than I do."

Doc inclined his head, assessing the younger man, then gave an approving nod. "That's mighty noble of you. But I don't need money, either."

"Donate yours if you want. I think you know that I wouldn't feel right if I didn't compensate you. What you do with your cut afterward isn't up to me."

"Fine," Doc surrendered. "I know a few charities in town that could use some help. I'll make sure they get it."

Dak looked around at the bodies on the ground with grim satisfaction. "That was some good shooting for a Navy guy," he joked.

Doc grunted a laugh. "You think you're funny, huh? Anytime you wanna go shooting, we can put some money on who's better."

"Not sure I feel like losing," Dak hedged. He changed the subject quickly. "What do you think we should do with this property?"

Doc stared at the building through narrow eyes. "I'm thinking burn it to the ground."

18

Fernando Diaz woke to the sound of footsteps clacking in the hallway outside his room. Instinctively, he reached over for the Desert Eagle .44 he kept on the nightstand and pointed it at the locked door.

He lived a life smothered in paranoia, always looking over his shoulder, perpetually on alert.

Deep down, Diaz knew this would be his life when he took over the cartel from his predecessor. The old man had been wise to make him the second-in-command, and thus give him the keys to the kingdom when he kicked off. Otherwise, Diaz may have killed him, too.

That had been the plan, after all, but treachery at the top of the food chain would only make things worse later on. Diaz possessed the foresight to know that. By leaving his employer alone, he created a thin veil of trust within his organization. He'd also been shrewd in choosing his own second, Paco.

Paco was pure muscle, a true henchman if there ever were one. Unambitious, grateful, and loyal, Paco had come from utter poverty, working his way up just as Diaz had. The two had connected early on, and Diaz always promised Paco that should he become the head of the cartel, Paco would be his right arm—should he want the position.

The result had been a powerful combination, with Diaz as the director and Paco as the enforcer.

They knew each other so well, communication often occurred without anything being said. Even now, as the footsteps approached outside Diaz's bedroom, he recognized the stride, the weight of the footfalls, and the cadence as being Paco's.

Diaz lowered his weapon and slung his legs over the bed. *No sleep tonight,* he thought. *Again.*

Diaz hadn't slept well since taking over the organization. A small price to pay to be on top. He often wondered if that would ever change but figured it was an ongoing sacrifice.

Three firm knocks pounded the door, again confirming it was Paco who'd come to Diaz in the middle of the night. A quick look to his left at the clock on the nightstand told Diaz it was just past one o'clock in the morning.

"Señor Diaz?" Paco said, muffled by the door.

"I'm coming, Paco," Diaz answered.

He slipped on a pair of trousers he'd left on an ottoman at the foot of the bed and walked over to the door, still holding the big pistol. He unlocked the chain and the two deadbolts, peeked through the crack as habit dictated, and then opened the door for his lieutenant.

Dim yellow light poured into the room, glistening off Diaz's muscular, shirtless torso and illuminating the many tattoos he'd accumulated over the years.

"What's the problem?" Diaz asked. The man preferred to be direct. He noted Paco appeared to have been awake for some time. The lack of haze in the man's eyes, the posture, all pointed to Paco having not yet slept this evening.

"We have an issue at the processing facility outside town."

Diaz's eyebrows sank. "What kind of problem?"

"There was an attack," Paco said, hesitantly. He almost never gave information reluctantly—which meant the news was bad.

"What kind of attack?" Diaz asked, his nostrils gaping as he fought to remain calm against the rising bubble of anger in his chest.

"Coordinated. We don't know how many."

"What's the damage?"

Paco paused again, once more spiking concern in Diaz's mind. "Total loss."

Diaz couldn't hide the devastation from his eyes. He clenched his jaw in one last effort to stave off the rage pulsing through his veins. Turning away, he paced over to the balcony window and threw open the curtains. The moon hung low over the ocean, causing the crashing, foamy waves to glow bluish white. Stars twinkled in the deep blue blanket overhead.

"Where is Raul? Did he escape?" The question simmered with suspicion.

"We're checking, sir. We believe he was killed in the attack."

"Who is responsible for this?" Diaz roared. He slammed his fist against the wall.

"We're...not sure, sir. But an attack like that...it could have only come from another cartel."

"Not the cops?" Diaz knew the answer before Paco shook his head. "Of course it wasn't the cops. You're thinking it was another cartel." It wasn't a question.

"It's the only thing that makes sense," Paco offered.

Diaz processed the information, trying to fit the pieces together. Why would a rival cartel—which were few in number—risk a big move like this?

"Do you think it's connected to the attack at the Turtle?" Diaz asked, his eyes still fixed on the ocean outside.

"Could be. It would be naïve to think otherwise. Two big hits like this on the same day? They have to be connected."

Diaz nodded. "I agree. Do we have any more information on Davenport?"

"No, sir," Paco said with regret. "Nothing yet, but we're still looking."

"It's possible that this gringo is working with another cartel, though I don't recall seeing that very often. Usually, the only Americans I've encountered are either tourists or retirees. It's unlike them to get involved with our trade. They don't have the stomach for it."

Diaz knew Paco was right. He'd never encountered any pushback from Americans, or other expats. And tourists certainly didn't get in their way, much less cause trouble like this.

If Paco were correct that the processing facility was a total loss, the revenue lost as a result would be catastrophic.

"Get the car ready. We're going to the facility."

Paco nodded and disappeared back down the corridor without a second's hesitation.

Diaz continued to gaze out the window, pensively watching the waves crashing onto the shore. Then, in a moment of pure rage, he picked up a nearby vase and hurled it out the window.

The vase had cost him ten thousand American dollars.

He regarded it with grim satisfaction as the porcelain tumbled into the darkness, then shattered on the rocks below.

Diaz sighed, as if that had calmed the storm in his mind. He turned toward his vast walk-in closet and padded across the floor to get dressed.

He had work to do.

19

When the SUV stopped at the front gate to the processing facility, Diaz couldn't believe what he saw.

The fire had been suppressed, for the most part, but there was nothing salvageable left of what had been the cartel's main source of cut cocaine. The metal building had collapsed upon itself, and now it was a huge heap of smoldering timber and hot metal.

Diaz opened his door and climbed out the back of the SUV. He walked absently toward the opening in the gate and stepped through, eyes sweeping left and right in case all of this was an elaborate trap, a way to provoke him and lure him into the open where he could be taken out by a sniper, or perhaps some other form of ambush.

"The men have cleared the perimeter, sir," Paco said from just behind Diaz. "No sign of those responsible."

"What about the workers?" Diaz's question pointed only to his concern about cheap labor. The people themselves were expendable. He could find more. And now he had to.

"Not sure yet, sir. They may have died in the fire. We'll know more when we can clear out the debris, but it's been too hot to start work on that yet."

"Get a bulldozer out here and begin immediately."

Paco knew better than to question the order. "Of course, sir."

"What about the vault?"

Hesitation filled the silent late-night air.

Diaz rounded on his lieutenant, glaring at him with a demanding stare.

"The safe was fireproof, sir. I'm sure it's in the debris, we just—"

"Yes, I know. We can't get to it because of the heat. Get the 'dozer here and clear out this mess. I want to know for certain if the money is gone or not."

Diaz strolled toward where the building once stood, passing bodies still frozen in their death poses, eyes vacantly staring into the darkness. Some of the men had died fighting the attackers, while others appeared to have died running, based on the positions of the bodies. He stopped and pointed at two men, separated by thirty feet, and lying in such a way Diaz knew they had been trying to escape the onslaught.

"Those cowards"—he said, indicating the bodies with a passing finger—"ran from the fight."

"It would seem so," Paco agreed.

Diaz changed course and walked over to the nearest corpse. He noted the entry wound on the side of the man's head; the exit wound pressed against the grass.

Diaz turned his head toward the fence and looked through it. "They had a sniper. A good one. The only way the shooter could have made that shot was from one of the nearby trees."

"You think he climbed a tree?"

"Only way to get this angle from that direction," Diaz explained. "If they'd been on one of the hills, it would have been much easier."

"Why choose a tree, then?" Paco asked. "Doesn't make sense."

"It makes perfect sense. This tells me that the shooter was ready to make a fast getaway. Up there," Diaz pointed at the closest hillside, "the shooter would have a long run back to the road and whatever transportation awaited."

"Yes. I didn't consider that."

"It also gives us another clue as to who the attackers were," Diaz added. "Have you inspected the dirt road back that way?" He tilted his head toward the gate.

"Yes, sir. I figured the first place to start would be out there. If it were a large group, they would have left many tracks in the dirt, and probably knocked down a good section of the tall grass beyond the perimeter, either parking their vehicles or spreading out before the attack."

Diaz wasn't surprised. Paco was a brilliant investigator, far too clever to be a part of the police department. What a waste of talent that would have been had Paco's destiny led him down that route. It was an alternate universe Diaz didn't want to be a part of. Much better to have Paco on his side.

"So, what can we deduce since there is no evidence of a large group presence here?"

"They were small," Paco answered sharply. "Minimal squad, maximum efficiency. Not sure I would do it that way. Dead of night, a rival cartel would have taken no chances. They would have come in hard and brought everything they had. That tells me they—"

"Aren't a rival," Diaz finished.

"Yes, sir."

"Excellent work, my friend. So, what are we thinking?"

Paco took the compliment in stride, as he did everything else. "A team that efficient would have to be highly trained, especially if there were so few of them. I'm guessing four to six, at most. Difficult to imagine fewer than that. Whoever it is, they're dangerous, and it's clear they're trying to send a message."

Diaz inclined his head and stared down the bridge of his nose as he considered the statement. "If it isn't a rival cartel, based on your assessment, who is capable of this?"

"I don't think this is local law enforcement, although they have some SWAT units that are solid. Still, notice how most of our men are here, in the front?"

Diaz had noticed that, and he indicated such with a nod.

"We have regular patrols here. There should be bodies scattered around the property, all the way to the fence."

"What are you trying to say, Paco?"

"I'm saying, the attack came from inside the building." Paco could see the confusion in his boss's eyes, along with the forthcoming question as to whether or not it was an inside job. "No, sir. It wasn't our own men. I'm saying the attackers were inside the building. I'm guessing when we get this rubble cleaned up"—he motioned to the building remains—"we'll find our guards dead from bullets, not fire or smoke. Same with Piñeda, I'm thinking."

"So, a small team of two or three snuck in, killed the men inside, and then shot their way out?" Diaz mused.

"Sounds about right, sir. Along with the sniper helping from the trees. I would say that once the attack commenced inside, it drew the attention of all the guards out here. They would have blocked the exits, or at least they knew to. For them to all be right here, they must have had a reason to abandon the other doorway, unless it had been blockaded to funnel the killers out through the front."

"That would make sense. Then they would all stand here and cut down whoever was coming out."

"Except," Paco countered, "it didn't work out like they planned."

"No. It did not."

Diaz stared at the smoldering wreckage. He pored over it, not wanting to guess how much product had been lost in the blaze. He couldn't make out anything that resembled the safe, but he knew the general location, and Diaz could only hope that Piñeda had been smart enough to lock it before the killers got to him.

"Let's assume the worst," Diaz said. "How much total product was in there? And how much money?"

Paco calculated the answer silently in his mind. "Based on the daily average, with the cocaine, the money, and the gold? I would say around five to six million. The gold bars alone were probably half of that. They average over half-a-million per."

"I know their market value," Diaz snapped. He knew enough to know how much cash Piñeda regularly kept on hand. It was Diaz's idea to keep some of the laundered money here, at the facility. It kept him from putting all his revenue in one place. The bookstore in town kept the second most, as it was the most discreet part of their business. The bulk of Diaz's cash and personal gold holdings, however, remained in his mansion, along with his other precious possessions.

One of the primary reasons he kept his home such a secret, was the value of cash, artifacts, art, and gold he kept in the gallery in his study. Diaz had gone so far as to purchase two other homes in the city, one an old colonial and another more modern, just to throw off anyone who might try to track him down.

He kept his public appearances rare, and almost always low-key. Diaz had been careful ever since taking over the business. He'd maintained the empire and grown it to new heights by diversifying their assets and venturing into new, legitimate businesses that provided both revenue and another layer of protection.

Someone had broken through all of it. They'd discovered the processing plant, razed it to the ground, and struck a terrible blow to Diaz's operation.

He calmed himself as he absently inspected the destruction. Things like this happened. It was why he'd wisely diversified the organization's assets. Losing nearly a third of their inventory, along with the gold and cash, angered him, but he took a small measure of satisfaction in knowing it could have been worse.

A new plan rapidly formed in his brain, and he faced Paco again. "Get in touch with Ricardo Flores. Tell him we have a problem. We need to move half of what he has at the bookstore over to my mansion."

"Yes, sir."

Diaz loved that about Paco. He rarely questioned his orders.

"Normally," Diaz demurred, "I would prefer not to put so much in one place, but it would seem someone is hunting down our operation, one place at a time."

"Who would do such a thing? Who even has the manpower for that?"

"I'm not sure," Diaz admitted. "Americans, certainly, but their War on Drugs is nearly over. More and more countries, even individual American states, are starting to repeal that antiquated effort. I don't think they're sending their people down here as often since nine-eleven. They have bigger issues to worry about now."

"Who then?" Paco asked, unwilling to offer his own theory.

"As we determined, another cartel doesn't have the operatives for something like this, at least no cartel I've ever heard of." Diaz lowered his eyes to the ground, glanced over at the pile of debris, and then back to his lieutenant. "I have a feeling once we track down this Peter Davenport, we will figure out who is behind all of this, and hopefully stop it from happening again."

"I'm on it," Paco said.

He took out a phone and started to make a call, but Diaz stopped him.

"And Paco," Diaz said, "after you get some rest, make an appointment for me to see the mayor. I have a business proposition for her."

20

Hector stood in the living room by an old couch with rough gray upholstery. The furniture looked like it had been ravaged by cats, with loose strands of curled fabric dangling from various points all over the surface. The coffee table, too, had seen better days. The dark wood showed scratches in multiple places and the stain had faded over time, giving it a more weathered look.

He looked over at the pictures hanging on the wall to the right, above an idle wood stove. The pictures displayed images of a family—happy, vibrant, prosperous.

Hector knew everything in this little house was fake. The furnishings, the pictures... none of it was real.

It was a waiting room for couriers like him.

The old, rundown home covered the clandestine activities going on within, and beneath.

Hector had never been through the white doors that stood twelve feet away. They supposedly led into the kitchen, but from there a stairwell led down into a basement built into the hillside. That basement was the entrance to an illegal underground gold mine operated by the Diaz organization.

He wondered what it looked like down there, down in the depths of the earth. He imagined it was a dark, bleak place that offered the young mind every possible reason to be fearful.

His father had worked in those mines for Diaz, and for the cartel boss before him. Hector choked back a lump of pain rising in his throat. He couldn't let them see him cry, or even get close to it.

He turned his head to the right, then left, noting the guards on both sides of the room. Hector's gaze fell to the guns strapped over the men's shoulders.

The guards were a new addition to the routine.

Hector had been coming here to collect gold for Señor Flores for as long as he cared to remember, but he never recalled seeing guards inside the building. One was always stationed outside, and never with his weapon in full sight of the public. Hector had assumed there were others hiding nearby, staying in the shadows in case there was trouble, but this additional security was a first.

The sound of footsteps coming from behind the white doors snapped Hector's attention back to the moment, and he let go of the questions in his head.

The boy heard voices saying something about Señor Diaz's orders, security, and...an attack? *Was that right?*

Hector hadn't heard anything about an attack, but he felt himself shifting uncomfortably. He wondered what the men beyond the door were talking about, though he didn't dare ask either of the guards, or even the handler, a man everyone called Silva. Hector recognized Silva's voice, and figured he was speaking to one of the miners, but there was no way of knowing, and Hector had no desire to see the other side of those doors. The only people allowed in there were the miners and Silva. *Unless,* Hector thought, *there was another guard in the kitchen, too.*

The door burst open, and Silva appeared. Sweat beaded on his skull, glistening on his scalp where a receding, buzz-cut hairline formed a sort of ring around the top of his head. His belly poked his blue button-up shirt out over his belt, and the gray slacks looked like they might burst at any moment.

"There you are, Hector," Silva said, washing away concern with a faux sense of relief.

Hector knew the drill. He turned around to face the door while Silva placed the precious ore in the boy's backpack. When the man released the gold, Hector felt the backpack sag under the weight and the straps tighten against his shoulders. He frowned, wondering why he was transporting so much today.

"It's a little more than usual," Silva said, clarifying the boy's unspoken question. The man's voice fluttered with a hint of nervousness. "You're one of our best, so I assume it won't be an issue for you?"

"No, sir," Hector said without turning around. "Not a problem for me."

"Good boy," Silva said. "Off you go."

Hector slogged over to the door, taking a second to get accustomed to the heavier burden on his back. One of the guards opened the door and let him pass onto the dilapidated porch. To his right, cars drove by on the street between the rundown homes. He looked ahead, down the sidewalk toward the city, where his destination waited.

The walk normally took him the better part of an hour, but today might be longer with the extra weight on his back.

He stepped carefully down the stairs and onto the sidewalk to begin the long hike to the bookstore.

Hector had grown to appreciate the sights and smells of the city's outskirts, or any area that didn't reek of squalor like his home in the tugurizadas. This area wasn't as pleasant as the countryside, or downtown where restaurants filled the air with delightful aromas, and where people appeared happier and less burdened by life.

He looked forward to his walks into the city despite the exertion required to get from the mining house to the bookstore. It certainly beat working down in the mines, and if Señor Flores kept his promise, Hector would never have to see the inside of one of those.

His mother had talked about leaving the slums, getting out of their derelict shack and moving into a proper flat somewhere in Chile. Hector appeased her with lip service and sincere nods, but he knew better. Lots of people talked about leaving the tugurizadas, finding a better life somewhere else. No one he knew had ever managed to make it a reality. It was a pipe dream, an unrealistic vision that perpetually dangled something glorious and terrible in front of their eyes—hope.

Hector might only be eleven, but he wasn't naïve enough to grasp on to empty promises. He gave his mother the money he'd earned, and he had no doubt it would help them. It would keep them fed for a month, which was all he could ask for. How many others didn't have that luxury in the slums? Every day, he saw people who were starving. When he passed dumpsters or trash cans in the city's alleys, and saw people scavenging through them, he recognized faces he'd seen in the hills of the tugurizadas, people desperate for a scrap of food that could get them through to the next day.

It was a hollow form of survival. And it certainly wasn't living.

The skyscrapers loomed around and in front of him as Hector entered the city. He'd been walking for half an hour and paused only for a second to rest and adjust the backpack cutting into his shoulders. He took a deep breath of cleaner city air and glanced back over his shoulder at where he'd come from and caught a glimpse of a face he recognized. The man with a shaved head and tattoos on both sides of his neck immediately turned his head and looked into a café as if considering making a purchase.

Hector knew better. It was one of the guards from the mining house. Why was he here? Had he followed Hector all this way?

There was an easy way to answer that question.

Hector tightened the straps on his pack and set off again, this time trudging forward with more purpose. After walking two more blocks, he stopped and whipped his head around. As he suspected, the guard stood about sixty feet back, once more pretending to be interested in one of the shops to his right.

Hector frowned. *Why is that guard following me?* The question lingered in his mind, and he ran through a series of quick answers.

If the man were going to attack him or take his bag, he'd have done it before getting into the city. Did that mean he was watching

Hector to make sure *he* didn't steal anything? *But the day before, Señor Flores said he trusted me.*

Hector decided standing still wasn't going to help, and might even make the guard suspicious, so he pretended to adjust the backpack again then kept moving.

As he walked, Hector wondered what was going on. He remembered something Silva had said from behind the closed white door. *He'd mentioned security, and what else? An attack.* Hector wondered what kind of attack, and who could have been so foolish as to bring a fight to Señor Diaz and his cartel. It wouldn't end well for them, or so Hector suspected. As far as he knew, Diaz had no intentions of letting another organization infiltrate Lima. Any who tried met a terrible end.

Fifty minutes after leaving the mining house, Hector arrived at the bookstore. He checked around, as he always did to make sure he wasn't being followed—save for the guard who now stood in plain sight halfway down the block.

Hector looked through the glass doorway into the bookstore and noted another guard waiting inside to the left, next to the checkout counter. "Another one?" he whispered to himself.

The boy pulled the door open and stepped inside. The familiar smell of paper filled his nostrils, blending with the welcoming scent of coffee coming from the back. Walking into the bookstore always entranced Hector, and he wished he could peruse the books someday, if only for an hour or two.

He'd learned to read years ago, but books were in short supply in the Lima slums. Hector feared if there were any to be had, people would simply use them for fuel on chilly nights when they were desperate to keep warm.

Still, perhaps someday Señor Flores would allow him to read some of the stories when he'd finished his work.

Hector acknowledged the gunman at the checkout counter with a timid nod. The man didn't offer a similar greeting, instead merely staring down at the kid with dark, threatening eyes.

The boy continued down the center aisle to the back of the shop, where the coffee café offered an assortment of freshly baked pastries and treats. Hector figured the food was meant to throw off any cops that might wander in by making it look more like a legitimate business instead of a cover for a drug and illegal mining operation.

Hector wondered who made the pastries, if it was one of the local bakeries or if they were made here, in-house. He didn't know who in Diaz's organization would be on baking duty, so he figured the treats were likely purchased and brought in.

Another guard stood in the back-right corner of the bookstore and a third in the opposite corner. Both men kept a keen eye on Hector as he approached the door leading into the back.

The boy knocked as he always had and waited until the inner guard opened the door for him.

It was the same as always and yet different.

Hector entered the manager's office and felt a swoosh of air as the guard quickly shut and locked the door behind him. The sudden sound caused the boy to start, but he regained his composure and walked through the money counting room toward the back office.

Instead of two people counting money, today there were six, all running the machines as fast as they could.

Hector saw Flores through the window in the office wall and could tell the man was stressed. Something weird was going on.

He approached the office but was halted by a guard who stepped from the shadows, leveling a submachine gun that pointed directly at Hector's face.

"Stop right there," the guard said in a gruff tone. "Turn around."

Hector did as instructed and slowly twisted around.

"I'm going to check your bag. Don't make any sudden movements, or you won't walk out of this building. Understood?"

Hector nodded sheepishly.

He felt the man unzip the bag and then rifle through it with his free hand. When he was done with the main compartment, the guard checked the other two pockets. Satisfied there was nothing worth worrying over, he zipped the bag closed.

"Wait here," the guard ordered.

Hector watched as the gunman entered the office and jerked a thumb in his direction. Flores took his eyes off the computer screen they'd been glued to and looked over at the boy. The look on his face wasn't the same as the day before. His bloodshot eyes hung dark circles underneath like sagging drapes under a window's trim. He wouldn't say it out loud, but Flores looked terrible, as if he hadn't slept in days.

The man motioned for the boy to enter with a wave of his hand.

Hector shuffled into the room and removed the backpack, setting it down on the table next to the desk where Flores had been working.

"You can go," Flores said to the guard.

The man said nothing, instead he simply walked out of the room and back to his post in the darkness.

"Sorry about that," Flores said, his voice cracked and tired. "Things have been a little crazy lately."

Hector wanted to ask what he meant by "lately", since the day before everything had been fine. Instead, he took his question in a more logical direction.

"Señor Flores? Is everything okay?"

"We're just experiencing a few setbacks with the business right now, Hector. Nothing for you to worry about. I assure you."

As if Flores hadn't said a thing, Hector ventured on, perhaps foolishly. "I heard Señor Silva talking about some trouble, an attack or something. There are more guards today, too, and one followed me all the way here."

The man's eyes darted to the door and then back to the boy, locking on him with a firm yet paranoid grip.

When Flores spoke, the kindness from the day before was gone, replaced with a dire warning. "Don't worry about that, Hector. Understand? We just need to be a little more careful right now. That's all. Now"—he put his hands on Hector's shoulders—"I need you to forget about anything Silva might have said. He's a fool, anyway. He doesn't know what he's talking about. Everything is going to be fine. Don't pay any attention to the guards, either. They're just a precaution."

The boy wanted to know why there were more money counters, too, and sensed that Flores was keeping something from him. There was, however, no way Hector could pry the truth from the man, and even at the age of eleven, the kid knew when to shut up.

"You won't be going down to the docks again today," Flores said.

Hector felt the hope of another big payday slip through his fingers.

"Do you think you can make the trip to the mine and back again?"

Hector's shoulders hurt and his legs ached. Today's haul had demanded much of him, but he didn't dare tell Flores no, especially not after his generosity the previous day.

"Of course, Señor Flores. I can do it."

The man met Hector's eyes, and for once it almost looked like Flores softened his gaze from the hardened look of deep concern. "Good," he said, patting the boy on the shoulder. "I will pay you double your normal day's pay for making an extra trip."

Hector's mood lifted and he felt renewed energy pulse into his veins.

"Thank you, Señor Flores. I won't let you down."

"I know you won't, Hector." A cell phone rang on the desk, interrupting their conversation. "One moment," the man said.

Flores picked up the phone, looked at the screen, and answered, "Yes? Oh? Okay. I see."

Hector couldn't gather anything from the short answers Flores gave to the caller, but it sounded urgent.

"Yes. I will send my best courier there right away." He ended the call and looked down at Hector. "Change of plans. I need you to take this package to Chocho. It's extremely important. Can you manage?"

"Yes, sir," Hector said with a quick nod.

"Good." Flores picked up a brown sack and stuffed it into the kid's backpack. It wasn't as heavy as the gold, to Hector's relief, and he was glad he didn't have to carry that burden again.

"Now, go," Flores ordered. "It isn't wise to linger here long. And don't stay at the docks long, either. Understand?"

"Yes, sir. I won't."

The boy turned and walked to the door under the careful watch of Flores and his guard. When he was gone, Flores looked to his counters. “Keep going. Diaz wants everything moved to new locations by nightfall.”

“What are we going to do about this place?” one of the men asked from the table to the right.

Flores leveled his gaze at the counter and clenched his jaw. “Our orders are to burn it to the ground.”

“What about the couriers? You ordered all of them to return this afternoon with a second haul.”

Flores didn’t speak for several breaths. He’d received the orders from Fernando Diaz himself. He couldn’t go against his boss’s command, no matter how grisly. “Don’t worry about that for now. Just keep counting. We have to have this finished before the end of the day.”

Flores turned back to his computer and stared at the email from his boss’s ghost email account. The cryptic message was one he never thought he’d receive. It simply read, “Fire Sale.”

He knew what that meant.

Flores and the guard had to kill everyone there. Diaz was hitting the reset button on his entire operation.

21

Emelda Zepata moved through the corridor with long, purposeful strides. Fury boiled her brown eyes. She kept her jaw clenched; her lips sealed stoically. Her dark chocolate hair flowed to her shoulders and fluttered in the breeze as she walked.

The two assistants behind her—a young man and a young woman—struggled to keep up.

Mayor Zepata had received the news about her husband's murder, and where his body had been found, earlier that morning. While their romantic relationship had faded through the years—in no small part due to her political ambitions, and to his depravity—the two maintained the appearance of a normal marriage for the public eye. The truth was Emelda had her own trysts on the side, too, but she at least understood discretion. She didn't venture out into the red-light district to look for lovers.

The murder of her husband, however, had created a mountain of potential trouble should anyone in the media learn of his infidelities. Voters were fickle when it came to such things and were all too quick to pass judgement.

Emelda's plan was simple. She had to make it look like her husband had died of natural causes. A tragic ending to a remarkable life is how she would play it to the media and her throng of supporters. After all, one of the key components she'd run on was family values. Her wholesome appeal attracted constituents young and old, and part of that persona was aided by her husband's support.

The media, as well as the people, loved the story of how the two met—college sweethearts who'd been together for a quarter of a century. The Zepatas were a crowd favorite and she'd won the mayor's office easily against the incumbent. It helped that her opponent was an egotistical, insensitive type who'd long ignored the pleas of the people.

Zepata, as others before, had run on a platform of cleaning up crime, making the city a safer place to live, and to be more prosperous. She'd even preached that those in the tugurizadas would have a better life, though she had no clear direction on that front. The truth was she didn't need one. The people from the slums didn't vote, not typically. Sure, there were a few outliers, but most of them didn't even know when or where to cast their ballots.

Instead, Zepata made huge gains with the middle class in the suburban areas and with the corporate heads who'd been struggling of late with new taxes pressing down on them from the Peruvian government. She promised to be a voice against crippling the businesses of Lima and had made strong advancements in her first two years as mayor.

She rounded a corner in the high-ceilinged corridor, the events of the last few days still rattling around in her mind.

At least she had a game plan for this contingency.

She'd known of her husband's infidelities and had urged him to keep things low-key, and preferably in-house.

The two hadn't shared a bed in over a year, and she was fine with that. Emelda didn't care what he did, so long as he didn't get caught. That was the rule. Don't get caught. Why he'd been unable to follow that one simple directive was beyond her. And of all places, the Red Turtle.

She shivered at the thought, wondering how long he'd been frequenting that place. In a strange way, her husband got what he deserved. In the long term, this incident could keep her in power for years to come. No one would dare vote against the widow whose husband died tragically, and so young. It was a wave she knew she had to ride, and it would crush any opposition.

Her male assistant stepped in front of her when they reached the office door and pulled it open.

Emelda thanked him and entered, walking to the receptionist's chamber and then turning left into the mayor's office.

The receptionist wore a look of concern on her face. "Madame Mayor?" she said before the male assistant turned the doorknob to the inner office.

Emelda stopped and rounded on the young woman. "Yes?"

"Someone is waiting for you in there." The line came with a looming sense of hesitation.

"Who? I don't have any appointments for another hour." The mayor's confusion spilled over to her assistants, who immediately reached for their phones to check the calendar.

"It's...uh...." The receptionist stumbled for the words.

"Well, spit it out. I don't have all day, Corela."

"It's Señor Diaz."

Emelda lowered her chin and raised her eyebrows, both expressions of disbelief. It had to be another Diaz, though she couldn't think of one she'd been expecting.

"Which one?" the mayor asked.

The receptionist took a deep breath. "The one you're thinking."

Emelda let out a long exhale and then nodded.

She'd never met Diaz, but she knew who he was. Thus far, she'd been unable to curtail the cartel's operations. Their tentacles reached far and wide, and it was difficult to know who Diaz had in his pocket.

"Very well," Emelda said, flattening her navy-blue business suit. "I'll handle it."

She turned and nodded to her assistant, who opened the door.

When she walked through, she kept her shoulders back and head high, the picture of dignity.

Two men in black suits stood to her left, and another sat across from the mayor's burgundy leatherback chair.

"I half expected you to be sitting in my seat when I entered," Emelda said in a nervous tone she tried to mask with fake confidence.

"That would have been rude of me," Diaz drawled. "I wouldn't want to offend the mayor of Lima, now would I?"

The male assistant closed the door and stood off to the side in a corner, doing his best to stay as far away from Diaz's goons as possible. The female assistant did the same, crowding into the corner with him and folding her hands in front of her waist in an effort to look innocent.

The mayor strolled around the huge oak desk and eased into her chair. She made a show of the move to make it look like she was the sole power broker in the room, but she knew the truth. She and the man across from her were on equal footing, each wielding roughly the same amount of influence. While she certainly had political control, along with the adoration of her supporters, Diaz possessed far more financial assets—especially where cash was concerned. She knew he operated legitimate businesses throughout the city and that there was nothing she could do about closing those—as long as they didn't step out of line.

One incident, however, would give her all the authority she'd need to go in with guns blazing and shut down the entire cartel operation. The problem was it would be violent and bloody. Innocent people could be hurt, and the last thing Mayor Zepata wanted was for Lima to lose its international standing as a relatively safe place for tourists and business. Such a bloodbath would ruin the city—and cripple the nation.

She'd spent countless hours with the chief of police and Peruvian investigators, trying to figure out a way to take down Diaz and his clan without splattering the "international incident" headline all over the world. It needed to be done quickly and quietly, but so far, the opportunity hadn't presented itself.

Zepata pondered these things while she steepled her fingers with her elbows on her desk and stared into the emotionless eyes across from her.

"What do you want, Diaz?" she fired, doing her best to remain civil but also letting him know he wasn't welcome. This was the mayor of Lima's office. He couldn't just walk in here unannounced like he was royalty.

"You and I have a common problem," he replied.

At that, the skin above her nose tensed. "What are you talking about, Fernando? I seriously doubt we have anything in common, much less a problem."

"Ah," he raised a finger, wagging it in the air. "But we do."

He motioned to the guard behind his left shoulder. The man stepped forward and set a blue folder on the desk.

She stared at the item for several seconds then met Diaz's gaze once more. "What's that? An offer?"

"Something like that," he answered coolly.

Zepata wondered if she should open the file, worried that he might have laced it with a poison that would absorb through her skin. She'd heard of such things before, and even stories of people who'd died by those means.

"If you're concerned about the folder," he said, noting her concern, "you shouldn't be. It's not going to hurt you. It's what's inside you should consider."

She may as well have trusted a venomous snake telling her it was a pig, but what choice did she have? Fernando Diaz was in her office and was, apparently, interested in striking some kind of deal. As preposterous as that sounded, she reached across the shiny surface of the desk and dragged the file closer.

When she opened it, her eyes flashed wide with a range of emotions: fear, anger, confusion, resentment.

"Where did you get these?" Zepata asked as she pored over the graphic photos within.

"My men took them the night of the killing," Diaz said. "I'm sure you know the Red Turtle is my establishment."

"Is it?" she feigned ignorance. "I wasn't aware of that."

He shook his head, grinning devilishly. "Come now, Emelda. You may be a good politician, but you're a terrible liar, at least to me. Maybe not to your constituents, but I am not so naïve. I know you know. Let's leave it at that and dispense with the games."

Her face flushed with anger, but she raised her eyes and locked with his gaze. "What do you want? For me to resign? Are you threatening to blackmail me? You think the press will listen to you and run this story? Is that your angle?"

"I don't want to go to the press with this any more than you want me to," Diaz defended. "There is no reason why we can't handle this like adults."

"What is that supposed to mean?" Zepata tilted her head slightly to the right. "Your goons killed my husband. I should string you up outside this very building. The people would thank me for it."

"Perhaps," Diaz conceded. "I don't think the ones who work for me would applaud that action. That aside, my men didn't kill your husband. His death was not the work of anyone in my organization. Myself included."

He noted the disbelief on her face and continued. "I was alerted to the incident at the Turtle the night of the murder. My cousin, Antonio, was also killed."

Diaz watched the mayor's expression change to one of bewildered curiosity.

"Are you trying to tell me," she began, "another cartel has moved into town? Because if you think I'm going to sit by and watch you and some other mob wage a drug war in the streets of Lima, you're a fool."

An easy smile crept across Diaz's face. It was an unnerving, unnatural expression that Zepata could have gone her entire life without seeing.

"I don't want a war in the streets of Lima any more than you do, Mayor. I can see from the look on your face you don't believe me, but I grew up in this city. I do not wish to see it crumble. I know you hate me and what I do, but this is truth."

The mayor watched him for nearly a minute, calculating the man's body language, his tone, the way his lips moved with every word. She didn't believe him, but what reason could the top drug kingpin in Lima, and probably all of Peru, possibly have for coming here to her office? He was desperate, crazy, or stupid.

Zepata's eyelids narrowed as she bet on the first. Then she looked to her assistants in the corner. "Could you two please step outside for a moment? I need to speak to Señor Diaz in private."

The two hesitated, sharing concerned glances with one another, then nodded and left through the door.

"You two," Diaz said to his guards. "Join them in the atrium. The mayor has requested privacy."

The men didn't question his order, even if they felt it unwise to leave him there with an elected official. She would pose no physical threat, but that made her request all the more confusing.

They walked through the door and closed it behind, leaving the mayor and Diaz alone in her vast office.

She stood and walked around the corner of the desk, stopping halfway to raise her leg and sit on the edge.

Diaz admired her toned legs as the skirt slid up just slightly. "You are a woman who takes care of her appearance," he said. "A shame your husband didn't appreciate that."

She crossed her arms, looking down at him without amusement. "My husband didn't appreciate much. Especially when it came to me. Still, I can't have his murder at a brothel dragging my reputation into the mud." She slid off the desk and sashayed over to a bar in the right corner. An assortment of tequilas, whiskeys, and vodkas festooned the marble surface. "Drink?"

He nodded but didn't look back at her. It was a show of trust, and one that she didn't miss. "Tequila, please," he said. "Neat."

"The only way to drink it."

She poured the light golden liquid into two tumblers and brought them back to her desk. This time, she sat on the front edge, close enough that her perfume danced through his senses. She leaned forward and handed him the drink, her blouse dropping loosely before him.

He played coy and accepted the drink with a modest thank-you. If she were trying to seduce him, this wasn't the time. Perhaps she'd misread his intentions, but he decided to let her speak.

"*Salud*," she said, raising the glass as she sat upright once more.

"*Salud*," he echoed.

After a long swig, she lowered the glass to her side, letting it dangle from her fingers in the sultry way only a woman could do. "So, you need my help."

"Oh?"

"It wasn't a question, Fernando. There isn't a reason in the world Lima's biggest cartel boss, only cartel boss," she corrected, "would come to the mayor's office...unless you were desperate."

She waited to see if the barb would set.

To her surprise, it bounced off Diaz without effect. "You're not wrong," he confessed, taking another sip. "We have a common problem, after all."

"And what is this mysterious common problem the two of us have?"

"There is someone causing trouble here in Lima. They killed my cousin, and your husband."

"Which we've covered," she interrupted.

His head bowed once. "Last night, someone attacked one of my processing facilities. My primary processing facility," he added. "I lost a lot of money."

She arched her right eyebrow as if his statement carried no consequence. "And? You came to me for help because your illegal business was attacked?"

He maintained patience despite wanting to grab the woman and throw her out the window to the sidewalk three stories below.

"We conducted an investigation. My men learned that an American named Peter Davenport was at the scene within thirty minutes of the killings."

"An American?" She sounded genuinely surprised—and interested.

"We looked deeper into it. He's former United States Navy. Was a physician. His wife died some years ago from cancer. I'm not sure why he came here, but after he left the United States, there are few records about him."

"And you think I might have some kind of access to that?" She huffed. "You'd have better results down at the public records office, Fernando."

"I don't know if this Davenport killed Antonio and your husband," he said, ignoring her last comment. "But I'm certain he had something to do with it. I cannot continue to accept losses like last night's. And you cannot afford for these pictures to go public. And before you ask, of course I made copies. I don't see why this unfortunate turn of events can't be used to our mutual advantage."

Zepata took a deep breath then downed the rest of the tequila.

"What do you have in mind?"

The sickly smile crossed Diaz's face again. "I need your cops to stay off my back while I try to find this gringo. And I need them to help in the investigation. If they find anything related to the murder, I want to know about it."

"That's a big request," she demurred. "Many of the police officers in the city would sooner see your body thrown in the sea than offer any sort of help to you."

"Understandable. Still, it is part of the deal. Make it happen."

She sighed. "I'll do what I can. What else?"

"That's it. My men need to be able to conduct their investigation without being harassed, and any resources you can lend will be...appreciated."

The mayor flicked her eyebrows up. "And how will you show your appreciation?"

"You have an election coming up next year. Elections can be expensive, especially if your opponent has a generous donor."

Her flirtatious look turned sour.

"Then again, I imagine the election would be an easy win if you had someone like...me backing you. Not only can I provide clean money for your campaign, but I can also discourage the competition."

She inclined her head, easing a Mona Lisa smile across her lips that only parted to allow a single word out of her mouth. "Done."

22

Dak sipped a cup of coffee from across the street as he watched the boy leave the bookstore and head in the opposite direction from the way he'd come earlier.

The kid was smart; Dak had to give him that. The boy had detected the armed escort twenty yards behind him on his journey from the mine, stopping subtly a couple of times to check if the man truly was tailing him or not.

The fact Hector spotted the man and then stopped again to check if he was still there meant something had changed. Previously, when he'd bumped into the kid, Dak had seen no evidence of any sort of escort. Diaz must have been spooked. In his paranoia, he'd evidently ramped up security measures, which Dak fully expected.

He wouldn't be surprised if the cartel kingpin were hiding out in his mansion at that very moment.

Hector disappeared into the mob of pedestrians along the sidewalk, and Dak found himself facing a decision. He could go in now, take out everyone in the bookstore, and then head down to the docks, but based on the direction the boy had gone, Dak figured Hector was on his way to the waterfront.

Was he taking a delivery to Chocho?

Dak didn't have the luxury of thinking about it for long.

He sighed, turned down the sidewalk, and started for the harbor.

With every passing second, he knew that Flores and his men were cleaning more money, moving more product, and endangering the people of Lima with their operations.

Dak had learned, though, that to resist the path before him usually led to trouble. It was a level of spirituality he'd delved into in recent years, mostly to help him deal with anger issues. Instead of being frustrated over not making a red light, he'd learned to allow that as part of his destiny, the path that he must take for his own good. The more he'd started looking at life that way, the less irritated he'd become at things that previously drove him nuts.

Now, seeing the boy leave the bookstore and go in the direction of the waterfront felt like a sign to Dak that he needed to follow the boy. He didn't know why. And he didn't have to. He merely accepted it and followed the path.

The walk to the shipping yards wasn't a short one, and Dak found it surprisingly difficult to keep up with the young boy despite having longer legs and being in better condition.

There was truly no substitute for the energy of youth.

When the boy arrived at one of the gates to the harbor, Dak had to hang back and watch from the shadows of an old machine shop across the street. Once, Hector looked back while the gate guard called someone on his radio. Dak pretended to be talking on a phone and turned away from the kid before the boy could recognize him.

Dak watched the kid's reflection in the shop window until the guard allowed him to pass through. Then Dak turned and watched as Hector climbed into a golf cart and was whisked away to the left, going parallel down the street.

With a frustrated sigh, Dak waited for the light to change and then crossed the street. He slowed as he reached the guardhouse and stole a quick look around. After surveying the busy shipping yard, Dak approached the guard.

The man looked up from a clipboard when Dak stopped at the window.

"Yes?" the man said, forgoing any pleasant greetings or social conventions.

"I'm here to see Chocho," Dak replied. "I'm supposed to go to Dock 79."

The guard studied Dak for several seconds. The man wore his suspicion on his face without the slightest effort to suppress it.

"Name?"

"Eduardo," Dak lied. "Eduardo Perez."

The man scanned his clipboard then shook his head. "I don't have you on the list."

"Exactly," Dak said.

The man's forehead wrinkled at the comment.

"You don't think a man like Señor Diaz would be stupid enough to put the name of one of his top enforcers on some shipping guard's list, do you? Or would you prefer I call Señor Diaz and tell him"—Dak noted the name on the guard's tag—"that Jose at the docks is giving me a hard time? I'm sure he won't mind being interrupted from his extremely busy schedule."

Fear crept into the man's eyes, and his demeanor immediately did a 180. "No, Señor Perez. I wouldn't want to bother Señor Diaz with such a small issue. I'm certain he doesn't want to be interrupted."

"Things have been strange lately," Dak continued, pushing the ruse along. "I've heard there's been trouble. Señor Diaz thought bringing in a little extra muscle might be a good idea. He's lucky I was available."

"Yes. I see your point." The guard turned in the direction the golf cart went and sighed. "I just sent someone over to seventy-nine a few minutes ago. It's been busy like this all day. If you give me a moment, I'll get you a cart, too."

"Not necessary," Dak insisted. "I can walk."

"It's a long walk over to that area. The cart can be back over here in five or ten minutes."

"I'll be there by then," Dak said coolly. "Keep up the good work. I'll be sure to tell Señor Diaz you were very helpful."

The man let an uneasy smile slide across his lips. "Thank you. I appreciate that."

"Don't mention it."

Dak walked through the gate as though he owned the place, then veered left and picked up his speed.

Halfway to the far end, he sped up again, this time to a brisk trot. Hector had already been inside for over five minutes, a fact that caused Dak to begin worrying. There was no telling what the cartel thugs might do now that they felt a threat coming. Hopefully, whatever they were doing didn't have anything to do with the kids, but that was an assumption Dak wouldn't make.

Fear pushed his legs faster. He couldn't let something happen to the kid. Dak wasn't sure why he cared, he didn't know the boy, had only bumped into him on the street. But a deep sense of obligation tugged at Dak's heart. There were millions of kids like him, billions, who lived a life in their respective slums much the same way Hector did. Dak couldn't help them all, so why worry so much about this one?

The answer, to him, was a simple one. He hadn't met them, heard the hunger in their voices, or seen the desperation in their eyes. These tangible, emotionally gripping experiences bound Dak to the boy in a way he couldn't fully understand—and didn't need to.

He might not be able to help every kid in the world escape a life like this, but he could help this one.

Dak slowed when he reached the last row of warehouses along the thoroughfare and stopped at the corner. He leaned around the building and looked across at the massive building. It stretched from one end of the shipping yard to the other. Most of it appeared to be in ill-repair, and many of the docking bays looked as if they hadn't been used, or weren't usable, for years.

He spotted the number 79 depicted in flaking, faded paint and paused. Catching his breath, he studied the location. No guards outside surprised Dak, as did the absence of the golf cart. Dak figured the driver must have dropped the kid off and returned to his regular duties.

Shuttling Diaz's guests, Dak assumed, was only a side gig.

Dak checked behind him again then darted across the lane to a closed door. He was about to check to see if it was locked when a familiar feeling flooded his brain. His senses tingled, and his skin crawled with it.

This is too easy, he thought.

Someone at Chocho's level would have some kind of security out here watching the door, even if it were just a lone guard, especially with the recent attacks on Diaz's other assets. The man had sent a guard along with Hector from the gold mine all the way to the bookstore. Dak had also detected other such goons trailing behind other child couriers. Diaz would be on high alert, and Dak knew better than to believe this was just random.

Everything about this felt like a trap.

23

Chocho peered at the boy through bloodshot eyes that hung over gaping nostrils that swelled and contracted with every breath. Four men with guns stood close by, surrounding the two in the middle of the room.

"Where is he?" Chocho fumed. "Where is this gringo who has been causing us trouble?"

Hector's eyes brimmed with tears. He fought against the fear clawing at him, but it was no use.

"I don't know who you're talking about," the boy said. "I swear it. I just came from the bookstore and Señor Flores. That's all."

"Are you certain?" Chocho pressed. "Señor Diaz suspects one of you couriers has been working with the enemy, telling them where to hit us, and when."

"What?" the boy protested. "I wouldn't do that. I don't even know that much. I go to the bookstore and to the docks. That's all. You have to believe me."

Even as Hector defended himself, the boy recalled the man from the night before—the American who'd shown him kindness, even given him some of his food. The taste of that delicious treat had long washed away, and now the only thing Hector could sense was the musty odor of the dock house and the salty air that cleared his nostrils.

Hector tried to avoid looking into the man's eyes, but he found the task nearly impossible. Chocho's drug-induced, glazed-over stare held the boy in an almost paralyzed state.

The man raised a pistol and pointed it at the boy's face. It wasn't the first time Hector had ever gazed down the barrel of a gun, not even the first time this week. He felt terror, confusion, and the overwhelming sense that he was dreaming, that none of this was really happening.

In that moment, Hector realized everything his mother said about the cartel was true. The warnings she'd issued about working for Flores and moving up the ladder all hit the boy with a gut-wrenching realization.

"You better not be lying to me, boy. Why do I feel like you're lying to me?" Chocho sneered.

One of the guards nearby laughed and made a joke about the boy looking like he was about to wet his pants, which caused the other three guards to chuckle along.

"You have to believe me, Señor Chocho," Hector pleaded. "I have never stolen anything. I'm always on time. Just ask Señor Flores. He'll tell you."

"Then why won't you tell me the truth about the gringo?" Chocho pressed. "Where is he? Tell me and I will let you live."

The boy sniffled at the question, fighting back the tears that had already broken through the walls in his eyes.

"I see gringos every day," Hector explained, choking on the words as they passed his lips. "There are many here in the city, Señor Chocho. How am I supposed to know which one is the one you're looking for?"

Through the drug-infused rage coursing through the man's veins, he somehow found enough common sense to listen to the boy's explanation, despite every irrational sense telling him that the boy knew more than he was letting on.

"Set the bag down and stand over there in the corner," Chocho ordered, keeping the gun aimed at the kid's forehead.

Hector started to loosen one of the straps from his shoulder when Chocho stopped him. "Slowly," the man growled.

The boy nodded and resumed removing the bag.

"Point that gun somewhere else, Chocho," a voice said from the shadows behind him.

Chocho spun around and aimed in the direction he thought the voice came from, but he saw nothing in his office or in the corners.

Suddenly, a shadow passed over the sunlight creeping through the hole in the ceiling. A silhouette dropped from above—a terrifying sight to the unsuspecting cartel thug.

He couldn't react fast enough with his weapon in a feeble attempt to raise it and fire. The interloper's right knee crashed into Chocho's collarbone, instantly breaking it with an audible pop. The attacker's weight drove both men to the ground in a heap.

Dak rolled off Chocho, who shouted obscenities in Spanish as he clutched at his shoulder and clavicle with the hand that had held the gun.

The guards, taken by surprise, hesitated for a second, which gave Dak all the time he needed.

He raised his pistol and fired at the closest gunman, drilling the man's chest with two center shots—and a kill shot through the forehead.

The other three gunmen aimed at the attacker. One's sights hovered just over the top of the boy's head.

Dak sensed the danger to the kid and lunged forward. He scooped up the boy and dove into the office as the guards rained bullets at the two.

Rounds shattered the office's glass windows and pummeled the metal siding. To Dak's surprise, the bullets didn't pierce the metal, though he knew that shield would only provide temporary shelter.

He and the boy were cornered now, with no way out.

"Are you hurt?" Dak asked, keeping the boy low and out of sight.

Tears streamed down Hector's face, but he managed to shake his head once. "No," he whispered in a trembling voice.

"Good. I'm going to get you out of here." Dak issued the promise without a plan as to how he was going to make it happen.

He searched the office for something he could use but found nothing.

Glass shattered above them and fell to the floor all around. "We need to get behind the desk," Dak said, pointing at the old metal relic. "Crawl into the hole under it. You'll be safe there. Okay?"

Hector nodded.

"Ready?" Dak asked. The boy bobbed his head. "Go."

Dak poked his gun around the corner and looked down the sights. The guard nearest the exit was creeping forward and was in the open. Dak squeezed the trigger at the same time the gunman did, Dak landing a single shot in the man's thigh.

The guard yelled in pain but managed to get two more shots off that sent Dak scrambling backward for cover.

He surveyed the office, noting Hector had made it to cover under the desk. That would only give them so much time.

"You're going to die, American!" Chocho shouted through the haze of gun smoke filling the room. "You should not have come here! You and the boy are both going to die!"

Another round of gunfire exploded from outside the office, but none of the bullets punctured the siding. Dozens of rounds zipped through the now destroyed window and whizzed over Dak's head. He checked to make sure the boy was keeping low under the desk and was momentarily relieved to see the kid crouching there, holding his knees with both arms.

Dak could taste the burned powder, could almost feel it against his skin. They were sensations he'd felt so many times before. For most people, fear would take hold of them in such a scenario, but to Dak, the smoke wrapped around him like an old blanket. This was his element. And while things looked bleak, he knew there had to be another way out, at least for the kid.

His eyes landed on an air-conditioning unit fixed loosely into a window. The glass above the machine was covered with cardboard, duct taped to the window's frame. The unit itself had been similarly sealed into place. The old air conditioner's white plastic body displayed signs of aging, being dusty and stained from years of service. Dak only spent a second wondering if the thing even worked anymore.

Not that it mattered. The machine was about to give the kid a way out.

The decision made, Dak put the plan into action. He popped up and fired through the opening of the window again, catching one of the gunmen advancing toward the office in a low crouch.

Dak turned his pistol at the man, but the rounds that followed missed as the guard dove for cover behind a stack of wooden crates.

Chocho and the other unwounded guard stayed behind a metal table they'd flipped over to use as a shield.

Funny, Dak thought, because he was going to do something similar.

He squeezed off one more round and then retreated to the desk. He slid behind it and faced the boy.

"Okay," Dak said. "I'm going to get you out of here. But first, I have to flip this desk over."

Hector looked at him with wondering eyes. Before the kid could ask how, Dak sprang up, planting his hands on the left edge of the desk. He grunted, shoving the thing up and onto one end.

The second the desk landed with a bang; more shots rang out from the other part of the dock house. Dak crouched low next to the boy, watching the underside of the desk as the top caught every bullet sailing its way. None pierced the hard surface, and with his suspicions confirmed, Dak initiated the next part of the plan.

"You're going out the window," he said to Hector. "Once you're outside, run. Run all the way home if you can. When you get there, don't come out. Not for anyone except your mother. Understand?"

The boy nodded through his trembling and wiped the tears off his face.

"You're brave," Dak said with a wink. "And you're going to be okay."

Hector tried to believe him, but Dak could see the doubt in the young man's eyes.

"Wait here," Dak ordered with a grin.

Then he turned, slid over to the air conditioner, and grabbed the machine by both sides. The desk blocked his view of the gunmen, but that worked both ways, and there was no possibility Chocho or his men could see what Dak was about to do.

Dak focused all his energy on the window unit, squeezed both sides, and then pulled back.

The air conditioner slid out of its housing easier than Dak anticipated, and he found his momentum carrying him backward with the heavy unit falling with him.

He turned at the last second and slammed the machine onto the concrete floor amid broken pieces of plastic and bent metal.

"All right," Dak faced the boy again. "Out you go."

He rose, stabbed the pistol around the makeshift shield, and fired the last rounds from his magazine.

His salvo narrowly missed Chocho, who'd risen from his cover and taken aim at Dak's position. While the shots didn't hit a target, they forced the gunmen back down long enough to get the kid to safety.

Dak stuffed the pistol in his belt, then grabbed the kid. "Time to leave," he whispered. Holding the boy horizontally, Dak eased the kid through the window feetfirst. Once his shoes touched the ground on the other side, Dak gave him a nod. "Run, just like I told you."

Hector hesitated, uncertain if he were being a coward by running or if he could somehow help this kind man who'd been willing to help him.

"Don't worry about me," Dak said. "I have them right where I want them." He disarmed the boy with another wink, then urged him to go. "Better get out of here, kid. I'll see you around."

Hector wasn't sure if that was true, but he obeyed and took off at a sprint back toward downtown Lima.

Dak slid back over to the desk and waited. He ejected the empty magazine from his pistol and replaced it with the spare one he'd brought. Pressing his back against the desk drawers, he waited and listened.

"What are you doing back there, gringo?" Chocho asked. "You think your fortifications can stop us? Sooner or later, you're going to run out of bullets. Then what will you do?"

Dak listened to the antagonist but paid him no mind. Chocho was trying to distract him, perhaps even using a little crude psychology on him, but it wouldn't budge Dak. He'd been in this situation before.

He looked up at a television hanging in the back corner. The screen, surprisingly, hadn't been damaged in the firefight. In the reflection, Dak had a good angle on every enemy in the other room.

The dead man was off to the left. The one he'd hit in the leg remained crouched behind a chair. Then Chocho and the last guards hid behind the overturned table.

As Chocho spoke, Dak saw him motioning to the two guards next to him to move up.

They were going to try to surround Dak and kill him at point-blank range.

Dak drew the knife at his side from its sheath and stood up, keeping his head just below the upper edge of the desk. He watched silently as the two guards approached.

The gunmen crept to the door and then stopped, taking shelter behind the corner. Chocho and the wounded guard fired another volley at the desk. The bullets thumped against the surface, ringing Dak's ears.

He winced and waited, knowing what was coming next.

The gunfire stopped, and Dak saw the men slip into the office, splitting in two directions to flank the intruder on both sides.

Dak waited until the last second, when the two gunmen were inches from the big desk. The one on Dak's right stepped on a piece of broken glass. The crunching sound sent the American into action.

He stepped to his right just as the guard's pistol came into view. Dak stabbed his blade through the man's wrist, pushing it until the knife's tip punctured though the other side.

The gunman screamed, but his misery had only just begun.

Dak grabbed the guard as the other rounded the desk's opposite corner. Spinning the cursing guard around, Dak grabbed the guy by the neck and shoved him forward as the second guard fired his gun instinctively.

The human shield caught every round, his body twisting and jolting in mortal pain with every bullet that bored through his skin.

The second guard shifted to his left, making a deadly mistake. If he'd moved right, he could have lived another ten, maybe fifteen seconds, but he stepped right into Dak's trap.

The American already had his pistol extended, and as Chocho fired from his position in the main room, Dak took one step behind the desk and toward the gunman. He fired a single shot into the man's nose and tucked behind the makeshift shield as the two guards fell in a tangled heap on the floor to his left.

Four more loud pops echoed from the other room, and then it fell silent.

"You could have done this the easy way, Chocho!" Dak shouted. "All I wanted was some information. Now, you're just going to die, and I'll get it from someone else."

"You think you can threaten me, gringo? You don't know who you're dealing with!"

"Yeah, yeah," Dak responded with sarcasm. "You're like the third person to tell me that in the last couple of days. I don't think I have to tell you what happened to them."

"Why don't you come out from your little hiding spot and we can talk?" Chocho offered. "I'll even let the boy go. He doesn't need to be a part of this."

"I agree, Chocho. He doesn't. But you missed your chance. Unless you tell me where Diaz's mansion is, the only way you're getting out of this place is in a body bag."

Chocho laughed, and Dak saw him motioning to the wounded guard who still sat on the floor behind an old office chair. The man's lower half was fully exposed, and Dak was certain the man was bleeding considerably from the bullet hole in his leg. It shouldn't have been a mortal injury, but without medical attention he would continue to bleed and eventually lose consciousness.

"Your last guard is hurt," Dak said. "And I heard the way your collarbone popped when I landed on it. I imagine you're in quite a bit of pain right now."

Chocho lashed out with a slur of profanity.

"That bad, huh?" Dak shouted. "I've heard a broken collarbone is one of the more painful bones you can break. Never wanted to try it myself."

Dak watched in the screen's reflection. Chocho was making wild gestures at the guard on the ground, but the man's sluggish response didn't exactly fill his boss with a ton of confidence.

"He's useless," Dak said. "You may as well shoot him for me. I'm going to do it if you don't."

"Shut up!" Chocho yelled back. "You're a dead man! Right now, Diaz has his men on the way here. You screwed up, gringo!"

Another three gunshots forced Dak to stay down, but Chocho's plan became evident immediately. Dak watched the man's reflection break for the exit to the building. It was sloppy and uncoordinated as he compensated with every step for the pain shooting through his shoulder and neck. He slumped to one side, looking back over his shoulder as he limped toward the door.

Dak spun around the desk and aimed. He fired a single shot as he stepped to the office doorway. The bullet zipped through Chocho's hamstring. With the next step, the cartel enforcer collapsed to the ground and rolled to a painful stop—no doubt aggravating the collarbone injury in the process.

Dak stalked through the door and into the main room. The guard to his right squirmed, clutching his leg with one hand and desperately tried to reach for his pistol with the other.

Without so much as a sideways glance, Dak extended his gun to the side and fired two shots into the guard's chest, then a third in the head.

Dak kept walking toward Chocho, who clawed at the floor trying to drag himself to the door with one good arm and one functional leg.

If the situation hadn't been so serious, it might have been funny. But Dak didn't laugh or smile or even crack the stony expression on his face.

He reached Chocho seconds before the man could grab the gun he'd dropped mid-run and stepped on the thug's hand.

Chocho screamed in pain as Dak drove the heel of his boot into the back of the hand.

He swore again, this time using a few choice terms Dak had never heard in English or Spanish.

Dak squatted over the man and pressed the gun to the side of his face, pushing the still-warm muzzle into his cheek.

"Where is he?"

Through the almost unbearable, stabbing pain in his shoulder and from his leg, Chocho found enough strength to grin up at Dak. It was a sickening expression, and for a second, Dak believed he was staring back into the eyes of pure, unadulterated evil.

"You will never get to him, gringo," Chocho said. "But I will tell you where to find him, so he can kill you himself."

"Touching. I didn't take you for the sentimental type."

A slur of swearing bombarded Dak's ears, and he pressed down on the injured clavicle with his knee, sending a shockwave of new pain through the wounded man's nerves.

"Where is he?"

Chocho begged for Dak to stop then. Even the most hardened, evil monster in the entire world would bend if enough misery were applied.

"Okay, gringo. I'll...tell you," Chocho spat, struggling to find breath between the words. He gave Dak the address to Diaz's compound on the edge of the city and explained how to get there.

"That doesn't seem very secretive." Dak's implied suggestion was that the lair of Fernando Diaz couldn't be that close to the city.

"Sometimes, gringo, the best place to hide is in plain sight." The statement was followed by a sickly laugh. The man's journey into delirium was complete. That, or shock had set in.

Dak stood up amid the disturbing laughter. Chocho's face twisted in an equally unsettling expression that landed somewhere between agony and ecstasy. With one twitch of his trigger finger, Dak put a bullet through Chocho's head and quieted the room.

Peering through the gray haze that hung in the dock house, Dak let out a long exhale. Finally, he had what he needed, but he had to make one last stop before he took down Diaz.

24

The sun warmed Dak's face as he trudged up the steep hill toward the center of the city. He stopped every few blocks to double back or turn down random streets in case someone was following him, though he never caught sight of a tail.

Police cars zoomed by about ten minutes after he left the shipping yard, and he heard more speeding down other streets nearby. They were, no doubt, responding to the call from the shootout that happened at Dock 79. Dak cynically noted the delayed response time and assumed it was because the police knew better than to get involved with a cartel gun battle until it was well and truly over.

They're certainly in for a surprise.

Satisfied no one was trailing him, Dak picked up his pace and made his way toward the bookstore.

People filled the sidewalks, heading to appointments or just looking around, peering through shop windows. Cars on the streets honked now and then in the midst of their stop-and-go lunch-hour rush.

All of it was a blur to Dak, and he barely noted the faces, clothes, or the models of cars that drove by on the street. The only reason he analyzed any of the faces at all was out of prudence. An attack could come from almost anyone. With so many people wearing sunglasses in the bright midday sun, he couldn't get a read on people's eyes, which were always his go-to when it came to detecting a person's intentions.

Still, even with sunglasses, Dak observed the body language of the passersby.

The walk back took longer than the journey to the docks, mostly due to his erratic path, but he arrived back at the bookstore without incident. He'd just come through the eye of the proverbial hurricane, knowing that the storm on the back end was often far worse than the initial onslaught.

He stopped at the corner of an alley across the street from the bookshop and scanned the perimeter. Dak noted the first guy standing at the corner of the next intersection. The man smoked a cigarette, flipping through his phone as if reading the day's news or perhaps checking social media.

Dak knew better. He could see the awkward bulge under the man's gray windbreaker. Only cops and killers were armed in this town, as far as Dak could tell, and he seriously doubted this guy was a cop.

Further recon revealed another cartel thug at the other end of the block. He sat at a café, sipping a cup of coffee while he pretended to read through a magazine. This guy's problem was that the magazine was about interior design.

Dak rolled his eyes at the carelessness. "You have to be kidding me," he muttered to himself. The least the guy could have done was pick up a sports magazine, maybe something outdoorsy, or even a science publication. Anything but the one he held in his hands. Almost any alternative would have been believable.

Most people didn't think about that kind of thing, though, and Dak knew the henchmen were likely assigned to keep watch of the street and pretend to look busy doing something else. His first instinct must have been to grab a magazine, any magazine, and pretend to be busily reading it while covertly looking over the top to make sure trouble wasn't coming their way.

Dak also noted the guard standing just inside the bookstore, through two sets of doors. The man's silhouette darkened the glass just enough to make him visible, but there was no denying the man's purpose for being there.

Diaz had ramped up security.

Dak smiled at the thought, relishing the damage he'd already done to the cartel's operation. While the upgrade in security measures made things more difficult, it was a signal that Diaz had grown desperate to protect the remaining segments of his operation from further destruction.

The bookstore was only one of several other distribution centers in the city; that much Dak figured. But as he analyzed the location and the way it was being guarded, it grew more evident that the shop had to be one of the more important, if not the most important, part of the entire operation. If he could take it down, he'd have cut off one of Diaz's legs to go along with the arm he'd taken at the facility the night before.

The biggest mistake the security personnel made was keeping themselves too far apart. Dak understood the men's logic of guarding the corners of the block. The men must have figured they would stop anyone who looked American from getting close to the shop.

The problem with their strategy was obvious to Dak, who had studied and learned battle tactics from throughout history.

One of the biggest ones that stood out in his mind was the blunder of the Maginot Line on the eastern border of France—a series of tunnels connecting huge guns that pointed toward Germany. The defenses had been intended to protect France in the event of another world war with the Germans. What André Maginot, the French lawmaker who'd advocated for the increased defenses, hadn't anticipated was the Nazis going around the line by way of Belgium.

In this case, Dak wasn't going to go around the guards. He was going to walk through the front door right between them. Before entering the building, though, he had one other task to complete.

As he scanned the building, Dak discovered the thing he was looking for within thirty seconds. A gray box hung from the bookstore's exterior wall. He couldn't see the wiring conduits from his position, but he knew they were there. All of the building's power ran through that box, metered and distributed into the shop.

Dak set down his tactical bag and retrieved a plastic baggy with a narrow strip of gray clay inside it. After removing the clay, he fished a receiver from the front pouch of his bag and attached it to the explosive. Satisfied the unit was complete, he took a remote detonator from the backpack and slid it into his pocket.

The guard in the building would be problematic, but only for a moment. Dak only needed to get by him without raising an alarm, and then he could put his plan into action.

He picked up his rucksack and cinched it tighter against his back. He waited patiently, doing his best to look disinterested in anything until traffic slowed, then immediately broke across the asphalt at a brisk walk, keeping his head down until he reached the opposite sidewalk.

He never glanced at the guards at either end of the block, knowing that if he did, they might recognize trouble and sound an alarm.

Dak stayed calm, keeping focused on the gray box in the adjacent alley until he was beyond the entrance and out of view. Then he sped up, running the remaining forty feet to the electrical box on the wall.

The smell of ripe garbage hung in the alley's still air. The stench plumed from two overflowing dumpsters only a dozen feet away.

Dak breathed through his mouth to quell the scent and quickly wrapped the explosive device around one of the gray wires running into the meter box. He glanced over his right shoulder to make sure no one was watching, then finished connecting the looped piece of clay.

The task took less than a minute but felt like twenty. With the miniature bomb in place, Dak quickly turned and started back toward the bookstore's entrance. As he neared the building's front corner, he slipped a hand into his pocket and thumbed the remote detonator, rubbing the button to feel its location.

Dak only slowed briefly at the corner to take a breath then depressed the button on the fob.

A muted pop came from behind him as he casually rounded the corner, as if he were just a curious shopper looking for a book.

He pulled on the door and stepped inside, then put his hand on the next door, twisting his body to remove the hunting knife from its sheath at his hip. As expected, the bookstore's interior was almost completely dark, and the guard inside was shifting from his position in front of the doors, moving toward the rear of the shop.

The smell of books and coffee washed over Dak as he entered the shop, but he only noticed the scents for a second.

The guard was in the middle of shouting to someone in the back when he felt the swoosh of outside air blow over him.

Dak took a long step forward as he bowed his head. The grip on the knife in his left hand tightened. He figured there were at least two guards in the back, hovering around the entrance to the manager's office.

Upon feeling the rush of outside air, the guard at the front whirled around. All he could manage was a gruff "What the—"

Dak moved swiftly. With his hunting knife already brandished, he slid the dark blade across the guard's neck before the man could raise his gun. The guard instinctively grasped at his throat as blood began to pulse out of the wound. Dak slashed the gun's shoulder strap and freed the weapon from the man's arm in a single move and continued forward into the darkened bookstore.

Men shouted from the back, unaware that the front-door guard was already on his knees, feeling the last of his life's essence seep through his fingers.

Dak went left, choosing to circle around at a wide angle to flank the henchmen in the back. He raised the dead guard's submachine gun and pointed it straight ahead. *Should have brought the night-vision goggles,* Dak thought with mild regret.

He crouched low, moving up the aisle with the pistol leading the way. The men in the back had stopped shouting at each other, which told Dak they'd left their posts—probably to go to the front to investigate. That changed nothing about his plan.

Dak rounded the end of the bookshelf and stabbed the gun forward. The men, as he suspected, were gone. He stepped quickly, moving to the corridor's edge. He spotted the outline of the office door in the back but didn't go that way. Instead, he focused on taking out the two remaining guards in the shop.

He didn't have to search long to discover the first target. The muscular guard moved steadily forward, almost sauntering to the front of the shop. The gunman must have figured the guy at the front was trying to fix the power issue.

When the henchman reached the end of the aisle, he looked beyond the front display table to the entrance and spotted his comrade lying facedown in a pool of dark liquid.

Dak crept rapidly down the aisle and caught the guard from behind just as he was about to speak. Whipping a hand around the man's mouth to silence him, Dak thrust the bloody knife through the back of the guard's skull. He felt the body go limp almost instantly and lowered it quietly to the floor.

Dak ducked back out of sight a second before the third guard stepped out of the aisle and into view. He stayed there for a second until he heard the gunman call out to the one on the floor in the doorway. Peeking around the corner, Dak watched as the goon moved hurriedly to the body.

With the guard in the open, Dak rushed around the display table and raised his weapon. He was about to slit the man's throat when he bumped into the table. Dak winced as one of the upright display books fell over on its face with a whap.

The guard reacted quickly, shifting his stance to a defensive position as he rounded on the intruder. He kicked out with his left foot, but Dak twisted to the side and fired the gun three times into the man's chest, then once through his head as he stumbled backward into a tall bookshelf. The stunned guard's face paled as he died, his wide eyes instantly glazing over in a vacant stare. His body tipped forward as books from the upper shelves toppled down onto him, littering the floor around the prostrate body.

Dak knew the men in the back of the building would have heard the gunshots, not that it mattered. With the sudden power outage, whoever was in the manager's office would have immediately been on high alert, and they probably would have seen everything via the cameras positioned in the corners. Dak knew his little trick with the power wouldn't knock those out since most security cameras had battery backups.

He looked directly into the nearest lens, peering into it as he would an enemy's eyes, and then turned away.

Dak locked the front doors first in case the guards outside decided to try to reinforce the others, then he spun and hurried to the corridor in the rear.

He slowed near the metal door. Within the confines of the short hall, he was shrouded in darkness. The security camera above and to the right of the door would yield few details, not that he cared. He'd already let them see he was coming.

Muted shouts came from within the office. A panicked voice issued orders in a flurry. Dak grinned. Whoever was in there—probably Flores—was telling his goons to clog the doorway and kill the next person who came through. He recalled the cardboard standup of a famous author standing in a nearby corner and returned to the main room to retrieve it.

He dragged the life-size cutout to the metal door and propped it up within the doorframe. Then Dak set down his bag and retrieved another strip of clay. This time, he pressed the explosive along the door's seam, where the deadbolts kept the back room secure.

After he attached the receiver, he pulled a small disc out of another pocket in the tactical bag. Satisfied he had everything he needed, Dak set the gear bag around the corner and returned to the door again.

He rapped on it four times then called out to the men inside. "Flores? Are you in there? I have a delivery for you."

No response came.

"I hear you in there, Ricardo. I just want to talk. Okay," Dak corrected, "that's not entirely true. I'm also here to kill you."

Still silence.

"Okay, Ricardo," Dak said after waiting a few seconds. "If you're not going to come out, then I'll have to come in. Can you guys see okay in there? I know the power went out. Kind of dark in here. I'm guessing there aren't any windows in there, so you guys are probably stuck using cell phone lights or flashlights, huh?"

Dak noted narrow streams of light under the gap at the bottom of the door and smirked. *Yep.*

"All right, Ricardo. I'm coming in. You might want to tell your men to stand back."

Dak knew the cartel lieutenant would do nothing of the sort. If anything, he might urge his men forward.

With the warning issued, Dak moved back around the corner, found the detonator in his pocket, and pressed the button.

25

Dak covered his ears the second before a loud bang rocked the bookstore. Smoke tumbled out of the hallway and into the shop.

He heard a creak signal that the door swung open, and then all hell broke loose. Loud clicks and muffled pops echoed from the back room. Bullets zipped by, ripping into books, shelves, and display stands. The men inside the office had equipped their weapons with suppressors, a fact Dak was thankful for even though his weapon didn't have one.

He waited as Flores and his men emptied their magazines. Then, when silence had descended over the bookshop, Dak pressed the little disc in his hand three times then whipped it around the corner and through the open door.

He ducked back out of sight as the metal device sailed over the fallen cardboard cutout and waited again.

A brilliant flash of white light flared out of the corridor. Men shouted and swore. From the sound of it, one or two stumbled and fell over something inside the office.

"My turn," Dak whispered.

He spun around the corner with the submachine gun and fired. Dak squeezed the trigger again and again, blasting a deadly salvo of bursts into the room where the gunmen crouched in a huddle, surrounded by gun smoke. The men inside held guns with flashlights attached, and a cell phone light in the back glowed bright, illuminating everything and everyone within. The haze swirled and danced in beams of light, like ghosts entranced by the lure of more souls to beckon.

Henchmen fell rapidly, one after the other under the barrage. Dak marched forward, a reaper come to collect his bounty. He stepped over the tattered remains of the cardboard standup and continued forward, pausing at the door. Inside, all of the guards were dead, piled up on the floor where they'd made their desperate stand.

Dak hesitated. His instinct was to turn on the flashlight atop his weapon and peer into the corners of the room to make sure everyone was eliminated. Something, however, stopped him in his tracks. It was a feeling, nothing more, at first. His gut instinct had saved him many times in the past, and now that same creeping sensation warned him that he wasn't safe yet.

He waited, silently, and listened. His senses heightened, and he let himself feel everything around him. The acrid smell of burned powder filled the air, much like a scent from his childhood when the family would shoot off fireworks on the Fourth of July. He pushed aside the nostalgia and focused on his hearing. If someone else was in the room, turning on his light and stepping inside would be a mistake. He hadn't come this far to be ambushed.

Dak stood perfectly still, waiting, listening. The sounds of traffic outside the building barely registered as a low hum through the walls of the bookstore. He held his breath, and then, there it was. He could hear the telltale sound in the dark stillness. Someone was just around the corner, trying to contain their breathing against the adrenaline of the gunfight and impending death.

The sound came from just around the right-hand side of the door. Dak eased the gun forward, allowing the barrel to poke through the opening.

A hand snatched the weapon and jerked it forward, but Dak had anticipated the move, knowing that would be the enemy's reaction. Dak let go of the nearly empty gun and raised his pistol as he twisted around the doorframe.

He pulled the trigger as the target came into view, but the man ducked to the side and fired his own pistol. The bullet clipped Dak's jacket, but he managed to turn his body fast enough to avoid catching the round with flesh.

Dak countered with a kick from his right boot to the back of the man's hand. Normally, that blow would have been enough to knock the pistol out of an enemy's hand, but this man retained his grasp on the weapon. The opponent absorbed the attack and quickly kicked out his own right foot, catching Dak in the midsection a moment before he could pull the trigger.

The blow knocked the wind from Dak's lungs, and he doubled over for a second. He barely had enough awareness to draw the blade from his belt and swing it up at an angle as the gunman tried to adjust his aim.

The knife's sharp edge slashed through the man's wrist, cutting deep into flesh. He yelped, and the gun dropped instantly from impotent fingers—their tendons severed.

The man's eyes blazed in a drugged-up swirl of anger and fury. He pulled back the wounded appendage and grabbed at it as he retreated a step.

Dak summoned his strength as he fought to regain his breath. He stood upright and lunged forward, still gasping for air. He couldn't let the enemy get the upper hand.

The opponent retreated farther, stepping backward into the darkness without watching where he was going, which turned out to be his undoing. His heel caught on a power cord and tripped him, sending him stumbling backward toward a table. The man's lower back struck the edge and he fell back onto the surface. He tried to grab a knife to his left, but Dak pounced before he could grip the handle.

The American drove the tip of his blade through the man's wrist, between the two bones, and into the table's surface—pinning the arm down.

The man screamed at the new pain, writhing around as if that would help. It only made things worse.

He swore and cursed the gringo, spittle spewing out from his lips with every word. Dak stood over him for a moment, watching the man suffer while regaining his breath. When the air sucked back into Dak's lungs, he calmed himself, looked back toward the door, and then inched closer to the man.

"Shh," Dak urged. "I need you to be quiet now."

The man cussed at him again.

Dak tilted his head at an angle, his face a portrait of mocking pity. "I can make it hurt more. Or I can make it hurt less. Which, is up to you."

The man let out another haunting yell as he struggled against the knife pinning him to the table. He kicked his legs, swinging them wildly as if that would somehow fend off the gringo.

"If you don't settle down, I'll have to shoot you in the kneecaps," Dak warned, speaking English since he didn't know the Spanish word for kneecaps.

Another grunt escaped the man's lips, along with more expletives.

"You know," Dak said, returning to Spanish, "I don't care for the things you're saying, about me or my mother. So, I'm going to tell you what I want. If you cooperate, I'll make this easier for you."

The man's nostrils flared with every breath. He clenched his jaw, a reaction from the anger and against the pain in both forearms.

"I've seen your brand of mercy," the man blared. "You're the one killing Diaz's men. And now you're here to kill me, too."

"Ah. So, you must be Ricardo Flores. I must say, I'm surprised, Ricky. I didn't expect much fight out of someone like you. Usually, your kind spend their days ordering others to do the dirty work for you. Well done. And that kick back there?" Dak motioned behind him to where the fight occurred. "Impressive. Very few people catch me off guard like that."

"Go to hell."

"Oh, Ricky. That's not very nice. This might have gone differently had you cooperated in the first place. We could have all sat down and had a nice chat." Dak waved a hand at the dead men on the floor. "But now all of your men are dead. And you have a knife sticking through your arm." He glanced down at the handiwork. "I have to admit, that looks painful. Is it as bad as it looks? Or is it one of those things where you stop feeling it after a minute?"

Flores barked another profane phrase.

Dak shook his head. "Such language, Ricky. I hope you never spoke to your mother like that."

"I never had a mother. She left me in the tugurizadas when I was six." The bitter words spilled from the man's mouth like acid.

"Oh, well I'm sorry, but I'm not interested in your backstory. I only care about one thing right now, and that's finding your boss. Tell me, Ricky, where can I find Fernando Diaz?"

Flores tightened his forehead, frowning with confusion. "Diaz?" He laughed. "You want to find Fernando Diaz? You don't know? Diaz is looking for *you*, gringo. He's got all of his men scouring the city for you. And now, he has the mayor on his side. So, all the cops in the city are looking for you, too."

Dak's expression changed in a blink.

Flores noticed and forced a delirious grin. "You didn't know?" He laughed a thin, sinister laugh. "You have made a terrible mistake, gringo. You killed Diaz's cousin. That was bad enough. But then you went and killed the mayor's husband. Now the entire city is looking for you. It will be all over the news before nightfall. Then where will you go? Where will you hide? You won't be able to escape. And neither will your friend, the doctor."

Dak tried to remain stoic, but he couldn't hide the surprise that flashed through his eyes in the moment Flores mentioned the doctor.

"Oh yes. We know about Davenport. Right now, Diaz's men and the police are searching for him. It's only a matter of time until they find your friend. Of course, it won't matter who finds him—the cops or our men. We both know the doctor won't see the inside of a jail cell. His body will be torn apart and left for the dogs. And no one will ever consider meddling with the cartel's affairs again."

Dak immediately regained his composure, pushing away his concerns for Davenport. That was something he'd deal with soon enough.

He stepped to the side and inspected the knife still sticking through the man's wrist. "You know," Dak began, "most people would be nicer to someone who held their life in the balance. Like right now, for instance." He scooped up a pistol from the floor and aimed it at his captive's knee. "Now, if you're done threatening me. I'd like to get back to asking the questions. And remember, Ricky, I can make things hurt more, or I can make them hurt less. Tell me, where is Diaz's mansion?"

Flores laughed again through the pain, wincing with every breath. "Find it yourself."

"Oh, I already have the address. I know how to get there. I just want to make sure my intel is good. So, I'm giving you a chance to be honest with me." He lowered the pistol closer to the man's knee.

Flores responded by kicking wildly again, but Dak lifted and lowered the gun accordingly, matching the man's movements.

"You'll get tired of doing that in a few minutes, Ricky," Dak pressed. "When you do, I'm going to shoot you in the knee if you don't tell me what I want to know. Just imagine what your life will feel like, never really being able to walk normally again, without pain. You're going to have your hands full with the other injuries you've sustained—pardon the expression." Dak chuckled at his own wit.

Flores cursed him.

"Okay, fine." Dak adjusted his aim and squeezed the trigger. The suppressor on the weapon puffed with a click, and the man's left shoe exploded.

A new scream filled the office, echoing and reverberating in a cacophony of anguish. Dak slapped the man across the face to shut him up, but the whimpering continued for another minute.

Beads of sweat rolled off the captive's face, and Dak knew Flores was probably going into shock.

"No more soccer for you, Ricky. Now, please. Tell me where Diaz lives, and all this pain goes away."

"You're just going to kill me," Flores spat. "I'm not stupid. Is this what you did to the others? Interrogated them? Tortured them? Then killed them?"

Dak nodded. "Yeah, pretty much. But hey, you work for a cartel. How did you expect your life to end? Sipping margaritas on a beach somewhere? Or perhaps you thought you would get by for a few years, live it up, then catch a knife in the back. That's how this usually ends for your kind, right?"

Flores shook his head. "You think you're so smart. You will not leave Peru alive, gringo."

"Fine," Dak relented. "You want me dead? What will happen if I go to Diaz's place? He'll have an army there, right? No chance I can get to him. So, you give me the location, I go there and get killed, and your organization continues to operate as before. All you have to do is tell me where he is, and I'll be dead along with your comrades."

Flores considered the offer, and Dak could tell he was mulling it over. The man chewed his lip, both as he weighed the possibilities and because he was trying to stay conscious.

"Fine," Flores said. "You're correct. Diaz and his men will kill you before you even get close. His mansion is on the coast, on the edge of the city." He relayed the location, and Dak found himself surprised by the fact it matched the one given him by Chocho.

"Thank you," Dak said. "I appreciate your cooperation."

"You're going to die a painful—" His words cut off with the click of the pistol and a bullet through his right cheek that exited through his skull. The head fell limp onto the table with a thud, hanging over the back edge just slightly.

Dak quickly scooped up another pistol and his own, shoving the latter into his belt. He surveyed the room and then strode to the door.

He stopped when he heard the sounds of the street filter into the shop. The gunmen from the street had either heard the commotion, been called, or were checking in as part of their routine. The reason didn't matter to Dak.

Quickly, he ducked down out of sight from the main entrance and scurried over to his gear bag. He slipped it on and stayed low, waiting for the gunmen to appear.

Dak didn't have to wait long. The men moved quickly down the aisles, giving no concern to the ambush that lay in wait. He heard them as they drew near, their pants rustling and their footfalls heavy. *Hardly Spec Ops.*

The men appeared at the same time from the two aisles at either end of the room. When they turned toward the hallway, Dak rose and extended the two pistols, one in each direction. His trigger fingers twitched again and again, unloading a wall of deadly metal at the two gunmen. Some of the bullets missed, which Dak expected. Firing two weapons at once in opposite directions looked easy in the movies, but in practice was an exercise in faith. Still, volume trumped all.

Books exploded behind the men, sending paper fragments fluttering in the air around them. Most of the rounds found purchase, though, and the men were struck down before they could offer a reply. They fell almost simultaneously to the floor atop torn pages and chunks of hardcovers.

Dak drew in a deep breath and lowered the pistols. He inspected his handiwork for a heartbeat and then tossed one of the pistols aside, deciding to keep one for later to go with the one Davenport had given him.

After stowing his weapons in his rucksack, Dak marched through the front door and out onto the sidewalk. He slid a pair of sunglasses onto his face and checked both directions. With no sign of trouble, Dak veered left, heading toward the cantina to find Doc.

He could only hope Flores had been lying about Davenport's fate.

26

Peter Davenport sat in his usual seat in the back corner of the cantina, waiting on his first beer of the afternoon to be delivered.

He didn't have to wait long. The young woman running the bar rounded the corner with two glasses, one in each hand. The golden lager nearly spilled over the lips of both. When she set them down in front of her patron, though, neither glass lacked a drop.

"Thanks," he said in easy English.

She smiled and walked back to the bar while Peter stared at the glass. He always ordered drinks in pairs. While the casual observer might simply think his double-fisting was a quicker way to get drunk than ordering them one at a time, Peter alone knew the real reason.

He thought of her as he peered into the golden liquid. He didn't see her face in it or smell the scent of her perfume. He wasn't overcome with some grandiose spiritual experience in which he could hear her voice speaking to him.

But the beer reminded him of her nonetheless.

They would always have drinks together, one every single day, and usually not more. It was a ritual, a part of their relationship that had become a daily tradition both looked forward to.

In his previously hectic life, Peter had been on others' schedules. The navy told him where to be, what to do, and when to do it. The hospital had been a similarly structured environment where he had little choice regarding his schedule, other than the times he set aside for vacation or paid time off. All that time, he could feel his job pulling him away from the woman he loved and the relationship he'd embraced for so long.

Taking an early retirement had been the best decision Peter ever made. And with it, he decided that he and his wife should share a drink together every day around the same time.

He looked down at his watch and noted it was about that time, raised the glass, and nodded to the image of her he saw in his mind. A grim smile parted his lips. "Here's lookin' at you, babe," he said, augmenting the line from one of his favorite movies.

He took a sip and clenched his jaw to stave off the sadness that came with this toast every single day. No beer, no matter the brand or bar, ever tasted quite as good as it had when he was drinking with her.

Since her death, Peter hadn't missed an appointment, though he had increased the quantity of booze he consumed. Along with drinking his wife's portion, he almost always ordered another two or three rounds. He'd long forsaken concerns over moderation. He was a man waiting to die. What did he care for moderation?

He set the glass down and continued to stare at it. The front door opened and closed, briefly letting in a tall stream of light that would have momentarily blinded the other patrons—if there had been any there.

Peter had the entire bar to himself until the newcomer entered.

"Took you long enough, Diaz," Peter said, still keeping his eyes on the glass in front of him.

"You're a difficult man to find," Diaz replied coolly from the doorway. He took a deliberate step forward, then another, walking steadily across the bar before stopping halfway. Two bodyguards stood on either side of him, both with shaved heads and multiple neck and face tattoos.

"I would have expected more from a man with your resources," Peter drawled. He lifted the glass again and took a gulp. When he set it back on the table, the container was already half-empty.

"My resources have doubled since you killed my cousin. Tell me, Doctor, why did you do it?"

Peter huffed at the comment and twisted his head at a slight angle so he could meet Diaz's simmering gaze.

"That what you think? You think I killed your cousin?" Peter shook his head and returned his eyes to the drink. "I didn't kill your relative. You've got much bigger problems on your hands than me."

Diaz inclined his head and peered down his nose at the older man. "Yes. We are still trying to locate the one who went into the Turtle. I suppose you didn't have anything to do with my processing facility, either."

Peter noticed the bartender leave through the back door into the kitchen but said nothing. He was glad she'd been allowed to leave peacefully. For a second, he thought Diaz might harm her, or worse.

"I didn't say I had nothing to do with Antonio's death. I was there that night. We both know that. Otherwise, why would you be here?"

"*Verdad*," Diaz said, switching back to his native Spanish.

"And I got no reason to lie to you, Diaz," Peter growled the name. He avoided the subject of the attack, and apparently, Diaz forgot he'd mentioned it.

"Where are the girls?" Diaz crossed his arms, keeping his hands close to his waist.

"They're safe. But you won't find them. I suspect they're halfway to Santiago by now, if not already there. The Chileans will give them refuge."

"Girls are easy enough to come by," Diaz demurred. "Your little rescue mission has done nothing but given me a need to acquire more."

Peter's head bobbed up and down. "Yeah, I suppose you're right. But you'll have to spend money and resources to make that happen. And frankly, anything I can do to get in your craw is time well spent."

Diaz stood silent, his hands folded in front of him. He seemed deep in thought, as if his mind wandered to some far-off place or time. Then, after a long dozen seconds, he inhaled deeply before speaking.

"When I was a boy," he began, "my mother left, and my father... Well, let's just say he wasn't there much."

"Sorry to hear that," Peter groused with venom.

Diaz allowed his irritation at the interruption to slide off his shoulders, though his men tensed for a second.

"I learned how to survive. But when I was young, living in the tugurizadas, it was tough. I wasn't as big as some of the other kids. One day, I found a toy someone had thrown out in a dumpster. It was a toy fire truck. One of the wheels wobbled, but I loved that toy. I played with it every day. It helped keep my mind off the hunger pangs in my belly."

"Daddy didn't feed you, huh?"

Diaz steamed, but he remained calm on the outside. Mostly.

"He fed me once a day, sometimes twice. He usually wasn't there much. Then, one day, I woke up and couldn't find my fire truck. I looked everywhere for it. My father claimed he had no idea where it was, and as you can imagine, he wasn't very sympathetic to my plight."

"Sounds like he was a real nice fellow," Peter huffed.

Ignoring him, Diaz went on. "I was devastated. How could I have lost it? The fire truck had been beside my little bed on the floor when I went to sleep. Then, as I sat there in my shack, my mind turning in confusion, I realized what happened. One of the other kids had broken into my home and stolen my fire truck."

"Is that the big climax of the story?" Peter asked. "Because I'm starting to wonder if there's a point to this whole parable."

"*Silencio!*" Diaz roared. The cables holding back his fury finally snapped.

Peter just grinned and took another casual sip of beer.

After taking a few seconds to reset his mind, Diaz continued. "I started investigating. I knew that whoever took my fire truck was close by. It had to be someone in my immediate area, perhaps someone I'd seen regularly, or who had seen me. And so I watched, and I waited. It was difficult to remain patient, but I put all of my focus, all of my energy into discovering who stole the toy that belonged to me."

Peter briefly considered saying something about him not having much of a life but thought better of it. He'd fired enough barbs Diaz's way. For the moment.

"Then, one day," Diaz said, "I found him. It was another boy who lived across the street, only a few doors down on our block. The kid had been mean to me before, wouldn't let me play with him and his friends. He was a rotten child, and he had a reputation for taking things from others. I'd suspected him but had no proof until I saw the firetruck with my own eyes as he played with it in the dirt in front of his home. It was as if he was taunting me with it, telling me, 'Look, Fernando! I stole your toy! What are you going to do about it?'"

"What *did* you do about it?" Peter asked, genuinely.

Diaz shrugged. "I waited until he was asleep that night. Then I took my father's machete, snuck into the boy's home, and retrieved my fire truck."

"You killed the kid?" A twinge of shock trickled through Peter's voice. The story had taken a dark turn, though he had a feeling it might.

"No." Diaz shook his head and let his eyes float to the floor for a second. When he raised them, they might have been the eyes of the devil himself. "I cut off his right hand while he slept." The evil look in his eyes dissipated, and Diaz shrugged. "I left his shack amid the screams and confusion. He never saw my face. But deep down, he knew who did it and why."

"That's a fascinating and disturbing yarn, Fernando. A little harsh, don't you think?"

"Hmm. Not at all. I seriously doubt that boy ever stole anything from anyone ever again. He certainly didn't steal from me anymore."

"Ah." Peter finished the lager in one last gulp then set the glass down next to the other. "Well, maybe you can teach an old dog new tricks after all."

"So it would seem. And now, I'm afraid it's time to teach another old dog."

Peter nodded. "Yeah. I know. Your story about the kid and the firetruck was a weak attempt at making a correlation with my setting those girls free. Except you didn't love them the way you loved your toy. And the irony is you stole them from someone else. From family. From friends. Perhaps from a boyfriend or fiancé. I guess you never paused to consider that, did you? And now you're upset because someone cut your hand off." Peter paused and turned his head to meet Diaz's gaze again. "Maybe you're worried someone is going to cut off your other hand. Or something worse; if you catch my drift."

Diaz sucked in a breath through his nostrils and then exhaled slowly. "I suppose we see things differently. Either way, killing my men, destroying my business, taking my property...It's all the same to me. I cannot tolerate this sort of encroachment."

He motioned to the guards, and the two immediately raised their weapons.

"So that's it?" Peter asked. "You're going to kill me?" He huffed a laugh. "By all means. Your bullets will be way faster than Father Time, I'll tell you that."

"No," Diaz corrected. "I'm not going to kill you. Not yet. First, you have to suffer. And there's no sense in wasting good bait when there's a bigger fish to catch."

27

Dak did his best to look casual as he walked down the sidewalk, but his heart pounded in his chest. He was far enough away from the bookstore that no one would connect him with the killings there. He doubted any witnesses had paid attention to him leaving the shop, and he hadn't noticed anyone who appeared to notice him. Most were simply going about their day. Others, those who had an inclination about what really went on at the bookstore, chose to ignore the man leaving the building for fear they might receive Diaz's retribution for even looking at the guy the wrong way.

They had no idea of knowing what Dak had just done, and he knew it would stay that way until the next delivery person showed up at the shop.

He hoped it wasn't a kid, but Dak knew the odds were fifty-fifty. Regrettable, but there was nothing he could do about it. Flores and his operation were a major arm of the Diaz empire, and that arm had to be amputated.

Dak looked at his phone again, thinking perhaps he missed a message or a return call. A blank screen stared back at him, reflecting a shadowy figure of himself on the surface.

"Why are you not answering?" he wondered out loud.

He sidestepped to the right, nearly bumping into a middle-aged woman with grocery bags hanging from both hands.

"*Lo siento*," he offered with a bow of his head. He didn't turn to face the woman, though, and kept walking toward the cantina.

He typed another message. "Doc. It's me. I have the coordinates for what I'm looking for. You don't have to help if you don't want to. This last part I'll handle on my own."

Dak hit the send button and saw the text bubble turn blue on the screen. He sighed with worry and picked up his pace to the point he was almost jogging.

He stopped at the next intersection and waited for the light to turn. He peered around at the setting—the cars, the people, the shops. None of them seemed to be paying any attention to him.

As he panned across his surroundings, Dak's head turned to the right until he noticed the tech gadget store mere feet away on the corner. Huge flatscreens hung in the display window, showing off the newest television models and their incredible capabilities. Crystal-clear images of a female news anchor filled the screen.

He was about to turn away and walk across the street when Dak froze. An image appeared on the screen in a box in the upper right-hand corner. Dak's jaw tightened as he stared at the composite drawing of a white male who looked somewhat similar but not completely like him.

"Great," he muttered.

The words on the screen underneath the anchor declared that this man was wanted for the murder of the mayor's husband. The text changed to reflect the anchor's words. "If you have any information on this man's whereabouts, please contact the police immediately."

Dak pursed his lips and nodded. "That's just perfect." He knelt down and set the backpack on the ground at his feet. After unzipping the main compartment, he pulled out a gray baseball cap and fit it low on his skull. Between that and the sunglasses on his nose, he figured he could evade any suspicious citizens or overzealous cops long enough to find Doc.

Temporarily satisfied with his disguise, Dak picked up the bag and crossed the street.

He kept his profile low as he moved in and out of foot traffic. No one seemed to notice him, and if they did, he would have known. People tended to point or stare or make a fuss about someone they recognized—whether a celebrity or threat.

Dak finally arrived at the cantina and stopped at the crosswalk, peering at the bar from across the street. Something wasn't right. He'd had that feeling before, the sense that he was walking into a trap or that things weren't what they seemed.

He searched the windows in the building above the cantina but saw no silhouettes amid the curtains. The sidewalks here were less busy than the ones he'd been on just minutes before and appeared the same as they had been on Dak's other visits.

No goons or cops lurked along the street, waiting to spring their ambush.

Yet Dak couldn't get over the impending sense of concern tightening in his gut.

He looked down at the phone again, but there was no response from Doc. Something was wrong.

A distant fear crept into Dak's mind. They'd been careful, for the most part. He'd realized there would be cameras in the bordello and knew enough to keep his face out of sight. Doc had been even more cautious, wearing a mask when he rescued the girls from the brothel. *No one could possibly know who I am or how to find me, unless....*

Dak hurried across the street and over to the cantina. At the doors, he waited for a second, collecting his thoughts. *There could be a dozen armed thugs through those doors, waiting to blast you to kingdom come.* The thought didn't dissuade him, but Dak briefly considered looking for a back door. He shrugged off the idea. It was doubtful such a door would be unlocked.

He reached out for the handle with his left hand while twisting his body and shifting his right hand to the pistol concealed under his jacket. Dak took a deep breath, then pulled open the door, fully expecting to see a horde of enemy gunmen standing inside with weapons drawn.

Instead, he found the cantina nearly empty, save for the bartender and a single patron sitting at the counter.

Dak felt both a wave of relief and renewed panic crash over him. He stepped inside and surveyed the room but found no trace of Dr. Davenport.

The bartender gave him a familiar, welcoming smile.

He stepped inside, almost unconsciously, and meandered over to the booth where he and Doc had met previously. Sitting on the table were two pint glasses. One full, the other empty.

Dak reached out and touched the side of the empty glass. He breathed calmly, but deep down a volcano erupted. He wanted to ask the bartender when they left, when Diaz's men took Davenport, but he didn't figure she'd give an honest answer. Maybe she didn't even know. They could have told her to step outside while they did their business. Dak forced himself not to be angry with her. She was just a young woman, probably no older than twenty, working at a dive bar in Lima. It wasn't her fault Doc had chosen this spot as his regular watering hole. And she certainly wasn't to blame for Dak coming here in search of a sword that the drug lord kept in his mansion.

He swallowed hard, forcing down his emotions so he could think clearly.

Suddenly, the phone in his hand started to vibrate.

Dak looked at the screen, surprised to see Doc was calling him. Perhaps the old man had gotten away, left in a hurry and didn't have time to finish his second beer.

Dak pressed the answer button and raised the phone to his ear.

"Doc?"

Silence greeted him at first, followed by a slow, rhythmic breathing. He thought he heard a car motor whirring in the background and occasional bumps on a road.

"Dr. Peter Davenport is...unavailable at the moment." The thickly accented English caught Dak off guard, but he immediately caught up to speed.

His initial concerns had been validated by Diaz's voice. The scenario played out in his mind, but he hoped the ending wasn't as bad as first thought. Had they killed Doc, or were they holding him as a hostage?

"Hello, Fernando," Dak said in Spanish. "I was wondering when I would have the pleasure."

"Oh, I assure you, when we do meet, the pleasure will be all mine, gringo."

Well, at least he doesn't know my name. Yet.

Dak didn't worry about Davenport spilling the beans, but there were other ways to uncover someone's identity. His immediate suspicion flashed back to the breaking news report on the televisions on the street corner. The mayor's husband was dead, and now all the cops in Lima were looking for the killer. There was no chance that all the havoc Dak had wreaked on Diaz's business and the ensuing manhunt were just a big coincidence.

"I see you've gotten into politics," Dak hedged. "Local politics, it seems. Nothing on a national scale yet."

"Ah, you are a smart man. Foolish with your decisions, and certainly dead, but intelligent in your deductive skills."

"Well, you know what they say, rats like to run together."

Diaz paused for a few breaths, and Dak imagined the man sitting in his car with a befuddled look on his face, trying to figure out the meaning of the phrase.

"I'm sure by now you realize that if the police arrest you, you will never see the inside of a jail cell. They have been instructed to bring you to me. I've also put out a considerable bounty on your head."

Dak blurted out a laugh at the last part.

"Seriously. Take a number, bro." His mind flashed a memory of Colonel Tucker's face, and then it was gone.

Another confused moment of quiet filled the call, so Dak clarified. "You ain't the first person to order a hit on me," he said, changing to English for effect.

"Ah, so you have some kind of a reputation for causing trouble." It was a statement, not a question.

"I guess you could say that. Funny how doing the right thing is viewed by others as trouble. Depends on your point of view, I suppose."

"Yes, well, you have caused me a great deal of trouble, Mister...." Diaz let the question linger.

"I'm sure you would love to know my name. Unfortunately for you, the old man doesn't know it, either. So I guess you'll just have to let a girl have a little mystery about her, huh?"

"A dead man with a name, or a dead man without, is still a dead man. And you *are* a dead man. There is nowhere you can go in Lima where I won't find you, but I know you're not going to run. You want to get back your friend, Dr. Davenport. I'm sure right now a plan is formulating in your mind to save him."

"Something like that. I mean, I already have your coordinates. Finding you won't be a problem."

"Perhaps," Diaz conceded. "I'm not so difficult to find as many would have you believe. Still, you surely know that I will be waiting for you. My men will be watching, every hour of every day."

"Good," Dak said. "Make sure you have as many of them on hand as possible. All of them if you can. Will make it easier to take down your entire operation in one go."

Diaz chuckled. The sound piled aggravation on top of the mound of rage building up in his gut. "Foolish American. Your false bravado will get you killed."

"Seems to be working out okay for me so far."

"Granted. But I think I have a way that both of us can get some satisfaction out of all this."

Dak already knew where this was going. "Let me guess. You want me to come work for you."

"You might not be as foolish as you seem, gringo. Yes. You would become my top lieutenant, next to my trusted bodyguard, Paco, of course. It wouldn't be right to take him away from his post after so many loyal years. You would be well paid, and I'm certain a man of your...skills could help rebuild my organization and thrust it toward new heights."

"That's a very kind offer, Señor Diaz," Dak said, a touch too loud. The patron sipping his beer at the bar heard the name and turned his head in Dak's direction with a terrified look in his wide eyes.

Dak twisted his head away from the man and continued. "But I'm going to have to decline your generosity. I don't work for the bad guys."

"I see. Well, then. You will have to die. Oh, and your friend? He's not going to die just yet. I'm going to make him suffer a very, very long time."

"If you—" Dak stopped himself when he realized the call had ended.

He squeezed the device in his fist then exhaled his anger. He knew what had to happen but didn't have a clue how.

28

The SUVs drove around the circular driveway and stopped in front of Diaz's four-story mansion. Round white pillars supported a portico over a massive entrance. The enormous home featured exterior slabs of gray stone cut into huge rectangles. An enormous roof slanted backward toward the ocean just beyond the cliffs. The structure was a tribute to opulence and contemporary aesthetics but was shielded from view of the city by a hillside peak that rose high between downtown Lima and the vast countryside to the south.

Diaz opened his door and stepped out, while Paco and the other bodyguard retrieved Peter from the cargo bay in the back. To their surprise, the man had remained relatively calm during the journey, though he'd been salty about pretty much everything. He complained about the bumps on the road, wondering how someone with such an expensive car couldn't afford to put some better shock absorbers on their vehicle. Then he went off on the car company itself, railing at them about their inability to put an SUV out that handled rough terrain better when, after all, that was their specialty.

Maybe he exaggerated a little just to get on Diaz's nerves, but it didn't seem to affect the man, and after ten minutes of driving, Peter settled down—slightly. He muttered the occasional insult, just to be persistent, needling at Diaz along the way, but his zeal for the task wore down by the time they reached the long driveway that led up the hill to the coast.

When the older man was standing upright, albeit a touch wobbly from being cramped in the back, he looked around at the setting.

The ocean stretched out to the horizon, foamy caps streaking through the deep blue like white tears in a blanket that ripped, sewed itself shut, then ripped again. Bright green trees dotted the hillsides —not as dense as most forests but enough to give the barren slopes some character and additional color to go with the gray rocks, brown dirt, and dark green grass.

Salty air filled Peter's nostrils, and he sucked it in with a grateful smile on his face.

"You gotta love that sea air, huh?" he said, letting go of the animosity that had filled his thoughts during the drive.

It was a strange thing to say, an awkward comment that bordered on camaraderie, though neither man—nor the guards, for that matter—had any misgivings about where they stood or what was about to happen. Still, the appreciation of nature was universal, and given the location, Diaz clearly shared it.

"Yes," Diaz agreed, taking in a long breath through his nose then exhaling. "It clears the senses, the mind. No better cure on earth than breathing in the ocean air."

Peter bobbed his head in agreement. "You certainly can pick the spots, Fernando. I'll say that. This is spectacular. Quite the view." He turned his head, taking in the vistas to the east, and all around until his gaze fell on the house again. "Shame it was built by enslaving the poor to hustle drugs."

"A man has to make a living." Diaz shrugged. "People like cocaine. It doesn't kill as many as heroin. I haven't dealt in heroin, though it seems my counterparts in Mexico have made a pivot in that direction."

"Yes," Peter conceded with a grumble. "When they realized they couldn't make real money from weed in the US anymore, they had to turn to something with better margins. Now the States has an epidemic on their hands. People are dying left and right."

"So, you see? My business is not so bad. Cocaine kills people now and then, certainly, but usually only those who have no self-restraint. If it weren't my powder, it would be something else that killed those."

Peter huffed at the comment. "Sounds like you've figured out exactly how to justify the suffering you've imposed on so many lives."

"I provide jobs for those who are most desperate. The people of the tugurizadas are free to find work elsewhere."

"Free? I doubt that. Well, except for the ones we set free the other night from your facility."

"And now where will they go?" Diaz asked. "What will they do? How will they buy food or take care of their families? You think you freed them, but you only returned them to the worst prison of all —poverty."

"You might be right, Fernando," Peter half agreed. "They might go back to the slums and live in squalor. Some may not make it. But what kind of life do they really have if they work for you, huh? It's not living. It's barely survival. At least they've been given the opportunity to look for something better. Maybe none of them take the leap. But that's the beauty of freedom. You can choose to stay where you are and be miserable, or you can pull yourself up by the bootstraps and make something out of nothing. You can build something."

Diaz chuckled. "Spoken like a true American. Look around," he waved a hand at his lavish estate. "No one understands this better than me."

"Yeah, well, I wasn't talking about building it on the backs of the poor or dealing dangerous drugs to people who have issues making good decisions. But whatever helps you sleep at night."

"I'll sleep when I'm dead," Diaz countered, his voice darkening like the sky at sunset.

It was Peter's turn to chuckle. "In your line of work, I imagine that impending moment looms pretty close over your head all the time."

"Yes. But it has its perks." Diaz motioned to the prisoner. "It is a shame you have to die, old man. Perhaps in another life we could have been friends."

"Son, I doubt there's a dimension or other life or alternate reality where the two of us would have been *compadres*. But who knows, huh?"

Diaz nodded. "Take him inside. Make sure he's adequately prepared for what's to come."

Peter didn't like the way that sounded, and while his curiosity begged him to ask, he kept the questions to himself. What manner of torture awaited him? There was no telling. He'd heard stories of the cruelty cartels exacted on their victims, especially those who had betrayed them or, as was the case for Peter, those who attacked the organization.

Paco and the other guard ushered Peter through the double doors and into the mansion. Inside, Peter was marched through the foyer where white marble tile lined the entryway until it met walnut floors. He'd never seen that kind of flooring design in this part of the world. Latin-American homes, from what he'd experienced, usually featured tiles, often in a reddish color. There were exceptions, of course, but that usually came from newer construction. The older homes, the ones from colonial eras that had been refurbished or even rebuilt through the years, typically retained the original flooring.

"Seems like a lot of house for a bachelor like yourself, Fernando. Not sure how you keep it clean." Peter passed an amused glance at the man, but Diaz only responded with silence, layered with a determined, fierce glaze in his eyes.

They walked over to a stairwell that split off to head both up and down. An elevator to the right of the staircase offered an easier way up to the fourth floor or down to the first.

"I don't suppose we can take the elevator," Peter said. "Stairs are hard on my knees nowadays."

"Get him down the stairs," Diaz barked, any semblance of politeness gone.

"You coming? Or you have more pressing things to do than torture me?"

"I have preparations to make. Your friend won't wait to attempt a rescue. He has nowhere to run now, except maybe back to the US. I have a feeling, though, he won't leave you here to die. He will try to ride in like an American cowboy to save the day and will be cut down by my men. Right now, I have fifty armed guards here at my estate. They have the high ground. There is no way for your friend to get here without my men seeing him. When he arrives, he will die." His lips spread into a sinister grin. "Of course, you never know. He may simply leave the country, abandoning you to your fate here with me. One never knows."

Peter clenched his jaw. "I don't think you realize who you're dealing with, Diaz." He struggled against the guards' grip for the first time since being captured. "This man is no ordinary man. He's not some two-bit mercenary I scooped off skid row. He has no future. His past has been erased. He's dealt with men far more dangerous than you or your contingent of thugs, and he's better trained, too. You're dealing with someone who comes from one of the most elite fighting forces in the world, and guess what? He has nothing to lose. So, if you think you're going to just pick him off with a couple of your hired guns, you should think again. Because I'm telling you right now, Fernando, fifty men ain't gonna cut it. I'd be surprised if you or any of them live to see the sunrise."

Diaz inclined his head as if considering the American's threat. He scowled at the insinuation then eased his expression to one of satisfaction. "I suppose we will see, Doctor. For now, you have a date in a room I've prepared especially for you. I hope you enjoy the amenities. They are...exquisite."

Diaz turned and walked away, heading toward what looked like a luxurious living room that overlooked the coast.

The men pulled on Peter's arms. They didn't have to drag him. He wasn't foolish enough to think he had a way out of this mess on his own. He could hold his own in a fight, even with younger men, but Peter knew it would be futile here. He was in the enemy fortress, surrounded by their goons. He figured he'd last five, maybe six seconds. And that was after he caught a bullet.

No misgivings of fantastical escapes filled Peter's mind as he trudged down the stairs into the mansion's bowels. The best he could hope for was that Dak might take a few of them with him.

29

Dak peered through his binoculars at the main gate leading up the hill to the Diaz compound. He'd been there in the bushes on an opposing hillside for hours, studying the layout of the mansion. After the sun went down and the dark of evening smothered the sky, he prepared a drone he'd bought in town, covering the lights with electrical tape and making sure the device would have enough range. Against the starlit evening backdrop, Dak flew the drone high over the hills, giving him a full overhead view of the estate's perimeter, the walls, and even a few of the guards on patrol, though those were more difficult to see in the dark.

He scanned the entire estate, all the way to its cliffside-front balconies, then descending along the rocky drop-off to search for a potential secret entrance built into the stone. Dak knew that last bit was a stretch, but he'd be remiss not to check.

His instincts had been correct regarding any sort of cave entrance cut into the cliffs, but he had found a potential weakness in the estate's formidable security measures.

A high fence wrapped around the property, encircling an enormous amount of acreage. The fence alone would have been an extraordinary expense to construct. On top of that, Diaz had included razor wire along the bottom and top, so the barrier looked much like ones Dak had seen at prisons. Except instead of being there to keep people in, it was designed to keep people out.

Dak wouldn't be able to use the same trick he'd used to get into the cocaine processing facility, but that didn't mean there was no way in.

The weakness, he discovered, was part of the natural design of the land. The fence stopped at the cliffs, and it appeared—at first glance—as if there were no additional security measures taken on the rock face along the shore.

Dak understood why. Scaling the wall up to the mansion would take an enormous effort, not to mention a unique set of skills. It would essentially be a free climb for someone going solo, which meant no cams or hexes to use with a rope as a safety precaution.

With a climb that high, the climber would have to be an expert, and in peak physical condition. Dak could only check one of those boxes, and it wasn't the expert-climber box. He'd done a fair amount of rock climbing, but nothing serious, and he never really rigged his own gear. In this instance, that wouldn't be an issue since he'd have no gear to set up such as ropes and harnesses.

Dak, however, had no intention of trying to free-climb the cliff from its base along the rocky shore. His plan was much simpler.

The patrols, from what he could tell, swept the area every ten minutes, with the guards overlapping at the front gate to tread where their counterparts had just been. Timing was key, but easy enough to work out. When the patrol turned around and started back toward the front gate, he could climb down onto the cliff face, traverse around the perimeter barrier, and then climb up on the other side.

It sounded simple in theory, but Dak knew plenty of things could go wrong, not the least of which was the potential for falling to his death on the jagged rocks at the bottom of the precipice.

From the recon, though, it looked like taking the route around the fence via the cliff was his best option.

He briefly considered seeing if he had any pilot friends in the area, old comrades with a penchant for adventure and who didn't shy away from a little danger.

The idea had been he could drop in with a parachute and land right on top of Diaz and his men. That plan had multiple problems, one being that Dak couldn't think of anyone outside Argentina who flew a plane, and he hadn't seen that guy in years. Another issue was locating a parachute, which was probably something Dak could handle but one more piece to an increasingly complex puzzle.

The last problem with dropping in from above was that it would give Diaz's men an easy target. Even with a low-opening-style drop, with minimal visual time, Dak knew that if one person saw the chute, the alarms would go off and every single one of Diaz's crew would rally to the landing zone.

With that idea out, he focused on the plan to sneak down onto the cliff and back up on the other side of the fence. There would probably be cameras, but he couldn't do anything about that. Had he been more prepared, and had someone else with him, he might have been able to override the video feeds, but without knowing where the hidden cameras were, that plan was dead before it could even breathe.

Having decided on his point of entry, and the method, Dak had one more thing to consider. He still had enough small explosives in his gear to create a diversion at the gate or at some other spot on the property. He scanned the perimeter photos from the drone, analyzing the farthest point on the land from where he would go in at the northwestern corner of the fence.

A diversion could draw most of Diaz's men away from where he'd enter the estate, but it also had the possibility of putting all of the enemy forces on alert. Rather than rallying to the trouble spot, they could well send more men out from the mansion and reinforce every patrol. That would make getting in much more difficult.

Dak had spotted ten guards rotating around the grounds but knew there were more inside the building, and likely some hidden in strategic places behind rocks, in trees, or simply lingering in the shadows.

While the diversion idea wasn't a horrible one, Dak chose to go without it. That meant everything was going to come down to stealth. Fortunately, he had plenty of experience with that.

He trudged down the hill and back to the old truck he'd rented earlier in the day and stowed the majority of his gear, only keeping a couple of the flashbang discs, two pistols, and his knife, along with two spare magazines.

That amount of ammo wouldn't be enough to take out all of Diaz's guards, but Dak planned on picking up more as he worked his way into the building. This would ensure he could move quickly and quietly.

Wearing an all-black outfit, Dak locked the pickup truck, leaving it behind a cluster of trees and bushes, and crossed the road, heading for the cliffs.

He skirted around Diaz's property, keeping out of sight from the fence and using the occasional tree or boulder for cover to take a quick look at the barrier wrapping around the estate. With every step, the sound of crashing waves grew louder. It took him nearly fifteen minutes to reach the point where the land dropped off to the ocean below.

Dak stopped at the cliff's edge and looked down then out. Only a few streaks of clouds stretched across the face of the night sky. One touched the edge of the half-moon. Stars twinkled in the grayish-black sky; the view dulled by the light pollution seeping into the atmosphere from the city.

Quite the view, Dak thought. *I'll give him that.*

The moment only lasted seconds, and then Dak set to work. To the south, he saw the lights of the mansion perched on a rise overlooking the sea. The building looked to be only six or seven hundred yards away, with the fence standing about halfway between.

There weren't many options for cover en route to the barrier, except for a couple of big shrubs and three scraggly trees. The rest of his path to the fence was barren, which meant between spots where he could hide, Dak would have to move fast. It was that or risk traversing across the cliff face a few hundred yards until he was beyond the fence.

He decided to pass on that second option. It was too risky, with too many possibilities of slipping or losing a foothold or a rock breaking free. All of those scenarios ended with him tumbling to his death on the shore below.

Staying low behind a rock about the size of an ottoman, Dak watched over the top of the stone, patiently waiting for the next patrol to walk by.

He remained there for nearly five minutes, knowing that he was somewhere between the shifts as they made their rounds on the perimeter. Finally, one of the armed guards came into view to Dak's left. The man's gray T-shirt made him easier to spot in the dark of night, though the night-vision goggles made seeing everything simpler.

The guard trudged to the top of the knoll where the fence met the precipice. He looked out across the ocean, perhaps even taking a second to admire the view. Then he turned, sweeping his eyes across the land beyond the fence. As the guard's head swiveled in Dak's direction, Dak lowered down out of view before the man could see him—not that he would have. At that distance, Dak would have been nearly impossible to spot in the dead of night and clad in black.

Still, he didn't want to risk it. After giving the guard five seconds, Dak emerged from behind the rock again, looking through his goggles in time to see the guard begin his slow walk back down the slope toward the front gate.

Dak checked his watch then moved out from behind the rock and crept toward the fence, staying low as he kept a watchful eye on the guard until the man melded into the darkness. When he was out of sight, Dak took off at a full sprint. He reached the first tree and paused, pressing his shoulder against it as he peered through the fence into the estate's grounds. With no sign of trouble, he pressed ahead, darting to the next tree, then repeating the process two more times.

Standing at the last point of cover, Dak stared at the fence post positioned just over the rocks. Fifty yards of open grass stood between him and his first goal.

He glanced at his watch again. The next guard wouldn't be coming by for another five minutes unless they changed up their routine every so often. He hoped that wasn't a possibility.

His mind made up, Dak sprang from the cover of the tree and ran as hard as he could toward the fence, veering slightly to his right toward the cliffs, but careful to give himself enough space that he didn't slip and fall over the edge.

He caught a flash of movement to his left and skidded to a stop about twenty feet short of the fence. A quick survey of the area sent chills shivering across his skin. They *had* changed the system, and another guard was walking up the hill toward the cliffs.

30

Dak didn't have time to inspect the cliffs to find the best place to drop out of sight. With only seconds to make a decision, he belly crawled over to the edge and lowered himself down onto a narrow ledge, carefully feeling around the rock face with his feet until he discovered another foothold. He gripped the rocks above and shimmied down another foot until he could no longer see the fence.

It was only after the first ten seconds on the rock wall that the danger of the situation truly emerged in Dak's mind. He broke the cardinal rule of being in a high place like this by looking down.

A hundred or more feet below, the ocean smashed into jagged rocks that jutted up from the shore. He knew that one mistake would send him to his death.

His forearms burned as he waited, watching the edge above for any sign of the guard. He had no idea how long he could hold this position; even in his prime physical shape, Dak had limitations.

A beam of light sprayed around in the darkness overhead, and at one point shone directly over where Dak clung to the cliffside. The guard's flashlight whipped around, scanning back and forth into the night, and Dak found himself holding his breath as if the gunman might somehow hear his breathing over the rhythmic sound of the ocean beating against the shore.

After what seemed like minutes, the beam of light vanished, and Dak pulled himself up high enough to look out over the cliff's lip. The guard was walking in the other direction, turning his flashlight from left to right and back again, searching for any signs of trouble.

Dak's concern had proved true. Diaz wasn't entirely foolish. Changing up patrol patterns was a good way to make sure intruders couldn't time their entrance.

For a few seconds, Dak felt relieved he hadn't been spotted, though that relief was short lived. He still had to maneuver across the cliff to the other side of the fence, which presented its own set of problems.

His fingers felt weak now, but he didn't trust the ledge where his feet were enough to fully let go with his hands.

Instead, he felt around to the right until his fingers brushed across a jagged piece of rock jutting out two inches from the main face. He grabbed it and then lifted his right foot, rubbing the boot around on the cliff until he found a thin ledge, barely wider than his finger. It wasn't much, but it was enough as long as the chunk he gripped with his hand held.

He tugged on the rock, allowing much of his weight to bear on it, but the handhold didn't budge. Satisfied, Dak shifted his weight, and felt his way over to the next ledge with his left foot.

The slow process dragged on for minutes as he carefully, deliberately navigated the rock face. Halfway, he looked up and noted the position of the fence looming directly overhead. The razor wire atop it gleamed dimly in the moonlight. Dak knew that even with the change in patrols, he'd only have a few more minutes until the next guard arrived.

When he was clear of the fence by several feet, Dak reached up and grabbed on to a rock sticking out from the edge where the cliff met sod. This section of the wall leaned in at a slight angle and provided several good footholds that were nearly as wide as his boots. All he had to do was pull himself—

The crag jutting out from the cliff face snapped. The sickening sound sent a wave of terror through Dak's body as he felt his weight shift backward. His left hand pinched a thin fragment of rock no wider than an inch. Instantly, he shifted his right hand close to the left, and squeezed the lip with every last ounce of energy he could muster.

The effort spared his life, as he regained his balance and pulled his body close to the wall once more.

Dak swallowed hard against his rapid breathing, and he waited a second before reaching up for another hold.

He froze at the sight of another flashlight beam. The guards on this pattern were coming by more frequently than when he'd timed it before. Had Diaz's men noticed the drone circling around the property? He doubted it since he'd been unable to see the thing with his naked eye and flew it entirely through the camera's view. The sound, although loud, wouldn't have been heard by the guards over the constant crashing of the waves on the shore and the sea breeze blowing inland.

Dak breathed calmly, at least able to rest by leaning his body against the rock and only using the tiny ledge at his chest for maintaining balance.

The guard's beam whipped around in the other direction, and Dak knew he had to make his move.

This time, he found a narrower, but more stable, ledge and pulled himself up, boosting his body over the top with one last push of the right foot. He rolled to his feet, ignoring the relief spilling through his body, and stealthily approached the guard walking back toward the mansion.

Aside from noting that the guard was heading back toward the house instead of the gate, Dak also saw that this guy wore a black baseball cap.

Dak had planned on taking out the guards, but now a new idea popped into his head.

He crept up behind the guard, then he rose quickly, wrapping his arms around the man's neck and head. The guard resisted for two seconds, then Dak snapped the man's head to one side while pulling on the neck. A low pop shuddered through the guard's body and he immediately went limp—his neck broken.

Dak allowed the man to slump to the ground gradually. Then he took the man's submachine gun and slung the strap over his right shoulder. He removed the radio from the guard's right shoulder and attached it to his own before placing the earpiece in his ear. Now, Dak could hear everything going on with the security detail. The last item he commandeered was the guard's ball cap, and he pulled it down low over his forehead to help conceal his face.

After looting the dead guard's body, Dak dragged the man over to the edge of the cliff and rolled the corpse over. Dak stopped watching the guard fall when he was halfway to the bottom and turned his attention to the mansion, a few hundred yards straight ahead.

Dak held the submachine gun just above his hip, letting the flashlight sweep side to side just as he'd seen the guards do while he made his way toward the house.

He realized that it took the same nerves to calmly walk directly into an enemy stronghold posing as a guard as it did to be in the midst of a raging gunfight. It took focus to keep from walking too quickly toward the mansion. The temptation to do so pushed hard against his mind. Dak denied the natural instinct. Sure, he could get to the house faster if he picked up the pace, but then one of the other guards would see something out of the ordinary. *Why would one of their comrades be moving faster than normal?*

He looked ahead, studying the layout of the mansion with every methodical step. A couple of SUVs sat in front, parked on a circular driveway. The foyer of the house was only one floor, but it merged with the rest of the house that climbed three stories over the ground and contained an additional basement floor cut into the cliff.

Business, Dak assumed, *had been good for Diaz. Well, until this week.*

Thirty yards from the front door, Dak paused when a voice came through his earpiece.

"Number Three, report in," the voice ordered in Spanish. The man sounded like he'd been repeating the same phrase for days, and Dak knew that might not be too far from the truth.

After no response, the voice requested that guard number three report in. That was Dak's cue he was guard number three.

"All clear on the north end," Dak responded in Spanish, hoping the wind coming off the ocean would conceal his accent and tone enough to pass for the real guard.

He started walking again, suddenly aware that he'd stopped, and waited for a reply as he moved toward the mansion and a door on the side.

"Copy that, Three," the man said after what felt like minutes.

The man went through the chain of patrol guards, checking in with each one as Dak neared the house.

A timber pergola stood over a patio where stacked limestone blocks wrapped around the sitting area, blocking off a small portion from the wind. A fire pit sat quietly in the center of the patio's paver tiles, surrounded by black lounge chairs with turquoise cushions. A cigar ashtray sat atop a stone tray being held by a sculpture of a Greek goddess.

Strange tastes, Dak thought, though the humor burned away as another guard stepped out through the side door and positioned himself next to it.

Dak knew there would be a guard there. He'd looked closely at images of this point of entry, and every one of them displayed a guard on duty. The man must have gone inside to relieve himself, or perhaps there'd been a shift change. Either way, Dak was far from surprised to see the guy take his position.

Keeping his head low so the bill of the ball cap covered most of his face, Dak approached the patio via a stone-tile walkway.

The other guard didn't address him until he was already around the short wall and on the patio tile.

"How's it looking out there?" the guard asked. The guy sounded stoned, and Dak half wondered if the guard had been smoking a joint out here. If he was going to do it, this was the place. He was out of view of the camera over the door by standing directly under it, but why risk it unless he was feeling anxious about the night's work? There was little doubt Diaz wouldn't approve of the men responsible for his protection getting high while on duty. No doubt, the stories of what had been happening at the cartel's places of business had reached most, if not all the guards. Anxiety would be spiking. Maybe that was why the man took the chance with a little weed on his smoke break.

"All clear," Dak answered in Spanish.

"No sign of this ghost the others are talking about?"

Dak shook his head, still approaching the doorway.

"No, but if he comes this way, he's going to be a dead man."

The guard laughed and nodded. "You know it."

Dak listened closely to the rhythm of the waves crashing below. The patio acted as a sort of amphitheater, enhancing the sounds by several decibels.

"You okay, bro?" the guard asked as Dak drew near. "Something wrong?"

"Not with me," Dak answered. He raised the submachine gun, and as the waves crashed against the rocks below once more, squeezed the trigger.

Red liquid splattered against the side of the mansion next to the door and the big guard slumped against the wall, then slid down to the ground. A streak of dark red followed the back of his head to where he stopped.

Dak glanced up at the camera over his left shoulder. He'd been just out of view when he fired the gun. He was surprised at how effectively the ocean waves drowned out the gunshot, to the point that his ears didn't even ring as a result.

He bent down and grabbed the guard by the ankles, careful to remain out of the camera's line of sight. Dak dragged the corpse over to the railing. It took some work, especially not to get blood on his clothes and hands, but he managed to dump the body over the edge.

With his head down and face covered once more, Dak returned to the door and pulled it open.

He stepped inside the basement and immediately caught the

smell of incense. He eased the door shut and took in his surroundings, sweeping the gun in every direction.

Dak nearly gaped at the spectacular room. *Diaz has built the ultimate man cave,* he thought.

A pool table stood in the center of the room. Beyond it, huge windows occupied the entire wall all the way to the far corner, where it continued around at a 45-degree angle. Four televisions hung from the inner wall, and two rows of leather lounge chairs faced them. A bar in the corner to Dak's right offered an assortment of liquors, as well as two beer taps and a small humidor atop the counter. An arcade version of old-school video games stood against the wall on the near side of the television viewing area.

Dak scanned the walls and corners for cameras but found nothing. A motion detector in the nearest corner to the door beeped with a red light, but that wouldn't help Diaz. Not right now. If the alarm had been on, it would have gone off already, or even when the guard stepped outside.

Feeling momentarily secure, Dak locked the door behind him and hurried across the room with the gun extended out, the brace tucked into his shoulder. He stopped at the corner where the wall bent at an angle in the other direction and peeked around it. To his surprise, the room continued on. A stone fireplace nestled in the center of the mansion's middle wall flickered with a gas flame, surrounded by a leather sofa and matching chairs. Another television hung just above the mantle.

Another guard stood by a door at the bottom of a staircase. A corridor shot off to the right, presumably leading into the southern wing of the mansion.

Dak pulled back from the corner and called out to the guard. "Hey, you think you can give me a hand with this. Looks like we got a loose wire over here!"

"Sure," the henchman answered. Dak took out his knife and watched the floor just beyond the wall. When the shadows drew near, he timed his attack and pounced. Dak surged from around the corner, instantly lining up his target with the knife. He thrust the blade's tip straight through the man's throat, jerked it out, and continued to the door at the end of the room. The guard hit the floor with a thud before falling onto his face.

Dak stopped at the door and listened. The gurgling from the guard ceased within twenty seconds, and then Dak heard a blood curdling sound.

Someone beyond the door grunted and yelped against...choking sounds?

He pressed his ear to the door and listened again. The unmistakable sound of water splashing and more choking, grunting, and swearing filled his ear.

There was no way to be certain, but Dak could swear the voice belonged to Doc. And unless he missed his guess, they were administering one of the foulest forms of torture known to man.

So much for going in nice and quiet.

Dak drew the pistol with the suppressor attached and put his hand on the doorknob. He wished he had a silencer for the other guns, but he was lucky to even have one. It might not matter. The second he went in, whoever was in the other room would defend themselves, and things could get noisy. He also had no way to know how many people were on the other side, but that didn't matter.

Dak had to get Doc out of there.

Twisting the doorknob quietly, Dak turned it until it wouldn't turn farther and then eased the door open. He didn't know what to expect, if there would be a guard next to the door, twenty guys inside waiting with guns pointed at him, or if there was a television on with a movie featuring a water-based fight scene.

He didn't have to wait long to get his answer.

Dak raised his pistol and stepped in quietly. What he saw took even a hardened soldier like him by surprise.

The basement looked nothing like the rest of the building he'd seen so far. While the lower floor's entertainment room had a refined, finished look, this portion of the downstairs looked more like a regular basement. Poured concrete walls enveloped a huge space, with concrete supports staggered throughout.

That didn't bother Dak.

What disturbed him was the array of torture devices lining the walls and occupying the floor. A wooden table fifteen feet away was splattered with blood stains, and leather straps hung from the head and foot of the surface to keep the victim in place.

Various blades and other sharp objects hung from a wooden rack to the right. A chainsaw sat on a workbench nearby, with a roll of black plastic underneath.

Straight ahead, on the other side of the room, four men stood around a wooden bench where a familiar figure lay on his back, tilted at an angle so the rest of his body was elevated slightly above his head.

Two of the guards held Doc down by the shoulders. A third held a bucket, dousing the man's towel-covered face intermittently with splashes of water.

The fourth stood watching at the foot of the bench, his arms crossed.

Dak had never been waterboarded before. He'd heard the horror stories, though. The sensation of drowning on dry land was enough to cause anyone to do a full body clench, even a battle-tested soldier like himself.

He heard Doc gurgle after the guard sloshed another wave of water over his face. Dak couldn't wait any longer.

Rage boiled inside him, and he nearly lost the frail thread of control reining in his emotions.

He kept his cool enough to stay quiet as he crept forward. The men were far enough away that they hadn't noticed him enter the room. The realization caused him to change his approach. He stood up straight and tilted his head down enough to cover his face while still allowing him to see where he was walking.

Then, Dak walked across the concrete floor with his pistol held at an angle behind his back.

Twenty feet from the waterboarding bench, Dak tilted his head up. The guard watching with his arms crossed turned at the sight of movement. He obviously thought it was just one of the other guards coming in to report, or perhaps to watch for a little entertainment.

The man's surprise at seeing the American approach splashed over his face. And his reaction was much too slow.

The guards had foolishly set their weapons on a table ten feet away, perhaps thinking the guns would get in the way as they performed their task.

The watcher reacted first, lowering his hands and taking a step toward the table to retrieve his weapon.

He was also the first to catch a bullet through the side of his head as Dak raised his pistol and squeezed the trigger.

The weapon clicked loudly, and the guard dropped.

Immediately, the other three turned—and found themselves staring down the barrel of Dak's pistol.

Dak fired rapidly, taking out the bucket man first with three shots to the chest. Then he executed the others in short order, one with a bullet to the back-right corner of the skull and the other with two chest shots and one through the right eye.

The bodies fell haphazardly onto the floor even as Dak continued forward. When they were all still, he lowered his weapon and checked back at the front door.

No sign of trouble.

Doc coughed through the soaked towel, and Dak spun around to yank it off him.

The older man looked up, his gray hair drenched and his face dripping with water. Confusion filled his eyes for several, finally clear, breaths, and then resolve replaced the bewilderment.

"Took you long enough," he coughed. "I was starting to think you were just going to leave me here."

Dak grinned at the old man and helped him off the board. Doc hunched over for a second, planting his elbows on his knees as his head cleared and the blood returned to his extremities.

"Sorry," Dak offered. "I got a little delayed getting in here. Seems they've ramped up security."

"Yeah, no kidding." Doc looked around at the bodies. "Nice work, though. I guess you Delta guys know a thing or two."

Dak nodded and motioned to the table with the guns on top. "Help yourself. We're going to have to shoot our way out of here. And get a radio from one of these guys," he added, indicating the guard nearest his feet.

"If there's one without tissue and blood on it," Doc grumbled.

"I shot that one in the chest," Dak said, pointing at the bucket man. "Take his."

Doc stood up, grabbed two of the pistols from the table, then stole a radio from the recommended guard.

When he was ready, the two looked toward the door. It was the only way in and out of the basement torture chamber.

Doc shot a sidelong glance at Dak, his expression calming into one Dak had never seen.

"Hey, kid," Doc said.

Dak turned to him.

"Thanks for coming for me. I owe you one."

Dak shook his head. "You don't owe me anything. And we're not out of this yet. Still more than forty guards out there in the building and on the grounds."

The older man cracked his neck to the side. "I've been wanting to do this to Diaz for a long time. Now, it's time to dance with the devil."

31

Dak opened the door and stabbed his pistol through. He checked the immediate area, including the entertainment room as far as he could see it and the corridor leading away from the stairwell.

There were likely other guards down here in one of the other rooms, and perhaps they wouldn't bother him, but he had to be certain.

"Watch the stairs," Dak ordered in a whisper.

He took off down the hallway, opened the first door, then the second, and so on until he'd inspected each of the rooms in the long corridor.

No one was there. All he found were empty bedrooms that looked like little more than college dorms, each with a couple of beds and dressers. Dak realized that many of Diaz's guards lived on site, here at the mansion, and likely didn't leave very often.

"He really does keep everything close to the vest," Dak muttered. Then he spun and returned to where Doc stood at the base of the steps.

Their radios crackled.

"Number Three, you missed your loop. What's your status?"

Dak responded with a short, "Sorry. Had to piss. All clear and resuming patrol now."

He waited with a foot on the first step. The two men shared a concerned glance, and Dak got the distinct feeling that his ruse was done.

"Three, you just had a break twenty minutes ago."

Dak bit his lower lip and started up the stairs.

"They're onto us," he said over his shoulder. "Things are about to get messy."

"Good," Doc said. "I don't mind getting a little dirty now and then."

At the top of the stairs, the men paused just out of sight of a guard standing at the front door. Dak stuffed the pistol back into a holster and drew his knife. He motioned to the guard, communicating to Doc to shoot the man if his plan didn't work.

The guard seemed to be in a rhythm of turning one direction, then the other, as if danger could come from any direction within the mansion. He didn't know how right he was.

When he pivoted toward a circular dining room across the foyer, Dak made his move.

The American sprang from the stairs, gliding across the floor in near total silence. When he reached the guard, he grabbed the man's face and slid the blade across his neck, cutting deep into the flesh.

Dak spun and drew his pistol, propping up the dying man against his shoulder for the benefit of the guard he spotted upon emerging from the stairs.

The stunned gunman blinked rapidly in disbelief, which gave Dak enough time to fire a shot through the guard's gut.

The man doubled over and fell to his knees.

Doc hurried around the corner and found the second guard clutching his abdomen with both hands, blood pumping through his fingers. The older man picked up the guard's suppressor-equipped pistol and put the bleeding henchman out of his misery with a click and a bullet through the skull.

Dak let the first guard slump to the floor and moved ahead toward a living room at the front of the mansion.

"Where you think he is?" Doc asked.

"Where any king would be," Dak answered. "Highest point of the castle."

"Fourth floor? You going to take the elevator?"

"Definitely not." Dak watched the corridor for more guards, but the head of security wasn't issuing orders. In fact, the channel had gone quiet. Too quiet. "You think they switched channels?"

"Maybe," Doc hedged, "but I don't know if they're smart enough to do that."

Shadows outside the building flashed through the front doors and windows, giving the two Americans their answer.

"Looks like the cavalry is here," Dak said.

"More than one, too," Doc groused. He raised his weapon and waited as multiple footsteps echoed down the corridor from around the corner in the living room.

"In here." Dak motioned toward the dining room.

Doc nodded, and the two sprinted through the open archway into a darkened room with a round pedestal-style table. Ten white chairs sat around the lavishly decorated surface. A basket in the center spilled fruits, vegetables, and wildflowers out onto the table.

"Interesting taste for a cartel guy," Doc noted.

"Yeah," Dak agreed.

Then the two pulled hard on the bottom edge of the table and flipped it over with several small crashes and one big one.

"At least they'll know where to find us," Dak joked as he crouched down behind the table.

The overturned furniture was large enough for four or five people to hide behind, and the two had managed to turn it to face both points of entry into the dining area. One led into a kitchen. The other into the foyer.

The front door opened and guards spilled into the entryway, joined by others from the opposite direction.

The first men into the room spun and looked into the dining room in time to catch the first volley.

Dak and Doc unloaded on the guards, firing rounds liberally through the opening, cutting down six guards in the first five seconds. Three more joined them in death before the reinforcements wised up to the bullet funnel they were running into.

Four took up positions at the left corner of the archway near the door. Two more huddled on the opposing corner, while footsteps tracked away, which Dak knew meant the men were going to try to flank them from the kitchen.

Dak motioned toward the new danger while reloading a new magazine into his pistol. Doc acknowledged with a nod and shifted his position to get a better angle into the kitchen.

Dak poked his weapon around the table and aimed at the fourth guard trying to crowd into the near archway corner with the other three who'd come in from outside. A quick twitch of the trigger landed a bullet in the guy's shoulder. He yelped and staggered out of his semi-hiding spot, only to receive two more rounds in the chest. He tripped over the body of a comrade and fell to the floor, writhing only half a minute before giving in and falling still.

More shadows ran by the window outside.

"Sending everything they got," Doc noted.

"Yeah."

The first guards appeared in the kitchen, creeping around a marble-slab island, using it and the walls for cover.

Doc aimed and fired. The first shot missed, but the second caught his target in the leg. Two more men popped up and returned fire, sending Doc back down behind the makeshift shield.

He winced at the sound of bullets thumping against thick oak. "Been a while since I've done something like this," he mused.

Doc leaned out from his protection again and fired, catching one of the gunmen off guard. The first round bored through the man's throat. The second plunged into his chest.

"How many did you say were here?" Doc asked, returning to cover as another volley of suppressed gunshots filled the air.

Dak peeked around the far-left edge of the table and aimed at the opposite side of the foyer.

One of the gunmen risked a look around the wall, and Dak sent a bullet through his forehead. The man dropped to the floor without fanfare, dead before he hit the tile.

"They may call for more," Dak realized. "Only fifty or so on the property, but I'm sure Diaz has more resources. I just hope he doesn't have the cops heading out here."

Doc laughed. "Yeah, I don't think we'd have enough bullets." He popped up and fired another round toward the doorway, picking off another of the emboldened gunmen who thought stepping out to take a shot was a good idea. "We're going to need to get out of here at some point."

Dak knew he was right, and with only so many rounds left, they'd need to do it sooner than later.

"We roll the table to the kitchen," Dak whispered. "Shields us from the guys in the front."

"But exposes us to the guys in the kitchen."

"I thought you already took them out." Dak looked at him with condescension oozing from his eyes.

"You young punk," Doc spat. "You move the table. I'll clear a path. Give me that sub."

Dak didn't have to be told twice. He passed the submachine gun over to his ally. Doc slung it over his shoulder and gave a nod.

"Now, son. While we still can."

Dak obeyed, lifting the single huge pedestal support for the entire table. The thing was heavier than he'd thought it would be. Still, he grunted through it and twisted the table to keep the surface pointing toward the front archway.

Doc fired slowly, methodically, into the kitchen as the two men walked toward the inner archway. One of the guards behind the island stood up to fire and received three shots to the chest as he managed to squeeze the trigger, sending four rounds into the ceiling over Doc's head.

Muted gunfire erupted from the foyer as the guards peppered the table with the contents of their magazines. Gunsmoke thicker than Dak ever recalled seeing filled the two rooms with a dense, hazy fog. The acrid smell knocked out any other odor in the previously pleasant-smelling mansion.

The thought pierced through the burning in his arms as he fought to keep the table rolling toward the kitchen. Another guard emerged from behind the island. Doc's reaction was a second slow, and the gunman reeled off two shots before Doc's response cut him down. The two enemy bullets glanced off the underside of the table next to Dak's shoulder as he carried the center stand, twisting it rapidly to make the thing go forward.

Dak let go of the table the second the edge crashed into the wall. His fingers ached, and his forearms felt warm and numb. He had enough strength in his hands, though, to lean around the table and empty his magazine at the three men reloading from the archway.

The three scattered then died on the floor with the others at their feet.

Doc burst into the kitchen, the gun brace nestled into his armpit as he swept to the right, left, and back again.

Dak rushed into the room to join him.

Another guard ran headlong into the kitchen, apparently unaware of the danger. Dak and Doc raised their weapons and mowed him down. The man's legs kept pumping as he fell to the floor, smacking his head against the wall on the other side of the kitchen.

"Now what?" Dak asked, watching the foyer archway from just inside the kitchen.

"This is your operation, kid. I mean, until a few minutes ago, I was a hostage. So, unless you think that was all part of my grand scheme, I think the next move is up to you."

"We've eliminated a third of their forces, give or take."

A guard popped around the corner in the foyer and fired. Dak ducked back behind the wall and waited, then squatted, jabbed his gun around the corner, and landed two shots into the wall, narrowly missing the gunman who stepped back with no time to spare.

"Somehow that doesn't make me feel better," Doc growled while firing another shot down a corridor at four more approaching guards. The men scattered for cover behind various pieces of furniture.

"I need to get up to the top," Dak said.

"Which means we need to get back to the stairs. Downside is—"

"If we get attacked from above. I know. But you know what they say about getting the high ground."

"Only way to get it is to take it."

Dak glanced at his new friend with a wink. "Cover me."

"You're a crazy SOB, kid. But you got guts. I'll say that."

Doc shuffled back to the archway to the dining room and stepped behind the table again. He fired four shots at the corner wall while Dak leaped from cover and into the open.

Doc's cover fire kept the gunmen in the foyer pinned against the inner corner, which made them easy pickings for Dak when he circled around. Six rapid shots took the remaining guards down, with only two of them able to fire wildly in Dak's direction. Windows shattered behind Dak. Curtains shredded. But he remained unharmed.

He moved fast, back into the foyer. After locking the front door to slow down any reinforcements, he called out to Doc, "Clear!"

Doc appeared around the corner two seconds later. Dak tiptoed up the first flight of stairs, rounding the corner with his pistol extended. Doc picked up another weapon from one of the several dead guards and stuffed it in his belt, then grabbed another for Dak. When Doc arrived on the first landing, he handed Dak the new gun.

Dak bobbed his head once in thanks and then continued up the stairwell. Just before they reached the next floor, the two paused and waited. Neither of them was naïve enough to believe they could simply climb to the top of the mansion without resistance. Both sensed trouble around both corners and stayed patiently in place until one of the guards shifted.

It was a slight noise, barely noticeable, but someone just around the near corner sniffled.

The sound was more than enough warning for the two Americans.

Dak reached into his pocket and took out one of the two metal discs he'd stowed there. He motioned to Doc to cover his eyes and mouthed the word "flashbang."

Doc looked at the device with confusion. He'd never seen a flashbang like it.

Dak pressed the center of the disc twice for a two second delay instead of the three he used previously, and then tossed it up the stairs. He turned away from the opening, and Doc copied him.

A snap followed by a white light blazed through the corridor above, spilling for a second into the stairwell.

Men shouted as panic set in.

Dak and his partner emerged from the stairs and onto the next floor. The open corridor on the front side gave a view of the living room below and the high ceiling overhead.

Three men on either side of the stairs grimaced, squinting their eyes shut and rubbing them furiously as if that would get rid of the problem.

The two Americans split up, each executing the gunmen at point-blank range.

"Wasn't very sporting of us," Doc said as he looked around at the three bodies.

"No," Dak agreed. "But effective."

"Where'd you get that little thing?" Doc asked. "I've never seen one of those."

Dak reached into his pocket and fished out the last of the discs. "Friend of a friend at DARPA. From what I hear, he has a few side projects. Garage stuff. You keep this one in case you need it."

He handed Doc the device. The old man palmed it then shoved it in his pocket with a grateful nod. He motioned toward the stairs when it was apparent no one else was waiting for them on this level. "Let's see what's waiting for us on the top floor."

32

Diaz fumed, pacing back and forth in the corner of his study. The wooden floors clicked under his brown Italian-leather shoes. He stopped every other trip to the window to look out on his property, though he knew there was nothing to see out there now.

The danger was already inside the building.

This American had caused him no end of trouble, and despite reinforcing his defenses, the man had managed to slip through all of them and breach the mansion's walls.

He wondered how that had been possible. They'd taken every precaution, and Diaz had brought in every able security guard he could muster from his local resources. The truth was Diaz's operation boasted far more firepower than under the previous regime, but much of it was still smoke and mirrors.

He used influence, leveraging fear in the public to make it look like he commanded an army. True, his organization was strong—and posed a serious threat to anyone willing to take them on, including the police—but with every guard this American killed, Diaz's pyramid of cards crumbled piece by piece.

Paco watched him from the doorway with a pistol in his right hand, his left holding the wrist.

"How did this *diablo* get by all my men?" Diaz roared. "Why is it so hard to get good help? Huh?" He turned to Paco, who remained stoic, unaffected by the barb that may well have been taken to be for him.

"I didn't mean you, Paco," Diaz added quickly. "You know that."

"I know," was all Paco offered in reply.

A panicked voice came over the security channel. "We have them pinned down in the—"

Then the voice went silent.

Diaz picked up the radio on his desk and pressed the button. "Hello? Do you have them?"

No response.

"Let me go after them, sir," Paco requested, his voice even and determined.

Diaz inhaled slowly, then exhaled to try to force the anxiety from his chest. It didn't work. He rubbed his head with both hands, then paced back to his desk. He picked up a golden straw and leaned over a line of blow, then snorted the rail in quick order.

He dropped the straw and jerked his head back, still inhaling. Then he snapped his head around and shook his arms like a prize fighter getting ready to enter the ring.

"I need you in here," Diaz countered. "What happens if that maniac gets through all my men?"

Diaz pouted. "All my men. How could a single guy, one gringo"—he raised his index finger near his face—"get through fifty well-armed guards? Huh, Paco?" Diaz drew his overtly large pistol and brandished it in the air. "You wanna tell me how that's possible, my friend? It's almost as if he has someone on the inside. You know?"

"Do you think we have a leak?" Paco asked without affect.

"Do I think we have a leak?" Diaz repeated. "A leak? I don't know. You're in charge of all that. That's what I pay you to answer." He resisted the temptation to lower his weapon at his old friend, but the formidable strength of the cocaine pulled hard at his instincts, shoving aside rational thought for manufactured righteous indignation.

"I don't believe we have a leak. If we did, I would have already handled it. Unless you think I'm the leak. If that were the case, we wouldn't be having this conversation."

Diaz cocked his head to the side, peering at his lieutenant with glazed bewilderment. "What is that supposed to mean, *amigo*? That you would have killed me? You think you can kill me?"

"I'm saying that if I were the leak, one or both of us would already be dead. You would have killed me had I attempted to assassinate you. Or I would have succeeded and you'd be dead. Or perhaps we would have killed each other. Either way, that isn't the present reality. We're both alive, and I'm trying to protect you."

Diaz absorbed Paco's explanation. Then he nodded, bobbing his head like it balanced on a pin. "Yes. I suppose you're right, my old friend. I'm sorry. The drugs. They sometimes make me think crazy things. Like everyone is out to get me."

"You're not entirely paranoid," Paco corrected. "These men are trouble. If they can get through all our forces, they can get to this room. Let me handle them personally."

Diaz thought about it, considering the scant few options he had left. His eyes wandered over to the sword above the mantle behind his desk. A fire crackled in the hearth. He'd just bought that sword mere days before. A prized possession, the old blade was rumored to be the very sword that Francisco Pizarro fought and died with. Now, the curse of the conquistador's fate seemed to be following the weapon. It was in a scenario much like this that the Spaniard met his doom. Men infiltrated his house, perhaps through help of his own people, and killed him in his home.

The story held a strange bond for Diaz, beyond the immediate correlation with the sword. Drug-induced fears coursed through his mind, and he found himself imagining wild, unfounded thoughts and theories. *Was it really the sword's fault?* He snapped his head around and looked to it again. The metal had deteriorated over time, but the weapon still held its shape, a reflection of its potency centuries before.

This trouble started after I bought that cursed thing, he thought. The blow ramped up the fears, the irrational thinking, and Diaz found himself working harder to convince himself the sword had nothing to do.

"Go," he surrendered, his voice despondent. "Bring me the head of this American. And when he's dead, kill the old man, too."

"As you wish," Paco said and left quietly through the door.

Diaz stared at the sword, working desperately to convince himself that there were no superstitious forces at play here, but he couldn't find a way around the coincidence. He shook it off and returned to his desk. This time, instead of diving into the cocaine, he walked around to the back and pulled open the center drawer.

Inside, two pistols lay at an angle as if bowing to each other.

The weapons displayed a shiny gold finish. Engraved images of Supay, the Inca god of death, adorned the sides, with flames etched around the grips.

Diaz picked up the weapons and studied them with appreciation, and resolve. The Desert Eagle was an intimidating weapon, but these two pistols—while not as powerful—were far more functional, though still showy in a much different way.

They had belonged to his predecessor, and now they belonged to him. A gift upon the old man's passing. He held the two pistols, one in each hand, admiring them as he might a priceless treasure.

Then, Diaz set the guns down on the desk and removed his suit jacket, revealing twin shoulder holsters. He slid the guns into the leather pouches and twisted his neck back and forth to loosen his muscles. If he were going to be in a fight, he would be ready.

He walked over to the bar in the corner and selected a bottle of Casa Noble tequila. For a second, Diaz held the bottle up, studying the label as if it might be his last drink on earth, then he pulled the cork and poured until the tumbler was half-full. After corking the bottle, he held up the glass and stared at the door into his study.

The fire continued to snap and crackle behind him. And for a moment, all was at peace in his world again. The death of his cousin, of so many of his men, and the dismantlement of his empire, they all faded away. Here, in this room, he would bring this American to his knees—and wipe him from the face of the earth.

Diaz raised the glass and took a sip, never taking his eyes from the door. The warm liquid splashed down his throat with a smooth, easy burn. Then he took another, longer drink, finishing the glass in one go. He waited, watching the door for the interloper to appear, but he did not come.

Diaz clenched his jaw, listening, watching, waiting. He poured another drink, about the same size as the last, and dumped it down his throat.

Then he slung the glass into the fireplace. The tumbler shattered on the hearth's back wall, breaking into hundreds of pieces.

His nostrils flared wide as he breathed in and out, waiting for his fate to arrive. "Where are you, American devil?" Diaz grumbled. "Come and meet your destiny."

33

Dak stopped at the landing between the third and fourth floors. More reinforcements tried to reach them, but with the high ground, Diaz's goons were easy pickings for the two former military men.

Bodies festooned the stairwell in a disturbing display of poor tactics and blatant disregard for danger.

Dak watched up above, but no attack came from the top floor. He figured the forces congregating up there were waiting for their quarry to appear, just as the men had done on the floor below.

That plan worked out so well for the cartel grunts.

When the guards stopped coming up the stairs, Doc looked back over his shoulder at Dak, "You think that's it?" He kept his voice just above a whisper, so quiet he almost couldn't hear himself speak.

Dak shook his head and pointed up the stairs.

Doc took a deep breath and nodded.

The two climbed slowly, creeping up the stairwell until they reached the next floor. Dak waited for a second then motioned Doc toward the left. He pointed at himself, then to the right, signaling they should split up and each take a different direction.

Doc acknowledged with another bob of the head.

Dak counted slowly with his fingers. When he hit three, the two men burst from cover and raised their weapons, ready to unleash hot metal.

Instead, they were surprised to find the corridor empty.

They looked both directions, guns extended, but found no target.

Four doors lined each side of the hallway going both directions, and to the left, another corridor branched out away from the main hall, leading toward the ocean.

Dak motioned with his hand for Doc to check that direction, while he went to the right.

Doc obeyed and crept down the corridor.

Dak stopped at the first door and twisted the knob. It turned easily, and he shoved it open, stepping inside with his pistol leading the way.

The bedroom featured a black contemporary-style bed with matching nightstands on either side and a window over the headboard. A closet and bathroom to the left offered more hiding places for a guard. Dak cautiously moved to the bathroom, then poked his gun inside.

It was empty.

He swallowed and spun around, wary that an enemy could have snuck in behind him. No one was there.

Dak returned to the corridor but found no sign of anyone. Not even Doc.

He considered backtracking to the room where Doc had disappeared, but the older man appeared once more, and flashed a *What are you looking at* glare at Dak.

Doc continued across the hall and opened the next door. Dak watched the man vanish inside and then looked toward the far end. None of the doors had light coming through the gaps at the bottom except the last one on the left. It would be on the back of the home, most likely giving it the best view of the ocean and of the city to the north. *If I were Diaz, that's where I would put my study.*

Dak skipped the next collection of doors and paused at the last one on the left. He held his gun low with the barrel pointing down at the floor just ahead. He smelled the faint scent of cigar smoke seeping through the doorway. *Strange time for Diaz to be smoking a victory cigar.*

Something felt off, and Dak glanced back down the corridor toward Doc, who emerged from the second room he'd checked and continued down toward the opposite end.

This part of the mansion felt more like the floor of a hotel. The many doors looked the part—ordinary, nondescript, uniform. The only missing items were the key card readers fixed to the side of the doorframes or on the doors themselves.

Dak returned his focus to the door leading into what he believed to be Diaz's study. He was about to open it when he heard a thump from Doc's direction.

He twisted his head around in time to see Doc fly back against the wall with a loud thud. His pistol clattered to the floor fifteen feet away. He'd already dropped the submachine gun earlier when the magazine ran dry, leaving him with two pistols.

Doc reached for the one in his belt, but one of Diaz's taller goons pounced from the room and snatched the gun away from Doc, tossing it to the side.

Dak saw the pistol tucked into the man's belt, but for some reason he was choosing to use his hands instead. He squeezed Doc's throat with one hand and punched with the other. His fist pounded into Doc's face one, two, three times before Dak could even mount a response.

"Hey!" Dak shouted, temporarily forgetting that by doing so he could spook Diaz.

The big man holding Doc turned, but he didn't move. Dak raised his weapon, knowing full well at that distance he didn't have any business squeezing the trigger. He'd have just as much a chance of killing Doc as he did the assailant.

Instead, Dak took a cautious step forward, then heard the faintest squeak from behind. He froze, then whirled around with his pistol extended, and dove to his right just before another guard fired a shot.

The long suppressor puffed with a click, sending the round just over Dak's left shoulder and into the wall.

A cloud of drywall powder plumed out of the fresh hole, and chunks of debris tumbled to the floor.

Dak rolled to his feet and raised his weapon, firing four quick replies at the gunman. This guard, however, was quicker than the others he'd faced, and the man retreated with a quick step back into his room. The bullets smashed into the far wall.

Dak spun around, whipping the pistol toward the area where he'd seen Doc and the huge goon, but the two men were gone.

With no time to puzzle over their disappearance, Dak rushed to the open door across from Diaz's study and waited with his back against the wall. He held his gun high and tight, counting down in his head. He evened his breathing and then spun around into the doorway with the pistol leveled in front of him.

The room looked similar to the one he checked before, though this one was longer, with a kitchenette to the left and a studio bedroom setup straight ahead. A bathroom to the right presented the only place the guard could be hiding.

Dak twisted that direction just as the hidden gunman appeared in the doorway. The man fired his weapon and sent Dak sprawling out through the main door again, barely avoiding two rounds that plunked into the wall just beyond the frame.

The guard pushed ahead, shooting again and again as if corralling Dak back into the hallway where he could finish the kill.

Dak scrambled back to his feet and waited for the gunman to show his face, but the man didn't come out.

Keeping the pistol extended with sights on the open doorway, Dak shoved his free hand into the pocket where he kept the flash-bang discs. When his fingers felt nothing but an empty pouch, Dak remembered he'd given the last disc to Doc.

He cursed his luck but cut himself off when he heard more footsteps coming up the stairs. This guard wasn't trying to kill him. Sure, if he got lucky with a shot, the guy would take it, but his primary function was to keep Dak occupied and in the corridor until reinforcements arrived.

Dak looked at the two doors just down the hallway from the end and briefly considered trying to get into one of them. If they were locked, though, he'd be exposed, an easy target out in the open.

He looked back at the room where the gunman was hiding and decided that was his best option, albeit one with immediate danger.

Dak took the spare pistol out of his belt and held it in his left hand. Extending the right, he leaped back in front of the open door and rolled, squeezing the trigger. The rounds sailed through the room and struck the far wall. Two hit the window and punctured it, sending webbed cracks through the entire pane.

The gun clicked, signaling the magazine was empty.

Step two.

Dak threw the pistol through the opening, aiming it in the direction the guard had retreated.

The second he let loose of the impotent weapon, Dak jumped through the doorway.

The flying pistol had briefly distracted the guard, and when Dak landed near the kitchenette, the man's head was turned, his eyes focused on the gun clacking to the floor.

Dak raised his second pistol and fired a single shot through the guard's forehead. The squatting man crumpled to the floor.

Without a moment to relish the victory, Dak returned to the door and looked out. Gunmen spilled into the corridor from the stairwell, all taking up positions facing his direction.

Dak muttered an intelligible complaint under his breath then checked the magazine. He'd counted eight men in the hall and knew more could be waiting out of sight. The contents of this weapon wouldn't be enough.

Then he looked down at the dead man on the floor. Dak retrieved the guard's pistol and a spare magazine from his belt, then returned to the door.

He leaned around and fired one shot, which missed one of the men in the front row by a few feet.

Their formation consisted of two rows, the front with men on one knee and the rest standing behind the first. They were exposed and would have been easy targets, but the numbers weren't in Dak's favor.

The second he unleashed the warning shot; the enemy unleashed a devastating salvo.

Dak ducked back into the room as bullets zipped by outside, destroying the wall beyond.

When the men stopped shooting, Dak searched the room for one of two things: a way out or something he could use to get the upper hand against the squad down the hall.

Even with two guns, he didn't stand a chance against the force waiting for him by the stairs. For half a second he wondered what happened to Doc. There was still no sign of the big guard or the retired doctor. Dak's shot in their direction appeared to have done enough to distract the assailant, giving Doc a chance to wriggle free, but where they'd gone Dak couldn't tell.

Besides, he had his own problems.

His eyes rested on the kitchenette. The electric stove would be no help. And neither would the sink, but he wondered if there might be something under the sink he could use.

His shifted over to the sink and opened the doors below. Inside, a bottle of dish detergent, a few sponges, a roll of paper towels, and a fire extinguisher occupied the space.

Dak smirked, stuffed one of the pistols into his belt, and took the fire extinguisher.

He knew he'd only get a few shots at this, and only one if he screwed up the first part, but a plan formed rapidly in his head.

It was a Hail Mary, and he didn't like the odds of success, but it was his best chance. If he stayed put and tried to wait it out, the gunmen would eventually close in and tear him apart. With a limited supply of rounds for his weapons, he couldn't try to outgun them either.

This was Dak's only shot.

He returned to the doorframe and paused, knowing that the men down the hall would fire on sight.

He peeked around the corner and lobbed the extinguisher down the corridor. With the quick look, he memorized the position of the eight men before ducking back through the door as they opened fire again.

A loud pop followed by a distinct spewing sound came from the hall. It was the sound Dak had hoped for; otherwise, he would have had to stick his pistol around the corner and shoot the extinguisher himself.

Fortunately, one of the enemy bullets had done the work for him, as he'd hoped, and when Dak poked his head around the corner, he witnessed the red canister dispelling its powdery smoke into the air, filling the corridor with the white fog.

The shooting ceased, and Dak moved knowing this was his one chance.

He stalked toward the fog, raising both pistols.

The extinguisher spent the last of its contents with a series of muted puffs, and then it fell silent.

Dak dropped to the floor and aimed down the hall, recalling where the men had been when he stole a quick look before.

He tensed his fingers on the triggers, and then squeezed.

The silenced pistols clicked loudly with every round escaping the barrels. Shouts from the other side of the fog told him all he needed to know. He kept shooting, shifting the sights on the guns slightly based on his recollection of the guards' positions, until the magazines ran dry.

Then he retreated, running back to the safety of the room before any survivors could return fire.

Dak waited for two minutes. The seconds ticked by as if being hammered out by a blacksmith at an anvil.

He breathed calmly then leaned back out the doorway and looked down the hall.

All eight men were down. Half of them writhed around, clutching at wounds. The other half lay still.

Dak held his empty weapon out toward the stairs, waiting for another round of guards to appear. They never did.

He exhaled and ejected the magazines from the weapons, dropping one to the floor. He replaced the empty well with the magazine he'd taken from the first guard and stepped to the door leading into Diaz's study.

It was time for the devil to pay his due.

34

Doc squirmed to wriggle free of the big guard. When Dak fired what looked like a bad warning shot, it distracted the attacker long enough for the older man to get loose and escape down the hall.

Unarmed now, Doc's choices were to take the big fella on with his bare hands, or try to hide and wait until he found something he could use as a weapon.

Even as a trained fighter, Doc knew his limitations. In an all-out brawl, he'd be able to hold his own only so long.

He looked back over his shoulder at the one Diaz called Paco before cutting down a side hall.

Paco was stalking toward him, like one of those villains from a horror movie. His long, methodical strides betrayed no sign of stress or concern, as if Doc's end were simply imminent.

Doc sprinted down the corridor then turned down the next. He checked every doorknob along the way, hoping he could find a place to hide, or at the very least a door he could lock behind him to keep his pursuer at bay long enough to formulate a plan.

No such luck.

Every door he checked produced the same result. *Locked.*

Evidently, the doors he'd found to be unlocked earlier were part of the ruse, to lure him or Dak into one of the rooms where they could be ambushed. Based on the brief exchange he'd seen with Dak at the other end of the initial hallway, that was exactly what Diaz's men were aiming to do.

No doubt about it, these locked doors were funneling Doc somewhere, and he wasn't sure he would like it.

At the end of the hallway, an open pair of doors allowed the cool sea breeze to blow through the passage. The smell of the salty air hit Doc's nostrils, and for a second he thought there might be a way out.

When he skidded to a stop at the door to the balcony, he immediately realized that was not the case and that his fears about being corralled to this spot were correct.

Doc spun around and clenched his jaw. He tightened his fists and stood in a fighting stance, waiting for the enemy to appear.

He didn't have to wait long. Paco stalked around the corner, never altering his pace as he approached the old man.

The guard's face remained stoic, a sinister visage of calm and death. The man's emotionless eyes were the most disturbing part. Doc stared into them as the guard approached, and it was as if Paco looked through him, to some distant point beyond. The retired doctor had seen that look only a few times in his life. People with eyes like that didn't associate what they were doing with any sort of moral compass. This man he was about to face was as cold-blooded a killer as any on the planet. He would end Doc's life without so much as a fleeting thought.

Doc's eyes begged to wander, to scour his surroundings for a weapon he could use to level the playing field, but there was none. He breathed through his nose, doing his best to calm himself as Paco approached.

"So, you wanna dance with the old man?" Doc asked, poking the bear.

Paco didn't reply. He just kept coming until he was within striking distance. Then, Doc lashed out.

He threw a jab, which Paco ducked easily to the side. Another jab missed as the big man dipped the other direction. Paco deflected the third punch and grabbed Doc's arm with his opposite hand, then jerked his opponent forward and jammed his knee into Doc's gut.

A curse escaped Doc's lips along with every gasp of breath in his lungs. He doubled over, dropping to his knees in front of the tall thug.

Paco tilted his head to the side, looking down at Doc as if he were a strange animal, then struck him across the cheek with a closed fist.

The blow knocked stars into Doc's eyes. He'd always thought that was a strange thing to portray in cartoons—when a character got hit on the head or face, they would see stars dancing around their skull for a few seconds. Now, he understood it. The twinkling visual disoriented him, and he clawed at the thin carpet to find a way to buy more time.

The salty air pouring in from the open doors helped clear his head, but by the time the dazed confusion started to dissipate, he felt a strong hand grab him by the right ankle.

Doc twisted around and looked up at the enemy. He kicked with his free leg, but he only landed one feeble blow to Paco's forearm before the big goon grabbed the other foot.

Writhing, twisting, and flopping around did nothing to loosen the big man's grip as he turned Doc around in a dramatic arc, dragging him on the floor. Then Paco backed toward the door, pulling Doc along with him.

Then Doc knew the man's plan.

Paco funneled Doc here, to this spot, so he could throw him over the balcony. The increasingly loud sound of waves crashing against the shore below only fueled the horror of that realization.

Doc kicked harder, jerking and pulling his legs to keep the man from dragging him any farther. When Paco backed out onto the balcony, Doc reached out with both hands and grasped at the doorframe, desperate to stop the killer's progress.

He didn't even slow the man down.

Doc's fingers slipped on the side of the door and was easily ripped away from the threshold. His nails scratched in futility at the tile on the balcony.

Then he stopped moving. Paco threw his feet to the ground and reached down to grab Doc by the shirt.

Doc threw a punch and kicked out his right leg. The punch hit Paco in the mouth, snapping the man's head to the side for a split second. The kick hit the man's shin and sent as much pain through Doc's leg as it did to his attacker's.

Paco's head twisted back around, and he faced Doc with a grim, slightly irritated glare. Blood trickled from his lip in a thin stream, inching its way toward the man's chin.

Doc threw another punch from his awkward sitting position, but Paco grabbed his wrist and yanked him up even as the older man attempted to scurry backward in retreat. Paco spun him around like a rag doll, and Doc felt his lower back crunch against the balcony's railing.

He winced at the sudden pain but regained his footing and tried one last time to punch his way out of the jam with his free hand.

Paco deflected the blow and then grabbed that wrist, bending both arms down and in at an awkward angle so the palms faced up.

Doc's nerves screamed in pain as the limbs were twisted to breaking point. He didn't give his opponent the satisfaction of hearing him yell. He clenched his jaw and swallowed against the agony, knowing that the end was almost here.

A muted pop from a gun somewhere inside the building, followed by a strange spewing sound, interrupted his thoughts, and for the slightest moment, it distracted Paco as well. The big man's head twitched slightly at the sound coming from the corridor, but soon it blended with the crashing waves, drowned out by nature's perpetual rhythm.

Doc used the interruption to his advantage and swung his leg up hard into the thug's groin.

His knee sank deep, and Paco's eyes flashed wide with nauseating pain. The fingers gripping Doc's wrists loosened just long enough for him to get his right hand free. The respite vanished in a breath, and Paco shifted his grip up to Doc's neck. The henchman squeezed the American's throat, cutting off Doc's windpipe.

Doc slapped at the man's face, but he might as well have been a fly buzzing around an elephant. The shot to Paco's groin had momentarily stunned the man, but that brief second of relief was instantly replaced by a fury he'd only seen a few times in his life.

There was nothing Doc could do to free himself. Paco had him pinned to the railing and continued to squeeze.

Darkness crept into the corners of Doc's vision. His lungs started to ache, begging for the vital air that would bring them relief, and life. He kicked his leg again, but this time his knee struck the outside of Paco's thigh, glancing off with no effect.

The shadows crowded Doc's vision, and he knew he was seconds away from unconsciousness. Then what would happen? Paco would throw him over the cliff, whether he was dead or not. *At least,* Doc thought, *I won't experience the terror of falling.*

As he braced himself to surrender to the shadows, Doc remembered something. In one last desperate act, he shoved his hand into his pocket. He fumbled for the device and finally felt the cold metal against his fingers.

He wasn't sure how the thing worked, but from what he'd seen, Dak pressed the center of it two times. He didn't know why, or how it worked.

With no time to deliberate, Doc made up his mind and took his chances. He pressed the disc twice and tossed it up into the air the same way someone would toss a coin.

The metal disc tumbled in midair for a second. Doc twisted his head to the left as much as possible, squinting his eyes shut with the last ounce of energy he could muster.

A bright light flashed pink against his closed eyelids. Even squinting hard, he couldn't believe how powerful the device was.

Instantly, Doc felt the fingers around his throat loosen. For the first time, Paco made a sound. It was a miserable, borderline pathetic sound.

Doc slumped down for a second against the rail, catching his breath in a couple of heartbeats. Paco rubbed his eyes viciously, desperately, in a vain attempt to clear his vision.

The only fire in Doc's eyes burned from pure rage. He stood up straight, his throat still tight from the choking. Paco staggered around wildly, swinging his elbows back and forth in a clumsy defense while he continued trying to regain his vision.

Doc knew all the man could see was black, and it would only be temporary.

He took a bold step toward Paco, timed his attack with fists up, and as the big man swung his elbows around again, Doc threw a single roundhouse into the man's throat.

The fist sank deep, crushing the larynx as Doc's knuckles snapped to a stop three inches behind the target.

Instantly, Paco forgot his blindness and grabbed at his throat. He gurgled and coughed then reached out with his right hand to try to fend off another attack.

It was too late. Doc was already behind him.

The American clutched the back of the big man's collar with one hand and his belt with the other. Then, like a bouncer kicking out a drunken reveler, Doc summoned every shred of strength he had left and forced Paco to the railing.

Paco resisted, sensing the danger, but his weakened condition prevented him from stopping the inevitable.

He dug in his heels in a last-ditch effort, but it wasn't enough against Doc's renewed strength. The older man shoved Paco until his waist hit the railing. Then, in one continuous movement, Doc fork-lifted the big man up, using the rail as leverage, and flipped Paco over it and down the cliff.

The retired doctor followed through, landing his elbows on the rail, exhaustion, pain, and relief all washing over him at once.

He watched the cartel lieutenant tumble quietly through the air, his body flipping head over heels, illuminated by the moonlight over the sea. Then it stopped abruptly as it smashed against the jagged rocks on the shore below.

Doc stared at the body for nearly a minute. The waves crashed over it, tugging at it with foamy tendrils, begging to carry it out to sea.

Then one of the waves succeeded, and Paco's body vanished in the murky soup of the ocean.

Doc slumped to the balcony floor and rested his head against the metal railing, finally able to catch his breath again.

35

Dak turned the doorknob and eased the door open. The hinges creaked only slightly in protest.

He paused for a second and then shoved the door open wide, anticipating gunshots from within.

The smell of burning wood mingled with the cigar he'd detected earlier. Across the room, the glass wall gave a spectacular view of the ocean and the moon hanging over it in the night sky. Dak waited, unwilling to risk venturing into the room until he knew where Diaz was.

Then, to his surprise, the man gave away his position.

"Come in," Diaz commanded in a demur voice. "Let me see this ghost who has wreaked so much havoc on my little business."

"I would hardly call it little, Fernando," Dak replied. "Pardon me if I don't step out into the line of fire."

"Yes, I assumed you would say something like that. Smart. I would do the same were our positions reversed."

The voice came from the right, the same direction the crackling sounds of the fire seemed to originate.

Dak lowered himself to one knee, looked back down the corridor, then poked his head around the doorframe.

Diaz sat behind his desk, a massive oaken piece that looked like it could have come from a palace somewhere in Europe. Dak briefly wondered how old it might be, and if it too, was something Diaz had purchased on the black market. Dak immediately noted the two pistols atop the desk, inches away from Diaz's hands.

The cartel boss raised his palms. "We can talk like civilized adults here, can't we?" Diaz asked.

"You're hardly civilized," Dak replied with vitriol.

"Oh, come now. You came into my home, killed my men. Even my best." A hint of regret tickled Diaz's voice. "And now you're here. To kill me, no doubt."

"Sounds like you have it all figured out."

"Yes, well, some puzzles are easier to put together. But"—Diaz raised a finger—"I know when I am beaten." He raised his hands high. "Come in. You can see my weapons are on the desk. If you would rather, I can pick them up and we can shoot each other, or I can leave them there and we can talk."

"I could just shoot you right now," Dak warned. He had the pistol sights on the man's head, though from that distance, hitting the mark would require a little luck. Still, he'd made that shot before.

"I believe you could," Diaz said, leaning back and steepling his fingers together. "But that's not why you are here, is it?"

Dak paused at the statement, wondering what his enemy meant by that. "No, I'm pretty sure I'm here to kill you." He still didn't trust that Diaz was alone and scanned the rest of the room to his left to make sure. The other side of the study featured bookshelves that stretched to the high ceiling, where antique tiles filled the overhead space. They were dark brown and glossy. The sculpted shapes of the tiles reminded Dak of old opera houses he'd been in before, with opulent decorations and reliefs hanging everywhere.

"No, you aren't," Diaz countered. "You're here for the sword. Aren't you?"

The question disarmed Dak in a way he couldn't have foreseen. *How did Diaz know that?* Dak wouldn't let the man know he'd been caught off guard by the comment, but it had certainly been a surprise.

"What sword?" Dak asked coyly.

Diaz laughed and made a show of it. "Come, my American friend. We both know the sword is why you're here." Diaz motioned to the centuries-old weapon hanging on the mantel behind him. "I'm not stupid. I can connect dots, as you Americans say."

Dak stood and slipped into the study, pulling the door shut behind him and locking it for good measure, just in case there were more guards he'd somehow missed.

"You see?" Diaz asked, splaying his hands out wide. "I am alone. In fact, I don't have many men left. The few who are still alive work in other parts of the city at my various businesses."

"What do you want, Diaz?" Dak asked, keeping his weapon trained on the man's head as he moved slowly toward the desk. With every step, the shot became more difficult to miss.

"It's not about what I want," Diaz said. "But what you want. You're here for the sword. Take it. It's yours."

"Why do you think I'm here for that old thing?"

"Because all of this started to happen when I bought that weapon. It is the sword of Francisco Pizarro himself, one of the most powerful conquistadors to ever set foot in the New World. There were rumors that it was cursed, that whoever owned the sword would face the same fate as Pizzaro." He chuckled. "I heard those legends, of course, and shrugged them off as only that. Legends. Now, however, I'm not so certain. And I'm willing to let you have it, along with the curse, in exchange for something."

"What would that be?" Dak asked, his voice low and grim.

"You have taken much from me, gringo. Money, drugs, gold, not to mention a significant portion of my workforce. I'll have to rebuild my facility, get new workers, and replace the girls you and your friend freed." He noted the surprised look on Dak's face. "Oh, your friend. He is down in the basement getting our best spa treatment."

Dak only offered a confused glare.

"Peter Davenport?" Diaz said. "You can pretend you don't know him, but we both know you do. He helped you pull off this entire operation. He's getting what he deserves, I assure you, but with one call from me, his misery will end."

"Ah," Dak feigned. "So, you want me to take the sword and leave, and you will let us both walk away? Am I supposed to believe that?"

"No. I wouldn't expect you to believe that. And I'm not letting Davenport go. The doctor must be held responsible for what he's done. He lives here now. In my town." Diaz's voice swelled, and he raised an angry finger.

Dak noted the lines of cocaine on the desk and the small pile waiting to be cut into more. He wondered how much of the drug the man had already inhaled, but judging from the crazed look in Diaz's eyes, Dak figured it was a lot.

"Well," Dak countered, "I guess that's where you're going to have some issues." He considered letting Diaz stew, believing that he still had the upper hand with Doc in his possession. One thing Dak learned long ago at the poker table was that if you knew you had a guy pinned on a hand, never let them know what hand you're holding.

In this case, he ignored that sage counsel and put it all out on the table.

"I already let Doc go," Dak said, lowering his weapon to his hip. "I think he found your little waterboarding spa treatment lacking. Seemed uncomfortable when I located him, but he's fine now. So, it's just you and me. And that sword you were talking about." He pointed at the weapon with his pistol.

Diaz suppressed his anger at the news of the doctor being freed. One more card stripped away from his crumbling house.

"The sword is priceless," Diaz offered. "You could make a fortune selling it on the black market. Or perhaps you're a collector."

"Keeping illegally obtained artifacts isn't really my thing, Fernando. I appreciate history, but I don't steal it. And I don't buy it from shady underground antiquities dealers."

Diaz's eyes twitched. "How do you know that?"

"Just guessing," Dak lied. "Somehow, I doubt you can pick up items like that at a Sotheby's auction."

"What do you want, gringo?" Diaz fumed. "Money? Gold? The sword? My mansion? What is it you want? Whatever it is, you can have it."

Dak shook his head dramatically. "You think I want to take over your operation?"

"No," Diaz said. "I'm offering you a job." He inclined his head, looking down his nose at the intruder. "I will need someone strong to help rebuild my empire. Clearly, I have security issues. Someone like you could fix that, could help make the organization stronger than it ever was before. And I will make you wealthier than you ever imagined."

"Hmm," Dak hummed. "That is a tempting offer, Fernando. Really, it is. Except that I'm here, holding a gun, and you are unarmed. I could simply kill you and take over everything."

"If only it were that simple." Diaz rose and paced around behind his desk. He looked up at the sword, then spun around slowly to face the interloper. "You killed the mayor's husband. At this very moment, her police are scouring the city for you. They will hunt you down, and when they find you, you will not see the inside of a jail cell. They will take you to her, and she will kill you. There is no escape from this situation except through me. I am your only salvation, gringo. Your only way out. I see no reason why we can't both benefit from this."

Dak inhaled slowly then sighed. "Yeah. That does make things a little trickier, doesn't it?"

"Yes," Diaz agreed with a nod. "It certainly does."

"Tell me something, Fernando. Why is it, again, that you think I'm here for that sword?"

Diaz grinned, believing he had finally turned the do-gooder into one of his own. "My operation was fine until I bought that cursed weapon. The day I brought it here was the day you attacked and murdered my cousin. Ever since, nothing but destruction has plagued me."

"And you think getting rid of it will rid you of your misfortune?"

"I don't see why not! There are coincidences, my friend, and then there are things that happen for a reason. I may not understand the reason, but that doesn't mean it's not there."

Dak listened but stayed alert.

"Please," Diaz continued, slowly walking over to the bar in the corner. "Let us drink to our new union."

"You make it sound like a marriage," Dak groused.

Diaz laughed. "An accord, then. Whatever you want to call it." He fixed two tumblers side by side and poured a light golden liquid from a decanter into them. "I hope you like tequila. This comes from one of the best agave farms in Mexico."

"I've been known to have tequila now and then," Dak said.

Diaz turned around, holding out the two glasses. Dak sensed something, a movement or a sound. He wasn't sure, but it was there, and he knew exactly what Diaz was trying.

Dak rounded toward the door, diving to his right as a guard aimed and fired a pistol. The bullet tore through a navy-blue-upholstered sofa near the window, narrowly missing Dak's foot.

He returned fire as he rolled to an end table and flipped it over to use for cover. It wasn't nearly as big as the shield he and Doc used downstairs in the dining room, but it was better than nothing.

The gunman at the door sprawled for cover amid the hail of metal spraying around him, but Dak's shots were erratic and plunked into the wall, nowhere close to his target.

Meanwhile, Diaz set the drinks on his desk and picked up the twin pistols, aiming them at the American who was exposed on the left flank.

"You should have taken the deal, gringo!" Diaz shouted.

Dak pulled the sofa closer to him and ducked low. The couch would only provide cover long enough for reinforcements to get there, assuming Diaz had a few more men in reserve.

No matter how bleak the situation, Dak always forced himself to look for a way out. He remembered the cave in the Middle East, where he'd been cast into utter darkness and left for dead by his team. He recalled the relief and utter gratitude for finding an escape to the light, and to a second chance at life.

Now, he squatted in the darkness again. It was different than the cave but similar in terms of desperation.

Diaz fired several shots, two cracking through the air just over Dak's head. Several more tore into the thick sofa. The guard at the door took his boss's cue and likewise ticked off six shots. Most of the rounds found the end table's surface. One hit the floor dangerously close to Dak's foot.

"It's a shame," Diaz said, stepping around the corner of his desk to close in on his quarry. He motioned with a twitch of his head to the gunman at the door. The guy stood up and started to advance slowly toward the intruder. "You could have been the second-most powerful man in Lima, gringo. But you went and made a bad decision."

"Oh yeah?" Dak grunted.

"Yes." Diaz stopped at the end of his desk, craning his neck to see if he could get an angle at the target from there. He aimed and squeezed the trigger. The bullet clipped the top edge of the sofa next to Dak. Cotton and fabric tore into the air and dangled over the side. "Now, I'm afraid the offer is off the table. You will die now. And then I will hunt down your friend, the doctor, and finish what I—"

A grunt and a gurgle interrupted the kingpin's monologue. He swiveled to the left and found the doctor with his arm around the guard's throat, squeezing hard.

"Any time, kid," Doc growled.

Diaz turned back toward where his target had been hidden, but before he could reset his aim, the sound of a muted pistol filled the room with soft puffs and clicks.

The bullets poured out of Dak's muzzle, drilling into Diaz's chest again and again, driving the man backward toward the fireplace.

He tried to raise his weapons in defense, but with every round boring into him, he was knocked farther back.

His arms hung impotently to his sides; the muscles unable to obey commands from their master any longer.

Dak stepped out from behind the couch and stalked toward Diaz. He raised the pistol, training the sights on the man's forehead.

Diaz wavered back and forth, as if he might fall in either direction. Shock covered his paling face as the blood drained from it and leaked out of multiple holes in his torso.

He coughed then looked down at the wounds with curiosity. He raised his glazed eyes and clenched his jaw. Diaz muttered a slur of profanity, then in one last desperate act, tried to swing one of his arms up to get off at least one shot.

Dak offered him no witty comment, no one liner to send Diaz off to Charon. He merely twitched his finger.

The bullet sank into Diaz's skull and out the back. Then the drug lord fell sideways, his face smacking against the desk on his way to the floor.

Doc twisted the guard's head to the side then snapped it back the other direction, breaking the man's neck. He let the guard drop with a thump and then took a deep breath.

"Looks like I got here just in time, kid," Doc huffed.

Dak nodded, his eyes now fixed on the sword over the mantel.

"That the thing you came here for?" Doc asked.

"Yeah," Dak answered, his voice distant and pensive. "I came for the sword, but it looks like I ended up taking care of some other business, too."

Doc stepped over the guard's body and walked over to the desk, bobbing his head in agreement along the way. "Yeah. Seems to me you have a knack for this kind of thing, vigilante justice and all."

Dak exhaled through his nose, stepping over Diaz's corpse. He reached up and plucked the sword gently from its supports. He admired it for a second then set it down on the desk, realizing that the dirt and oil on his fingers could corrode the metal.

"Maybe you're right," Dak said. "I thought I found myself a job, but maybe that job was meant to bring me to a greater purpose, helping people who can't help themselves."

"Could be," Doc said. "But what do I know?"

Dak met the man's steel gaze. "Thanks for saving me, Doc."

The older man snorted derisively. "Don't get all romantic on me, son. Besides, you got me out of the worst torture I've been through in my life. I'd heard stories about waterboarding, but nothing does it justice."

"So I've heard. Although Diaz said you were getting a spa treatment."

The two men shared a quick laugh and then made for the door, leaving the dying fire crackling in the hearth behind them.

36

Dak picked his way through the tugurizadas, keeping mostly to the shadows to avoid detection.

It had been three hours since he left the Diaz compound with Doc, and an hour since he left the older man at his two-bedroom condo in the city.

On the way to the slums, Dak noted a higher-than-average police presence on the streets of downtown, but as he neared the outskirts and the hills where Lima's destitute dwelled, the absence of any sort of law enforcement was conspicuous.

It was late. The moon had already made most of its journey across the sky, and in a few hours, Hector and his mother would wake up for another day of indentured servitude.

As he trudged through the dirty side streets and alleys, Dak pondered what Doc Peterson had said about his abilities. A "knack," his new friend had called it. The sword, safely guarded by Doc until Dak returned, had been difficult to get, and a worthy prize, but it paled in comparison to the real mission Dak had finished.

He'd taken out one of the most powerful drug cartels in this part of the world. While his ego tempted him to think he was some sort of demigod, Dak knew better. He'd been lucky a few times. Skilled? Sure. But no one ever won a fight without a little bit of luck.

A putrid smell washed over Dak that reeked of rotting food and sewage. His sense of smell, unfortunately, was exceedingly good, and walking through a place like this assaulted every part of that ability.

He fought away the stomach-turning odor until he was clear of it, then inhaled timidly for fear the smell would only be replaced by another. Finding fresh air in the slums proved to be a nearly impossible task, but some spots were better than others.

Dak slowed down and looked across the intersection at the house where Hector lived. The lights inside were out, and he knew the boy and his mother were likely still asleep.

He tightened the heavy bag against his shoulder, looked both ways, then marched across the street. Only a few vagrants were awake at this hour, smoking cheap cigarettes in the dirt or puffing on some strange concoction that smelled like someone had dipped weed into hairspray.

Once across the street, Dak looked around again, surveying the area. No one was around to notice him, not that they would have anyway. With his ball cap pulled down and his ordinary clothes, no one would remember him.

He climbed the steps up to the rickety porch that wrapped around half of the house and then tiptoed across to the door. The wooden planks creaked under his weight, and he worried that the next step he took could send him falling through the thing to the dirt below.

Fortunately, the porch construction was solid enough to hold him, and he reached the door without incident.

Dak loosed the strap on the duffle bag and lowered it to the floor, nudging it up against the bottom of the door.

He looked around again, making sure no one was watching him, then rapped firmly on the door.

HECTOR ROUSED from his shallow sleep. He looked around the tiny room but found no trouble. His mother turned over in her bed and blinked sleepily before returning to her slumber.

Hector rubbed his eyes. He'd heard something. *A knocking?*

For a second, worry consumed him. Had someone broken into his home again? They had nothing of value, save for the money hidden under the floorboard beneath Hector's flimsy mattress.

If someone took that, he and his mother would be ruined. And they would be resigned to life in the tugurizadas, which was no life at all.

Hector rolled off his mattress and onto the floor. He grabbed the only weapon he could find, the rusty machete his father had left them when he died.

Hector's old man had told him stories about that machete, how he'd used it in the jungles when searching for Incan artifacts, but he never came out with anything but tall tales and lots of bug bites.

The boy gripped the weapon with an unsteady hand and padded toward the door. He stopped at the doorway leading out to the porch and scanned the room. The kitchen/dining room/bedroom was empty except for his mother and their paltry collection of belongings.

But he knew he'd heard something. A noise had woken him, and now he couldn't go back to sleep without making sure they were safe. He was, after all, the man of the house now.

Hector stared at the door, uncertain if he should open it. If he didn't, anyone lurking outside would just come in the second he went back to sleep. If he did open it, he might get taken away, or worse.

He sucked in a gulp of air and reached for the door. Then, convincing himself to be brave, Hector pulled it open.

To his surprise, no one was there. A baby cried in the night from somewhere a block away, but no thief or killer stood on the porch.

He started to take a step outside to look around and nearly tripped over a duffle bag jammed against the threshold.

The boy looked down at the bag, peered out around the street, and then back to the bag again.

He knelt down and tried to move it. The thing was heavy, and bulky. His mind raced with wild thoughts, many of them warnings about what could be in the bag. *Was it an explosive?*

Curiosity got the better of him. Hector unzipped the bag and then pulled open the flaps.

A faint, shimmering yellow gleam caught his eye in the waning moonlight. He opened the bag farther and saw the source of the flash. A single gold bar sat nestled in a cradle of more money than he'd ever seen in his life.

He snapped his head up and whipped around, looking in every direction to find the mysterious deliverer.

Paranoia leaped into his mind, and Hector decided quickly to pull the bag into his home and out of view from any curious passersby.

Once the bag was inside, he closed and locked the door, then looked down at the contents again.

A piece of paper had been pushed off to the side atop the stacks of money. Hector bent down and picked up the folded paper. He pulled back the flaps and read the letter.

"Hector, I can't save everyone in the tugurizadas. But I didn't meet any of them. I only met you. You seem like a good kid, with your head and heart in the right place. Never forget what's most important—taking care of your family and helping others. Use this money to get you and your mother somewhere safe, somewhere clean, and start a new life. Leave Peru. You're not in danger, so don't worry. But if you truly want to start over, that begins with a new location. Use this money wisely. I know you will. I hope you enjoyed the pastry."

It was signed, *The Courier.*

The boy mouthed the word for pastry, then a broad smile swept across his face. His eyes widened with the realization. *The man from the street.*

He turned to his mother, who still slept on her side. With a mischievous grin, he tiptoed across the floor and tapped her on the shoulder.

"Mama," he whispered. "Wake up."

37

"Where are you?" Dak stood in the middle of Coolidge Park, a long cardboard tube tucked under his arm. A chill slithered through the air, shaking the skeletal trees surrounding him and jittering the few leaves still clinging to branches.

"I'll be there in five minutes," Boston answered. "My parents were doing something, so I had to wait."

"I don't like waiting," Dak countered. "Especially not out in a public place like this. And definitely not out in the open with few places to take cover."

"You sound paranoid."

Dak snorted. "Yeah, maybe I am a little."

He thought about telling the kid he would be too if he had the kind of people after him that Dak did, but he decided not to. There was no reason to scare the kid. It wasn't about scaring him. It was about keeping him safe.

Maybe Boston's early financial success in life, and relative fame, caused him some kind of detachment from reality, where he didn't think about the dangers around him, especially when dealing with someone like Dak.

The past haunted Dak. It followed him wherever he went. Last he'd checked, Nicole was safe, but for how long? He knew Tucker would eventually find her. Dak prayed the colonel never caught on.

She'd changed her name when she moved to Turkey. None of her coworkers at her tech startup would ever know her real name. It had been part of the plan before Tucker went off the rails.

After all, Tucker wasn't the only one trying to hunt down Dak. The enemies he'd made through the years all wanted him dead.

He winced. A series of bizarre memories scrambled his brain for a second, and then they were gone. He'd been in a building. Some kind of facility. It looked familiar, yet foreign.

The white metal walls offered no clue as to the location, but Dak didn't need a clue. He knew the place.

"Well," Boston said, interrupting Dak's wandering thoughts, "you don't have to be. I'm fine. Just leave the item where we discussed, down on the slope under the walking bridge. There's a rock there that overhangs the hillside near the shore. Tuck it under there."

Dak started walking before the boy had finished his request. "Anything else?"

"The money is already in your account. I made the transfer yesterday."

"I noticed. Thanks. Although that's a lot of trust to put in someone you just met and who's carrying a potentially priceless historical artifact. I bet this relic could fetch a big offer."

"True," Boston agreed. "You could have just skipped town, probably made a fortune on it. Which is why I sent you a little extra money."

"I thought maybe you made a mistake," Dak said sincerely. He strolled casually across the wide lawn that stretched from a carousel house all the way to the river, with winding sidewalks snaking through the grounds.

"Nope. Job well done. I hope it wasn't too difficult."

Dak glanced to his left, then right, crossing the promenade near the shore. "Nothing I couldn't handle." A part of him—most of him—hoped the kid hadn't seen any of the news coming out of Lima. Dak had seen it, and the mayor was doing all she could to both cover up the truth about her husband's death and make it look like she was the one responsible for taking down Diaz and his cartel.

The spot he'd seen online made him laugh out loud. Dak had sent a message to the mayor to let her know there would be no more trouble with Diaz, and that the man responsible for her husband's death was gone.

Of course, he didn't need to mention that *he* was the killer. That kind of info was on a need-to-know basis, and in his opinion, she didn't need to know. He hadn't lied. Dak left the country before the message was delivered to the woman. So, in truth, the killer was gone.

"Good to hear," Boston said. It didn't sound like the boy had any inkling about what might have occurred in Peru. "When you're ready, I'm working on a lead for another artifact. I don't have anything concrete yet, but I'll let you know."

Dak trudged down the gentle slope toward the Tennessee River. Dark ripples danced across the surface, all the way to the south shore and Ross's Landing. Dak found the big rock sticking out from the ground and sat down on the front lip of it as if taking in the chilly morning air. He peered across the river at the Tennessee Aquarium and the downtown Chattanooga skyline.

Then he bent over, sliding the tube under the rock with a casual look around to make sure no one was watching. The Walnut Street bridge loomed overhead to the left. On this cold morning, the only people on it were the truly dedicated: runners and a few walkers.

"Sounds good," Dak said, tapping the end of the tube so it would remain out of sight. "I have something I need to take care of in the meantime."

"Hobbies?"

"Something like that," Dak demurred.

"Well, glad to hear you're staying busy." Boston paused. "We're about to turn off the exit, so we will be there in a couple of minutes."

"I'm already on my way out. Good doing business with you, kid."

"You, too. And thank you."

Dak smirked wryly as he stood. He turned and hiked back down the little slope, crossed the concrete path, and made for the stairs on the other side of the parking lot, where Frasier Avenue fronted a line of shops, eateries, and bars.

"You're welcome."

He ended the call and stuffed the phone in his jeans pocket. At the top of the stairs, he turned and walked onto the Walnut Street walking bridge. A guy in a beanie, running pants, and a red windbreaker jogged by, turned around, and started back across again.

Dak found a good spot where he could see the rock down by the river and waited. As promised, Boston and his father appeared a couple of minutes later. The boy looked under the rock, and a funny thought struck Dak.

This kid was excited about relics and artifacts in the way others got excited about new toys at Christmas. *Boston McClaren hardly lives an ordinary life*, Dak thought.

He took the phone out of his pocket again, unlocked it, and stared at the wallpaper image for a long minute. Nicole stared back at him with a smile that could melt an iceberg. His chest tightened, and he forced himself to put the phone away before emotions overran him.

"I guess that makes two of us, kid," Dak muttered. "No ordinary life for me, either."

THANK YOU

First of all, I want to thank you for reading this story. I had a great time creating it, and I hope you enjoyed every minute.

There are millions of books you could have chosen to spend your time and money on, and you chose mine. So I appreciate that.

Thank you so much.

Visit ernestdempsey.net to get a free copy of the not-sold-in-stores short stories *Red Gold, The Lost Canvas,* and *The Moldova Job.*

You'll also get access to exclusive content and stories not available anywhere else.

While you're at it, swing by the official Ernest Dempsey fan page on Facebook at https://facebook.com/ErnestDempsey to join the community of travelers, adventurers, historians, and dreamers. There are exclusive contests, giveaways, and more!

Lastly, if you enjoy pictures of exotic locations, food, and travel adventures, check out my feed @ernestdempsey on the Instagram app.

What are you waiting for? Join the adventure today!

Ernest

OTHER BOOKS BY ERNEST DEMPSEY

Sean Wyatt Adventures:

The Secret of the Stones

The Cleric's Vault

The Last Chamber

The Grecian Manifesto

The Norse Directive

Game of Shadows

The Jerusalem Creed

The Samurai Cipher

The Cairo Vendetta

The Uluru Code

The Excalibur Key

The Denali Deception

The Sahara Legacy

The Fourth Prophecy

The Templar Curse

The Forbidden Temple

The Omega Project

The Napoleon Affair

The Second Sign

The Milestone Protocol

Adriana Villa Adventures:

War of Thieves Box Set

When Shadows Call

Shadows Rising

Shadow Hour

The Relic Runner - A Dak Harper Series

The Relic Runner Origin Story

The Adventure Guild:

The Caesar Secret: Books 1-3

The Carolina Caper

Beta Force:

Operation Zulu

London Calling

Paranormal Archaeology Division:

Hell's Gate